Mia

a novel

Leslie
Bazzett

SCRIBNER
New York Amsterdam/Antwerp London
Toronto Sydney/Melbourne New Delhi

Scribner
An Imprint of Simon & Schuster, LLC
1230 Avenue of the Americas
New York, NY 10020

This book is a work of fiction. Any references to historical events, real people, or real places are used fictitiously. Other names, characters, places, and events are products of the author's imagination, and any resemblance to actual events or places or persons, living or dead, is entirely coincidental.

First Scribner hardcover edition August 2026

Interior design by Kyle Kabel

Manufactured in the United States of America

1 3 5 7 9 10 8 6 4 2

Library of Congress Cataloging-in-Publication Data has been applied for.

ISBN 978-1-6682-2732-9
ISBN 978-1-6682-2734-3 (ebook)

For Michael

Mia

1

I awake drenched in sweat, alone in the big bed. For long seconds, I don't understand where I am, what day it is, what season, what country even. In panic, I wonder if my children are in their beds and need my protection—from what? But no, they are nearly grown, taller than me. By the quality of night beneath the streetlights beyond my windows, I gradually realize it's winter. I'm in Minneapolis. By myself. As I wait for my heart to calm, the dream recalls itself to me. Then, for a long time, I lie thinking of her with a hatred that turns inward, coiling back on itself.

She's younger in the dream than when I knew her; closer to her mid-forties, the age I am now. I watch her step from the narrow doorway of the mail service into dazzling sunlight, stride up the steep cobbled street on two strong legs. My silver bracelet flashes on her wrist, a package that I know is mine bundled under her arm. When she reaches the corner, where a wrinkled *campesina* sits on a wooden crate selling roses, she stops. For the duration that good manners stipulate, they exchange pleasantries in a Spanish that I comprehend without any stutter between words and meaning, as though it were my first language. What color? the old *campesina* asks when at last it's time to get to business. Orange, the American woman says. Ah, that's a nice color, says the *campesina* approvingly, her eyes disappearing within her wrinkles, as the younger woman smiles disdainfully—of course it's a nice color—gazing down the bridge of her fine nose.

Here the dream shifts. I am suddenly aware of my own presence, my gaze lingering on her face. Like a camera panning closer to its subject, I know now that it's me dreaming her: her perfect teeth, the lovely angle of her strangely unscarred jaw, her neck. From at once far away and near to her, I feel my heart leap and begin to race as she says, *They're for my daughter, these flowers*. And for a single beat—the flicker in which every person is capable of self-deception—I am suffused with extravagant joy. *She's remembered me! She's gotten me a gift!*

2

When I first met her, I was happier than I'd ever been. I'd finally triumphed over the mother who abandoned me, my whole ugly childhood. I had everything I'd ever wanted: a husband who adored me, two beautiful children, a stunning glass house high on a hill. More than anything, I had this year in Mexico, rising before me like a stark white sail.

A few days before leaving the States, Tom and I had thrown a party. Three couples we knew and their children. Because we'd rented out our house furnished, it was as I always kept it, full of flowers I'd cut from the garden, stacks of art books and polished silver dishes and leather trays holding keys. On every surface, a curated clutter, as if we were leaving in a rush for nothing more than a long weekend.

After the meal, we sat amid empty platters and wine bottles, talking about the country's problems, how envied Tom and I were for getting out. It was a time, much like the current one, in which it was almost compulsory to express disillusionment, a kind of resigned despair. Leaving was something our friends had floated more than once—first in reaction to the Iraq war, then the 2004 election. "I'm moving to Canada," someone would say at a dinner party. "No, I'm serious. I actually spent an hour looking through the Canadian immigration website."

Inevitably one of the children would ask in their tiny voice, "Are we really going, Daddy?" and the speaker's fierce resolve would crumble. "If only we could."

Not that it was our ideology that was taking us to Mexico; in a way, it was the opposite. Tom, an architect, had been asked to oversee the construction of an elaborate community aimed at wealthy Mexican and American retirees. Toward the end of the evening, when we were well into our drinks and sharing stories and laughing, Tom told everyone what had happened the night before; someone had rifled through our unlocked car. He felt violated, he said.

"*Really*, violated?" I scoffed, gesturing to the dishes stacked everywhere, the empty bottles of wine, like: *What do we care? Look at all we have; it's obnoxious.* "So they took a few dollars in change," I laughed, "so what? I just hope it was enough to get a beer or whatever, a bottle of mouthwash."

"Mouthwash!" someone barked out amid a ripple of laughter.

"And what about the fact it's wrong?" Tom cut in, in his pedantic way, a way I couldn't help feeling dampened everyone's joy.

"What about it?"

"It doesn't upset you, that we were robbed?"

"Not really."

"Wow. Okay, then."

I sensed people becoming embarrassed. It was silly to me, their unease. If Tom and I argued, it was only because we were so close, like one person split in half. Disagreements like this were just the sparking of our passionate connection.

"Should we maybe get some air?" my neighbor Jessica asked, touching my arm with that fatuous look of concern so many women have mastered.

When we stepped outside, the children were running along darkened lawns scattered here and there with signs protesting the war, little shadowy figures rushing past. With a stab of love, I saw my son whooping and pumping his fists as Jessica's twin daughters chased him.

"I can't stand it," Jessica said. "They're all going to miss this so much!"

It was only a year, I consoled her; we'd be back before she knew it. In truth, though, I was already indifferent to her, to everything. My house, my things. I'd learned this in girlhood, trailing my mother from town to town after she left my father, in and out of other relationships, our fortunes synchronously rising and falling. Rather than attachment, I had learned to cultivate a reckless joy in our inevitable leaving, the opportunity to remake myself, the defensive scorn of seeing people and places as disposable: *I never liked them anyway.*

"Still—a year! Poor Mavis and Etta, they'll be miserable without Henry."

Mavis and Etta, I thought, what names for two little white girls in eighty-dollar shoes; what could girls like that possibly know of misery? We had reached the end of the block and, without speaking, turned around. These sad conventions; these American ways of being, pacing to the end of a block and back like hamsters. *Soon it will all be different*, I told myself. *Soon everything will be new.*

And how I loved Mexico! From the beginning. I loved the freedom of it, driving around with no seat belts the way all the locals did, Ida and Henry straining through the open windows, their mouths wide with delight. I loved walking them to school in their tidy plaid uniforms, past makeshift shrines where women knelt and crossed themselves, through four-hundred-year-old squares with their sounds of pigeons lifting at once like a flurry of slapping rags, their church bells ringing nonsensically, fallen out of time.

After dropping them off, I'd wander the vast covered market buying the things María needed for the afternoon meal. The *tortillería*. The produce seller's stand, with its tall pyramids of shining fruits. The poultry store, with its bright stench of blood and bleach. At noon, I picked up Henry, waiting with the other mothers on a stone bench beneath a huge old pepper tree for the kindergarteners to be brought out. Ida, who was in second grade, would be done with the older children at two o'clock.

One afternoon, as I sat waiting for Ida, one of the younger-looking mothers arrived having just bobbed her hair. It made a stir as she strode through the gate, the other women springing forward to touch it, test its weight, its bounce, while she turned her head from side to side loudly criticizing herself—it was too short, wasn't it? It was ugly! *No*, they rebuked her, *don't say that! It's so pretty!*

I smiled to myself. Somehow it didn't bother me as much here, their competition masquerading as concern. Maybe it was the novelty of seeing it in a different context, being an outsider. I let the conversation wash over me, inhaling the reek of the littered arroyo that trickled beside the school, the ubiquitous smell of roasting corn and dust and the lavender soap that the maids dumped into the street each afternoon when they had finished cleaning. I checked my watch—nearly two o'clock—and lazily glanced up the hill beyond the wrought iron fencing.

It was then I noticed her: an older woman standing outside the gate a short distance up the hill. She struck me immediately as an impressive person. Tall and exceedingly slender, she was dressed in a faintly androgynous way. Tailored button-up shirt, dark slacks, her cropped silver hair combed sleekly back. She held a cane in one hand, an oversized black leather bag crumpled beneath her other arm. One foot poised above a milky stream of discarded mop water as if above a cool brook. In spite of everything, she possessed a very definite sort of elegance. She reminded me of an old greyhound rescued from the races, its body broken but its pedigree intact.

Her face turned safely in profile, I continued to study her. I had a habit of casting around for older women I found appealing. A way of reckoning with the inevitability of aging, maybe. Or the fact I hadn't seen my mother since I was a girl. I suppose I did it with all women—that brutal process of deciding in a few wordless seconds whether someone counted or didn't.

Into these chronic musings, she suddenly turned her face, and our eyes met. I tried to arrange my mouth into an expression of neutrality, as though I'd only just noticed her, to which she smiled in a way I couldn't read. My cellphone was in my hand, a rudimentary flip phone I rarely used. Self-consciously, I brought it to my face now, just as the school bell rang and the end-of-day pandemonium erupted, throngs of children flooding into the concrete breezeway, pushing and laughing. Right on cue, the ice cream man beyond the gate began calling out, his high voice cracking, "*¡Paletas y helados!*"

I spotted Ida among the fray, alone as usual. I could see her already speaking to me, a river of words that never paused, not even to reverse their flow when she reached me. I could put a cardboard cutout of myself in front of her, I often thought, and she wouldn't notice, so relentless was her focus on her own ideas.

Outside the courtyard, I stole a glance over my shoulder. The older woman had gone. Just as well. I had to return to the market—I'd forgotten limes—and as I continued on past our car, Ida seemed not to notice. She spoke fervently, touching her fingertips together in tense excitement. In this state, she would let me lead her anywhere, close at my side yet infinitely far away. I bought the limes at my usual produce stand, lingering for a moment to chat with the young seller. Then, as we were making our way out along a corridor that sold pottery, I suddenly caught sight of the woman from the hill.

"Ida, darling, hold on; can you wait here a moment?"

I hurried after the woman—to do what exactly? I had no idea. But I felt an almost primitive attraction to her. She had turned down another corridor. When I reached it, she was nowhere to be found, though, absorbed into the noisy thrumming of the market.

I doubled back, only to discover that Ida, too, had vanished. I looked up and down, my panic mounting as people brushed past me obliviously, talking, laughing. I retraced my steps. She wasn't at the produce stand. I moved along the tables selling toys, ready to break into a run if only I'd known where, everywhere seeing other mothers holding their own children's hands tightly. At an intersection crowded with plastic bins of flowers, I stopped, turning a slow circle as the claustrophobia of the market closed in on me, overwhelmed by my helplessness, my hampered Spanish, the limits of my belonging.

It was only a few minutes. Soon enough, I found her in the very corridor where I'd left her, crouching in concentration with several "fairy things" lined up on the concrete floor before her: tiny clay plates and pots, tiny straw brooms, tiny glass bottles, all of them handmade, smaller than a mouse might use. She seemed unaware of having been lost as I seized her shoulders in relief, kissing the fragrant crown of her head, her cheeks. Ida shook me off, maintaining her focus on the objects.

"I need these for my project."

It was what she'd been talking to me about, I realized. I glanced at my watch. We were late. "Maybe tomorrow, my love."

"*Please*," Ida pressed, staring up into my face.

I relented. I smiled at her. Yes, she could have them. Only now she couldn't decide which she wanted. I tried to hurry her—she could have all of them—at which she bristled and seemed to begin the process again, setting her mouth stubbornly as I pleaded and tried to reason with her: Daddy would be home already; María would be setting out the *comida*; we needed to bring her the limes.

At last, she handed me three things. I paid. We hurried to the car, Ida clutching the paper bag with her treasures. Inching up the steep Cuesta, caught behind a gas truck, I reproached myself for losing her, buying things for her and not for Henry, the trivial amount of money I'd spent and Tom's imagined disapproval at it. Somehow the small exchange had left me unaccountably frazzled, almost bereft. What did it say of me, of my weakness and need, that I had chased after this woman I didn't know?

As I was parking the car, I tried to extract some small measure of gratitude from Ida. "Do you like your new things, my love?" I always called my children by those names—*love*, *darling*, *sweetheart*, *angel*. When she nodded, I told her maybe it would be best if we didn't mention anything about the gift to Daddy or Henry.

3

The instant I stepped inside the house, I began to feel calmer, soothed by the smells of the food, the well-ordered, cheerful sounds of pots and plates being set out, water filling the sink. Where before it had been my job to make the household run, maintain its happy atmosphere, now I was a part of a system that functioned independently of my moods and actions. Each day, we ate in purifying sunlight, seated around a beautiful old Saarinen table while María shuffled in and out. She prepared whatever we wanted—chicken tinga, mole, enchiladas suizas, Spanish rice and beans, thick stacks of warmed tortillas with extra wedges of lime for Ida.

Her own portion she ate standing in the narrow kitchen, occasionally peering out at us through the pass-through. Tom's boss, the house's owner, had assured us we'd get used to being waited on. At first, we invited her to join us at the table—a suggestion that seemed to mortify her. She spoke not a word of English; it was difficult trying to explain ourselves in our limited Spanish. Over time, we variously asked, could the children help set and clear the table? Help her cook? Could we at least put a chair in the kitchen, to make her more comfortable?

No; she was adamant. "*Es mi vida*," she always insisted, her voice as close to stern as it was capable of being.

"Thank you so much," I said now, as she shuffled in to refill my water glass. "Please, let me do it, it isn't necessary."

"*Ay, no, señora*," she said, lifting the pitcher and smiling placidly. "*Es mi trabajo.*"

"Yes, but in the United States, it was *my* work," I told her in my plodding, careful Spanish. "In the United States, *I* cooked and cleaned."

"*Ay, no, señora*," she repeated, laughing lightly as though I were playing a joke.

When I insisted it was true, she uttered something quietly, addressing herself to Tom.

"Did she just say she's worked here for twelve years?" I asked in English.

"No, since she was *twelve years old*."

"Oh my God."

"Yeah."

"How long ago was that?" I asked Tom, holding a neutral expression because María had not yet gone back to the kitchen. Tom asked her in Spanish. Smiling in mild resignation, as though connoting to us the way things are, she said, "*Veintidós años, señor.*" After which she silently retreated.

Tom stared across the table at me. "I just did the math. She's thirty-four."

"That can't be right." She had six children; her daughter, who was pregnant and whom I'd taken to be closer to my age, worked here also on Wednesdays and Saturdays; her grizzled brother was our gardener.

"Can you believe it?" Tom said, turning to Henry. "María's younger than Mommy."

It bothered me, his appeal to Henry and not Ida, as if he was introducing him to a way men talk about women: María, plump and wrinkled, her graying braid trailing halfway down her back; me, slender and toned. But I didn't say anything; I disliked women who were overly strident around these things. Henry just sat there sucking his thumb, the damp noise of it, the lizard pulse at his throat as his tongue worked.

Tom said, "Did you think María was a lot older than Mommy, Henry?"

"Sort of," he lisped around his thumb. "María knows a lot more."

"Ouch!" Ida said. "Burned, Mom." We were all laughing except Henry, who continued to suck his thumb.

Reining himself in, with a tempering tone, Tom said, "I don't know, Henry, Mommy's pretty smart."

"Maybe Henry was thinking about a different kind of smart," Ida said. "Like with the spider and the tea."

I knew what she was referring to. One afternoon shortly after we'd arrived, I overheard María seeming to scold Ida and Henry in the courtyard, *Very bad, children!* When I rushed to the window, I saw her pointing at a huge spider. "*¡Muy mala, niños!*" she repeated, before, with a decisive slap of her rag, she killed it. More recently, when Henry became sick with a barking cough, she had brewed a tea from plants she'd picked in the fields near our house that immediately soothed his throat. But her most impressive act was when, late one afternoon, she called us from the kitchen balcony. We discovered her crouched beside the pot of red geraniums, her hands cupped in front of her like she was praying. A small disk of metallic green glinted between her thumbs and first fingers. She had caught a hummingbird. With an incline of her face, she gestured for Henry and Ida to come closer. Without squabbling over who would be first, in turn they stroked its tiny head with their finger as she instructed them, like an incantation, "*Suave, niños, con mucho cuidado*," obeying her with an absoluteness of which I had thought them incapable. I longed to touch it, too, but held myself back, clasping Tom's hand in girlish amazement. When each child had stroked the jeweled head, María opened her hands, the bird lifting weightlessly in the air like so much iridescent ash. Remembering these things, I was proud of Henry and Ida for regarding them as intelligence. *Maybe*, I thought, *the world hasn't ruined them yet.*

When we had finished eating, we dispersed into the languor of the day. Ida to the churchyard across the street where there was an ancient, rusted swing that she would ride, passing back and forth as she composed plays in her mind and songs under her breath. Henry into the garden with his action figures. Tom and I to the living room, slumped beside one another on the couch, surrendering to the inevitable torpor.

Tom picked up an old copy of *The New Yorker*. I listened to the pages turn. I asked if he had to go back to work, and he said he didn't. The project, bigger than anything he'd worked on before, encompassing not only houses but also communal buildings, stables, an outdoor amphitheater, had been slow to get going. Fifty years ago, its principal architect had designed the neighborhood in which we now lived, naming it Los Balcones for the way the houses were set into the steep bluffs like a series of terraced balconies. His own house—ours for the year—was both more modestly scaled and more elegant than the others in the *colonia*, descending organically along the slope of the hillside, flooded morning to night with sunlight.

I had strolled over to the wall of glass that opened onto the upper balcony, looking down on the sea of tile roofs and church spires, to my left a cluster of clouds. I could see people moving in the square, children in the playground in Parque Juárez, where we often took the kids on Sundays. A bird dove and then paused before me in midair.

"God, Tom," I said. By which I meant: *I love our life; I am overcome with joy.* And, perhaps hearing those unspoken things, he came behind me, resting his hands on my shoulders to turn me to him, and I lifted my mouth. We kissed for a long time, our knees touching. We caressed, standing before the window as if we were invisible, María was no longer moving about in the kitchen. That was how it was with us. That sudden igniting spark, in a few breaths the world falling away.

"Let's go downstairs," he said, looping his fingers through the heavy silver bracelet we'd bought together our first week here.

"Yes," I answered, agreeing with my body when Tom tugged the bracelet, like a handcuff, leading me away.

But when he silently pulled the covers back from our bed, I went on edge. A wave of repugnance swept through me. Not toward him but desire itself, as though hidden inside my body festered something rotten, a thing he touched whenever he was inside me. As always, I tried to banish the feelings, scolding myself, *Stop it; don't be frigid; Tom is a good man; he's the best man you've ever known; everything you have in the world is because of Tom.*

Moments later, settling myself against the pillows and lifting my mouth to be kissed, I felt a smaller wave of satisfaction, as though his desire were a confirmation of having done my job well. *You're a good wife, Sally. He still wants you.*

4

It ashamed me that I couldn't always take joy in physical love. I felt it as a failing, something that marked me as damaged. This was the dark secret I carried: that love and desire were antithetical; to desire, I must be treated with violence and debasement, in my imagination, if not reality. I knew it was because of my mother. The things I'd seen with her. The lessons I'd learned.

I was five when she left my father for another man, taking me with her to a depressed factory town several hours away from our home in Boston. Every other weekend, she would drive to the halfway point to exchange me. Despite my father's humiliation, the fact that they had fought and broken things and hit one another, he pleaded for her return. I waited in his station wagon, alone or with his girlfriend, while they argued at the side of the road, their screams occasionally reaching me over the din of passing traffic. Compared to the mean apartment we'd lived in with my father, our new house was grand, and for the first time, she didn't need to work. She spent the days wandering through the drafty rooms, applying and reapplying makeup, changing her clothes. She taught me to walk myself to kindergarten and back. I would return at midday to find her posed on the living room sofa, a drink set on the table before her, waiting tensely, though not for me.

She and my new father walked naked through the house, her hair disheveled, her wine-colored birthmark spreading above her pubic hair like a bruise of which she was incomprehensibly proud. I hated that birthmark. I had a similar one, a tiny echo just above my hip bone. On evenings and weekends, they played a game with each other, kissing noisily, pressed against door frames, him pinning her arms above her head or behind her back while she laughed low in her throat. On those occasions, my presence made him uncomfortable, and he began to banish me from certain rooms. He asked my mother to send me away. "Can't your mother take her?" he complained, referring to someone I barely knew, a woman who lived on the other side of the country. Hoping to ingratiate myself, I begged my mother for a pair of pants like his, a clip-on tie—or perhaps I was merely trying to erase my femininity, having already perceived its danger—but these acts only served to harden his dislike. Some weekends, his twelve-year-old son came to visit, and as the animal sounds of our parents filled the darkness, he would come into my bed, inexpertly touching me with a look that mingled intrigue and disgust. I both wanted and didn't want these moments, waiting anxiously for him to join me, unable to sleep if he did not.

After two years, my mother and I moved to a decrepit apartment above a family who fought morning and night. I slept in a small alcove off the kitchen at the top of a narrow reeking staircase, where each night I imagined my head detaching and floating away into a vast nothingness from which I peered down upon my abandoned body. Because she had returned to work, she got a puppy from the pound to keep me company, black and white with sharp little teeth. I dragged him, tied to a rope, along the ugly streets of our new neighborhood; spoke to him ceaselessly; shared my food with him. In the dingy afternoon light, in my mother's bedroom, I enticed him to lick me and did the same back. One weekend while I was at my father's, after it was discovered the dog and I both had worms, the dog disappeared. By then, my mother no longer drove me halfway. I rode a Greyhound bus alone the three-hour ride to Boston.

I longed for her to reconcile with the man who had wanted to send me away, the brother who had violated me, my father. But she had found someone new. She'd begun to roll joints and wear leather boots that laced up over her jeans. We moved to another apartment in a neighboring town, this one on the side of the highway. There was a bar I had to pass on my walk to school, and I would dare myself to look inside the door, standing in the shattered glass and dark slush of late winter. Once, I saw our former landlord there, his head propped sideways in his hands. "Come here," he said, "you've gotten so pretty." It was not an assessment that I shared. I had no friends in school. I was prone to violence, often awakened by nightmares. Half asleep, I would run along the still unfamiliar hallway to my mother's bedroom. If she was alone, she would make a grudging space beside her, telling me that I was too old to sleep beside her. I was seven. What I remember most from that time is the mixture of repulsion and longing I felt at her physical proximity—the scent of her skin, the tang of her breath washing over the pillow. I longed for her to hold me, but when she did, it seemed unnatural, given either resentfully or too ardently. If I asked her to, she would sometimes rub my back in hard circles. More often, she lay staring at the ceiling, ensconced in loneliness like a forgotten toy, and I curled away from her, clutching myself into a tight ball, telling myself, *There's no one, there's only you.*

It was a phrase I later repeated to Tom, the first time to appease his worry. We were planning our wedding, and I didn't want to invite anyone. Wasn't there anyone in my family, he asked anxiously, any friends from college? "No," I insisted. "There's no one. Only you."

In marriage, I changed my name to his. I followed him to Minneapolis, where I knew no one. We bought a modest house, and I rearranged and cleaned it tirelessly. Every weekend, I threw elaborate dinner parties. "The perfect couple" was how our friends referred to us. *Look at the two of you; it's disgusting.* In these moments, I would smile at Tom, touch his shoulder, laugh as if to excuse myself; how could we help it if we were still so in love?

When I was pregnant with Ida, out of the blue, a letter arrived. My mother had heard—she didn't say how, or where she had gotten my address—that I was having a baby. She was pleased, she wrote, because once I became a mother, I was sure to feel the kinship that was undeniably between us. She had only been twenty when she'd become pregnant with me. It hadn't been easy. But the bond between a mother and daughter withstands everything. Soon I would understand. We were actually so alike. *I know you will always love me*, she concluded.

I tore the letter into small pieces and carried them outside. It was early autumn, chilly. On the back patio we had recently installed, I set the pieces down and struck a match. I squatted there with my hands cradling my huge belly, utterly remorseless, as I watched them burn.

5

Nearly a week passed, and I didn't see her again. My days were filled only with my children, with Tom and María, the people I encountered in town. The handsome fruit seller with whom I'd begun exchanging shy hellos. The manager of the *carnicería* where I bought ground beef, who knew my name and had taken it upon himself to help me learn Spanish. Certain strangers, too, had become familiar. The men sprawled drinking in the doorways of the Cuesta, the maids trudging uphill. The amputee in his Yankees hat who sat outside the market. The old blind couple who danced for spare coins, him playing a harmonica, her banging a tambourine.

One night as we lay naked in bed, Tom told me he had to fly back to Minneapolis to reassure the American investors. He was anxious about what he would tell them. We had a way of calming one another, laughing at adversity. I pressed my body close against his. "What if you get fired," I teased him, "and Bill kicks us out?"

"Most likely that's what will happen," Tom said with a laugh. "We can always live in a yurt back home."

"Yeah, I don't think so. The kids—you know—we've become accustomed to a certain way of life."

"One day, my children, all of this . . ." He gestured into the darkness, both of us laughing at the absurdity of it, that this could be our life.

Underneath our banter, though, I was childishly nervous about being alone. In the fifteen years since we first met, we'd scarcely spent a night apart. What if María asked me something I didn't understand? What if the children were late to school? In Mexico, schools are gated; after the final bell rings, no student is permitted to enter. I had occasionally seen late parents cursing and banging in vain at the tall locked metal door, or children in their plaid uniforms trailing their mothers through town in the middle of the day.

The next morning, when I drove him to the airport in Léon, although the directions were hardly complicated, I kept asking him nervously, *Am I going the right way? When I return, I'll take this same route?* Enacting a particular kind of helplessness out of habit. I had lived my childhood in a similar state of disorientation whenever we moved to another street, another town or city.

That evening, we spoke several times via Skype, Tom reassuring me. The next morning, I wrote down the things María needed for comida, making a phonetic approximation of the words I hadn't yet learned. When I went downstairs to check that the children were ready, I found Ida still in her underwear. "Why aren't you dressed?" I demanded. With agonizing slowness, she began to argue about which uniform she was supposed to wear. There were two, depending on whether it was a gym day or not, the schedule shifting often with the seemingly endless string of holidays. María had washed and ironed the skirt; I could hear her moving about upstairs, and in desperation thought of enlisting her. Ida's Spanish was better than mine, and she respected María unquestioningly. But there wasn't time.

"Fine," I relented, "wear the one you want."

"So you agree I'm right?" she said, her eyes flashing brightly.

Hurrying them through the door and down the long, narrow stone staircase, I looked for other children in uniforms on the sidewalk and didn't see any. After all my worrying, they were going to be locked out of school. I'd have to take them to the market with me and everyone would know what had occurred, my incompetence.

Then, halfway down the hill, something wonderful happened: A battered pickup truck pulled over just in front of us, and a mother I recognized from school leaned out the window. "Come on," she called. "Throw the kids into the back with Adriana; otherwise, no way you'll make it!"

Henry's and Ida's eyes grew wide watching Adriana, in her spotless uniform and immaculately braided blond hair, clamber into the dusty flatbed. They glanced at me, not believing their good luck when I nodded my consent. I was already sliding into the passenger seat. As we pulled forward, the woman introduced herself in English. "Fabiola."

"*Mucho gusto, me llamo Sally.*"

"Yes, I've wanted to meet you." She laughed. "I've been curious, you know?"

Behind us, I could hear Henry screaming with joy each time we jostled over a pothole. I turned to smile at them through the window, Ida not meeting my eye but instead staring ecstatically into the emptiness before her. "This is like an amusement ride for them," I said. "And it's so kind of you to help us out."

"Please, it's nothing. We women have to stick together."

It was the sort of sentiment I would never have spoken; as a rule, I counted on no one but Tom, and least of all women. Still, I was touched, gratified at being thought of as something other than an outsider. "Your English is excellent, by the way."

"It has to be," she said with a dry laugh. "I work in the Fábrica."

The Fábrica Aurora was a former textile mill that had been converted a decade before to expensive shops and galleries that catered to wealthy tourists. I felt a flash of dissonance, wanting to commiserate as I would have done back home, to distinguish myself from the people she waited on. Ida loved going there, walking among the little studios where the artisans allowed you to poke around or to get a hot chocolate from the overpriced café. I sometimes took her as a treat, following the dirt path that ran along the arroyo beside school. We were by now crossing the little bridge. Fabiola pulled to a stop, and I thanked her again, the children already leaping from the truck bed and running across the dusty street.

I stood on the sidewalk, watching them scatter across the grass toward their classrooms, Fabiola's daughter stopping halfway to tie her shoe. A moment later, the secretary appeared with her heavy ring of keys, her heels clicking over the tiled corridor.

I ran my errands, exultant. When they were done, rather than go straight home I walked to the Jardín. On a bench in a narrow strip of sunlight, I watched the town waking up. The newsman arranging his papers along the low stone wall, lurid photos offering peeks at car crashes and drug killings. The shoeshine man still awaiting his first customer, singing to himself as he slowly lit his cigar. Some children ran up, too young for school or else too poor. The youngest carried a box of Chiclets. "What flavor," they clamored, "how many," falling against each other, their chins wet, mouths full of gum. "Hey, lady, where are you from?" one said in halting English before, laughing wildly, they ran away. I tilted my face to the sun. *Vivo en Los Balcones*, I smilingly recited to myself. *Vivo cerca de la Cuesta de San José, en una casa blanca. Tengo una buena vista*. As I was repeating this last phrase, a shadow fell over me.

"Oh, hello," I breathed, tenting my eyes to make out her backlit form. "I know you, I think, from the school?" I'd spoken in English, making my voice lift into a question though there was none; I'd recognized her immediately as the woman from the hill. She still hadn't spoken. "I'm Sally, by the way."

"Marvelous," she said. There was a trace of an accent, the way old film stars speak, *mah-velous*. "Sally! I've never met one of those before."

"Well, I'm honored."

She stared as if to say, *We'll see about that*. "You're very pretty," she finally said. "Whatever that's worth."

I laughed, liking her archness. She told me her name was Louise Nieman. We began to chat, the way people do in a foreign country when they discover they speak the same language, despite the twenty or so years' difference in our ages. She was curious how long I had lived in San Miguel and whether I liked it. Wasn't it nice now that summer had ended and so many of the tourists had gone?

She had an eager and engaged way of listening—not the way most people listen, as if already composing their answers, but as though a mutually delightful surprise were slowly being unwrapped. I found myself recounting to her the way it had stormed the day we arrived, releasing the heaviest rainfall I'd ever seen. In minutes, the Cuesta was gushing, brimming above the gutters. The four of us had run into the emptied streets of our neighborhood that always reminded me of an abandoned movie set, lifting our arms, the rain striking us like buckshot.

When I finally stopped speaking, I was flushing hotly. Louise continued to stare down at me, blinking slowly, assessing me. After an excruciating silence, she announced, "You're interesting. 'Rain like buckshot.' You must be a writer."

I shrugged as if to allow for that possibility, pleased by it. "But what about you, Louise? Have you lived here long?"

"Only a month, although I lived here before, with my husband—oh, ages and *ages* ago. No doubt before you were born," she added disapprovingly, then abruptly laughed, as if deciding I couldn't be held responsible for that, my relative youth. She still hadn't sat down. It occurred to me that it might be painful or difficult for her to do so, because of her leg. She was telling me that she had seen me around town. "You and your husband, holding hands. You must be terribly in love."

"Oh, yes, *terribly*," I repeated with a laugh, as though we were sharing a joke about love; there was something foolish about it. Almost immediately, I had a flash of annoyance, both with myself and her. I can't stand women bonding over the inadequacies of men. I started to gather up my plastic grocery bag, saying, "I should probably get going."

"Back to your maid and cook?" she laughed. And for the second time that morning, I wanted to differentiate myself from a certain kind of American, to disavow my apparent privilege. "I'll bet you live in Los Balcones," she went on. "Some beautiful modern house built by an American. Not that I hold it against you. It's magnificent, Balcones, no?"

Hearing her affectation, the *no* at the end of the sentence, I smiled to myself, gaining back a bit of ground, and was surprised when she said:

"Come have coffee with me."

"You mean—now?" I glanced toward the big café on the corner of the square, El Rincón, where a waiter stood in shiny black pointed shoes with his hands folded behind his back.

"That place is only for tourists," she said. "I know a wonderful place, I'm sure you've never been." There was something of a dare in the way she said it. A critique tucked within the flattery of her asking.

As I began to follow her away, already composing the clever things I would say, how I would arrange my face, all the ways I would endear myself to her, I was aware of adjusting my naturally deep stride, falling a step behind her because she limped and the sidewalks were too narrow to accommodate us side by side. We reached the corner where in the evening a group of men in matching vests sang bawdy songs, passing around a jug of red wine, then began the steep descent along Hernandez Macias.

I looked this way and that. Mostly I looked at the back of her head, expectantly at first, then mindlessly, studying its shape, the curving length of her neck. She had that ability, especially rare among women, of establishing a companionable silence. She seemed above the usual feints at getting to know you. She didn't ask what had brought me to San Miguel, or the circumstances that allowed us to live here, or what I did for work.

When we'd been walking maybe fifteen minutes, time and distance harder for me to gauge because of her limping gait, I realized that we were now in a part of town I'd never seen. The sun had risen higher and I was becoming hot. I took my sweater off and tied it around my waist. "This way," she said, leading me into a *callejón* so narrow that I could almost touch the houses on either side. I had a prickle of foreboding, not entirely unpleasant. We passed a toothless woman weaving straw dolls in a doorway.

I allowed myself to be led, yielding to her the way I often yielded to Tom or the children; that same fuzzy, pleasurable sensation of receding, allowing my desires to be subsumed by someone else's. Louise drew to a stop before a one-handed man selling peaches from a fraying straw basket. "How much?" she asked in a brusque, toneless Spanish that mortified me. I was always fastidious in my politeness. The man, unfazed, quoted her a price for the whole basket. She raised herself up, rummaging into the big black bag she'd had the day I first saw her. "I'll take one," she said without further negotiation, giving the man a single coin, with the same hand passing me the fruit. "Taste it," she commanded.

An oppressive smell of cooking hung in the air as I took the fruit from her, warm from the sun; a mingling of exhilaration and fear at the thought of eating something on the street like that, unwashed, her staring at me as I drew it close. As I was about to take a bite, it struck me: I had left my groceries in the park beneath the bench. "Louise, I'm sorry—"

She cut me off: "Save it for later, then."

"No, it's not that. I'm embarrassed."

She wasn't looking at me any longer. She'd taken a pack of cigarettes from her bag and was fiddling with it in a display of impatience. I reproached myself: What was I doing here, with this strange woman? I wanted to leave, get back to my groceries and on with my day. Yet for some reason, what I said was: "It's just that I don't have any cash with me."

"Don't be daft," she said. "What do you need cash for? I invited you."

And with that, we began again to walk.

6

Stepping inside the café that first time, my impression was of a deep shift in temperature, as if we were entering a cave or a chapel. That particular reverence of cool, dark places. The small, narrow room had an old-world sort of elegance, with round marble tables and bentwood chairs and worn Moorish floor tiles in shades of turquoise and cobalt. We were the only ones there.

I followed Louise to a table near the back. As we settled into our seats, her face bloomed into a broad smile. An asymmetry I hadn't noticed before. There was a faint scar above her jawline, around which the skin had the unnatural sheen of scar tissue; was this the result of the same accident that had damaged her leg? A new warmth had come over her, as though we were old friends. She began to reminisce about the man with the peaches, laughing about the look on my face when she handed it to me, asking solicitously did I like the café; wasn't it simply marvelous? I nodded and prattled my agreement—it was charming, so chic, the very sort of space I covet.

"Ah, so you covet spaces," she said, narrowing her eyes as if the fact were worthy of deep interest. I half waited for the dry remark, but her archness had vanished. "I knew you'd appreciate it. Mexicans have such an extraordinary sense of style. And wait until you taste the coffee!"

The waiter appeared, his hands clasped behind his apron, addressing Louise with studied deference. "*Bienvenidos, ¿qué puedo ofrecerles?*" She ordered for both of us in the same fluent but toneless Spanish. It struck me she was making a point to speak in this way, as though attempting a correct accent would be an insult rather than a courtesy. As soon as he'd gone, resuming the relaxed warmth of moments before, she began to talk about the first time she lived here, in '67. She'd arrived on the back of a motorcycle when she was just nineteen, she confided, and I calculated that she must now be fifty-nine.

"In those days, I used to walk everywhere, miles and miles, clear out of town. I met my husband here, Allan. He was an extraordinary painter. Everyone admired him, important people whose work already hung in museums. We were so poor we barely had enough money to eat," she said, laughing as though it were wonderful to be penniless, an extravagant gift. "I used to hunt for maguey worms and *jumiles*, which are small beetles. A woman named Nuria taught me how to cook them. She was one of Fernando Navarro's lovers—of course you know Navarro."

I nodded, though I didn't. A woman had stepped into the café, and I followed her with my eyes as she sat, setting her pebbled leather tote bag onto the floor. She was youngish, maybe twenties, with a scarf tied around her neck. She must have been a regular because, without taking her order, the waiter nodded in her direction and she smiled back her assent, then crossed her legs, reaching to remove a worn paperback and, tucking a thick strand of black hair behind her ear, starting to read. I could see the black marks of words on the page. I suddenly wanted to know what the book was; to be the book held in her hands, or to be her, so perfectly self-contained. Louise was animatedly speaking of her life with Allan, how they used to run far out along the Obraje road at dawn before that was a thing people did; the parties they threw that lasted until morning, everyone crowded into their tiny living room.

"Everyone came to our place, passing through. Burroughs, Ginsberg, Kerouac."

"What about Neal Cassady?" He had famously died here, passed out on the train tracks.

"Oh, sure," Louise said, as if it were of no account. "I met Paul Bowles here, too. Later lived with him in Morocco, in fact."

I gaped. "You *lived* with him?"

"You don't know the half," she laughed, pronouncing it in her old-Hollywood way, *haahf*. "Among our set, though, it was the Mexicans that most interested me. Fernando Navarro. Now there was someone worthwhile." She narrowed her gaze in the already familiar way. Her beauty could be almost startling, revealing itself in flashes, only at certain angles, like suddenly seeing a woman's shape beneath a dress in a gust of wind. "And Nuria you would have loved."

The declaration seemed to announce an intimacy between us: not *liked*, but *loved*. In its wake, I blushed. "A woman like Eve," Louise continued, "free and without shame," telling me how the two of them had roamed through the hills and washed each other's hair with a hose in the barren yard behind Louise's apartment, shrieking at the cold.

As she was finishing this memory, the waiter arrived with our coffees on a small silver tray. He set the cups down with exaggerated care, turning them slowly in their saucers, some inscrutable rotation that only he knew where to end. He was short and sturdily built, with dark Indigenous features, his crisp white apron reaching clear to his knees. Louise watched him and leaned back in her chair, resuming her air of superiority and reserve. Given her quasi-socialist affect and talk of having been penniless, this surprised me. And yet it seemed correct in a way I couldn't fully pinpoint. As he was straightening to leave, she said something to him in an undertone, gesturing, after which he smiled appraisingly at me.

"*Muy bonita, ¿sí?*" Louise said with disinterest, as if I were a photograph.

"*Sí, señora. Se parece a usted.*" She resembles you.

"My God, this coffee," I said, to mask the pleasure I'd taken at being mistaken for Louise's daughter, although it was truly the best coffee

I'd ever tasted. Glancing back into Louise's face, I saw that something had shifted.

"Sometimes I wonder if I should have come back. They say places change more than people do. Do you believe that?"

I didn't think people changed at all, but before I could answer, she said, "I lost him here, you know. My husband. Allan. I was pregnant at the time. I know, poor me, blah, blah, blah."

"I'm so sorry," I said, adding the customary platitudes that I didn't fully believe, how horrible life could be, how unfair.

"Why should life be fair?" she scoffed. "Fairness, justice, inalienable right; the inventions of privileged men to justify their status in a brutal world." She glared at me. "Of course, being back here, I see Allan everywhere. After I bought my house in Montes," she went on after a pause, "I hired a man to take everything across the border for me, things I'd had in storage in California. This is everything I own in the world, you understand, and . . . he doesn't show. Three days I wait for him, without a word. I'm sleeping on my hard tile floor without so much as a blanket. When he finally arrives—this idiot I should have known better than to hire, this friend of a friend—I immediately notice the boxes are jumbled together with other people's things, and some of my boxes are missing. And then one of my husband's paintings has a gash in it. There's a hole this big"—she gestured—"clear through it."

"Louise, that's awful."

"He had the nerve to tell me it was like that when he put it in the truck."

"What did you do?"

"I went mad is what I did. For weeks, I was out of my mind, cursing like a crazy woman, wandering the streets. I was going to kill someone."

Something in the way she said it made me think, *She could; she's capable of it.* The thought didn't horrify me. On the contrary, it allied me to her. Through her story, I'd perceived a set of shared beliefs: that life is volatile, and in the end, things are apt to be solved with violence of one kind or another. As much as I had struggled to eradicate this from my life, some unmovable part of me still accepted it as true and viewed anyone who didn't—even Tom and my children—as pitiable or weak.

"The things from that time are so important to me," Louise was saying. "The few I've managed to keep, anyway. Three oil paintings of Allan's, some notebooks he scribbled in, a few pieces of jewelry. One afternoon maybe a month after I arrived, I'm walking past a shop near Independencia, and I see my jacket hanging in the window."

"What do you mean?"

"He'd sold my things. The van driver."

I must have looked incredulous because Louise said angrily, "I worked in fashion for years, in Paris. This jacket was virtually one of a kind. I won't bore you with details. It was an Alaïa, size 32, black with bronze buttons. To see it hanging in a junk shop on the side of the road! The stupid girl didn't even know what she had."

"Did you confront her?"

Louise snorted. "It wasn't worth it. People like that."

I had a sudden reckless desire to find the jacket and buy it back for her, as if to dispel any suggestion that I, too, was a person *like that*.

"Your bracelet is lovely," she said, apropos of nothing.

I smiled, touching the bracelet I'd bought with Tom, the one he'd looped his fingers through, tugging me to our bedroom.

"May I ask where you got it?"

I shrugged. "The Tuesday market, I think?"

"You don't understand, do you?"

It was more a statement than a question. The waiter was approaching with our bill, and for a few breaths, I retreated into the impassiveness of his features. The high cheekbones and flattened nose, the deep wells of his eyes that seemed as if they had witnessed, unblinking, the whole violent panoply of human existence. "*La cuenta*," he quietly announced, setting it onto the table. Louise had turned sideways, her eyes brimmed with tears, and after an indeterminate pause, I heard myself ask if I could pay with a credit card, and the man apologize in his overly formal Spanish, "*Disculpe la molestia.*"

When I laid the fifty-peso note onto the table, Louise did not protest that she'd invited me, or remark on my lie that I didn't have my wallet. "I suppose you think me disgustingly bourgeois," she said, without looking at me. "Only a bracelet, you're thinking, a *thing*. I don't blame you. In any other circumstance . . ." Her voice trailed away.

"I'm sorry, I don't—"

"It was stupid of me to pack it in the moving truck when I could have worn it. A gift from my late husband."

All in a rush, I understood. "Oh my God, this is *yours*? Here, please take it," I said, falling over my words, "it's nothing, I have too many bracelets anyway."

She shook her head, no, she couldn't possibly. But I was already pulling the bracelet from my wrist, reaching it toward her with relief and even joy, releasing a tinkling laugh as I pressed it into her hand, as if to declare I was above desiring such things; I had everything I needed.

"Then I want you to have something in exchange," she said as she fastened the clasp.

"Don't be ridiculous! I'm only glad to be able to give it back to you. But it's so crazy, isn't it? Of all the people to pass through the market, that it would be me who bought it, and then wearing it this morning. It's incredible."

I remember I used that word precisely, then immediately smiled, as if I'd raised the specter of credibility only to signal my indifference to it, the relative unimportance of facts in the forging of deep connections. It was then Louise reached across the table. That was the first contact between us: her lean hands wrapping mine with surprising strength, all angles and bones; the acquiescing softness of my own hands in hers when she repeated:

"I want to give you something in return."

I laughed, tilted my head to my shoulder. *It's nothing.*

She smiled, showing her beautiful white teeth. "I knew from the moment I saw you. I thought, here's one of the good ones. Here's one of my own."

7

Undoubtedly there were a few more words exchanged between us. But in that way memory has of burnishing things to their essence, they are the last: *Here's one of my own.* Her holding my hands in hers, telling me that she wanted to give me something.

At one point, remembering where I first saw her, I had asked if she had a connection to the school. Not at present, she'd said, although she hadn't ruled out the possibility. She might teach English literature to the advanced students, or European history. The only impediment was having to walk to and from school—not that she lived far away, but the afternoon sun was so punishing. "It must be dreadful for you, too," she said with a knowing smile, "walking your little ones all the way up the Cuesta de San José."

I might have asked how she'd guessed I lived in Balcones, and knew I lived off of the Cuesta. Instead, I was self-deprecating:

"I'm embarrassed to admit it, most afternoons I drive."

"Never apologize for yourself. I'd kill for a car."

"Where do you live?"

"Montes de Loreto."

"No!" I said, worrying it had sounded gruff, as if I didn't believe her. Or, worse, that I was horrified by the notion of living in such a place.

She must have taken my surprise for unfamiliarity, because she laughed and said, "Believe me, it's not what *you're* used to. There's basically nothing there. I don't even have a phone."

I was eager to maintain her misperception; it was in Montes, after all, that Tom's development was being built, taking over a neighborhood that had been deemed negligible, a project I was certain she'd disapprove of. I said, "I'd be happy to give you a ride whenever you want."

"Don't be absurd," she said flatly.

"No, really, I'd love to! I love seeing other people's houses. And you could meet my daughter," I added, guessing Louise would be impressed by her. How quickly we offer up our children, without even a thought. I looked at my watch, alarmed at seeing it was nearly noon. "Ah, but I need to go. My son will be getting out soon."

"Go, then—off with you!"

As I was about to leave, on an impulse, I bent down to kiss her cheek. At the last second, she lifted her face to me, my lips glancing her mouth. I tried to pass it off, laughing and kissing the other cheek in the European way before rushing out.

As soon as I reached the sidewalk, I realized I had no idea how to get back. I hurried to a corner, looking helplessly for a landmark. Where was I? I went blindly down another street, as I would in a dream, dazed. At the corner—a miracle—I saw a cab and ran to catch it, breathlessly telling the driver the name of the school.

I was amazed when, after no more than a few turns, we began to speed along a familiar stretch of the Ancha. In relief, I leaned back, the wind picking up, stirring the heat in which people were going about their day beyond my window. Mothers and their young children. A stray dog limping along the side of a high stone wall, ribs jutting. I was intoxicated with belonging, as though I had arrived into a truer version of myself. I even chatted with the driver, my Spanish for once coming easily.

As we were pulling up to the school, I found a pen and a scrap of paper in my purse, scribbling *ALLAN NIEMAN* and, in smaller letters beneath that, *Fernando Navarro*. Then I handed the driver two twenty-peso notes, refusing any change even though the set fare anywhere in town was only thirty, brimming with confidence as I crossed the street to the courtyard. The children were just being brought out, all of them holding hands. Two tidy rows. Some—the ones who had been especially good, all of them girls—had little gold stars stuck to their foreheads.

When Henry reached me, I hugged him and kissed him, overjoyed.

"Why are you so happy?" he said.

I laughed. "How would you like to have lunch in the market?"

We went to the counter where I had only ever seen Mexican families sit, drinking mango *licuados* out of plastic bags tied around thick paper straws. When he'd finished, I walked him to the butcher's, the only shopkeeper I knew by name, so that he could see how handsome my son was and read the name of the town's best school on his uniform.

"Impossible, you cannot be old enough to be the mother of this young man," he said, rising from the desk where he always sat, rumpling Henry's hair. "*¿Quieres un chocolate, Henry? ¿Un caramelo?*" He took the sweets from the drawer. "Ah, but I see it now, he resembles you," he said, using the same phrase the waiter had used with Louise. "*Sí, en los ojos.*" Lifting a finger, he recited a little rhyming couplet: "*Más lejos ven los sesos que los ojos.*" The eye sees, but the mind sees farther. "Her Spanish lesson for the day," he told Henry, crossing his arms over the brightly colored sweater he always wore regardless of the weather. In an earlier life, he had taught English literature at a university in Guanajuato. He kept a stack of Great Books on his desk; when the shop wasn't busy, he would read over the phone to his wife. "You must help your mother remember," he said in Spanish, Henry nodding solemnly.

"Isn't José Luis nice?" I prompted him as soon as we'd left. "Don't you love it here?" I wanted him to confirm my feelings, that way we crave to hear our opinions in the mouths of our children. Yes, he said. He asked to visit the stall where they sold *luchadora* masks. This time, I didn't just let him look but bought him one, and a blue cape. We went to the library to wait for Ida to be done, to the outdoor pavilion where the old men sat all day playing chess. Henry danced around the fountain, kicking his feet high into the air, uttering Spanish phrases he'd learned from television, making the old men laugh.

It was only after we'd collected Ida and were halfway up the Cuesta that I remembered the groceries. For the remainder of the walk, I was plagued by thoughts of what María had done when I didn't come home; had she worried, been angry? Already our lives had become inseparable. From the trash we discarded, the bedsheets, the air itself, María knew when I had my period, when Tom and I had made love, when we were fighting. On a shelf in the laundry room, she kept broken toys we'd thrown away, wrinkled magazines, even torn underwear.

But when we arrived home, the comida was set out like always, and she was perfectly equable, without a hint of bitterness, saying only: "*Qué bueno que ya llegaron.*"

This, too, stoked my sense of belonging, the particular freedom of knowing your place within an established order. Still, I apologized: "*Lo siento, María. Discúlpame.*"

She shook her head in embarrassment. "*Ay, no. No hay problema, señora. Es una comida americana para los niños.*"

Ida and Henry looked at each other in surprise—an American meal? As soon as she had gone back to the kitchen, they began peeking under the lids at the strange assortment. Leftover green beans, zucchini with white cheese melted over it, two hard-boiled eggs cut into quarters. The main dish was spaghetti, coated in a textureless red sauce. Henry was the first to taste it. "It's good," he proclaimed. Ida took a minuscule forkful and narrowed her eyes in deliberation. "It's ketchup," she said. She waved her hand, saying in her actress voice, "Waiter, I'll have the pasta with ketchup sauce, and make it snappy." We all laughed, but they gobbled it up.

After the meal, we played a game in the courtyard, pretending to be characters from a favorite picture book, elaborating the story until it started to grow dark. Then I bathed them, drawing pictures in the suds on their backs; I let them eat cereal in their pajamas on the couch, watching a dumb Hollywood movie on television. It made us laugh, seeing the well-known faces open their mouths and Spanish come out. I had to admit, certain things were easier without Tom. I could do things when they suited me. I could give them my undivided attention, spoil them without reproach.

That night, though, I had trouble settling down to sleep. In the big bed, I kept to my usual side, listening to the faint tinny sounds of the mariachi bands roaming the Jardín below, the thuds of fireworks that sounded like distant thunder. I turned the light back on and read, page after page, without comprehension. I turned the light back off. I touched myself without real pleasure, only to release something, like voiding the bladder. Still, I couldn't relax. In my agitation, I had begun to recast the morning's events as a series of humiliations: my hackneyed attempts at storytelling, my meek docility in following her, my slowness in understanding about the bracelet. More than anything, I kept returning to Louise saying that she wanted to give me something. From earliest childhood, I had trained myself not to have expectations. *It's life*, I had insisted to myself when frightening things happened, when the boy from our neighborhood threw rocks at me and, one February afternoon, exposed himself, standing above a dirty crust of snow, his sweatpants bunched beneath his hands. *There's only you; nothing lasts; don't let yourself get soft.*

Finally I went upstairs, barefoot though the stone floor was freezing and there were sometimes scorpions. In the kitchen, I found a half-empty bottle of wine. Drinking straight from the bottle, I went to the living room and opened my laptop. The sound of it turning on was soothing. My homepage was the *New York Times*. An article caught my eye, about a woman who had pretended to be a 9/11 victim. There was a picture of her smiling next to Rudolph Giuliani. *She's fat* was my first thought, after which I laughed shrilly into the vaulted stillness. I wanted to confess my reaction to Tom; I could parse such things with him—my internalized self-hatred; the way prejudice persists even, maybe especially, among educated people.

I was about to open my email and write him. Instead, I typed "Allan Nieman painter" into the search bar, disappointed when nothing turned up. I tried various different spellings, different search parameters, all without success. Then again, I didn't know if he was American, the year he'd died, if he was, in fact, well-known; maybe he and Louise had different last names. Appeased by this last thought—of course that must be it!—I typed "Fernando Navarro." This time, my screen filled with images of artwork, a link to a Wikipedia page, a black-and-white photograph of him above a list of biographical information. On the website of a gallery in Mexico City, I found a portal of available work, a series of etchings inspired by a Kafka story with which I was unfamiliar. The first depicted a monkey in a tree, with two hunters aiming guns beneath him. The lower third of the image was a tangle of vines and blooms shaped like Chinese lanterns in which more monkeys were half hidden, screeching in fear or ecstasy. After several minutes, I clicked ahead to the next image. There were seven etchings in all. Farcical, obscene, they depicted monkeys in sailor suits holding phallic exploding champagne bottles; blowing noisemakers; crossing high wires; screaming, fucking, prancing with exposed swollen testicles. They revolted me. I couldn't decide if they were good.

After the second or maybe third time through, I realized I was shivering with cold. Back downstairs, I bundled beneath my covers. I couldn't get warm. Scenes from my childhood assailed me. The gaunt gray-skinned girl who told me she and Leo, the boy who had exposed himself to me, had "done it" in the dumpster. She was only nine and had that look of malnourished children. Her pointed chin, her crooked little teeth when she gloated: "He stuck his thing in me." The filthiness of it filled me. The stacked boxes from the liquor store holding our things. Ants in our cereal boxes. In the mornings, rats scattering from the trash outside. In my exhaustion, these scenes became tangled with the others. Monkeys fucking, screaming.

For hours, I lay unable to stop seeing them, to sleep. Near dawn came the sound of a couple arguing in the Cuesta, or maybe they were laughing. I could hear the woman's voice rise above his, the excitement in it. Then a shattering of glass. A pool of silence. Later the rhythmic clop of hooves over the cobblestones: the mounted policeman making his usual rounds.

The last thing I remember thinking is that when I walked Ida and Henry to school, when we discovered the mounds of horse manure, they would seem wholesome, comfortingly old-fashioned. And then the maids would sweep them away and splash the sidewalks with soapy water, and for a time, everything would smell wonderfully of lavender and masa and baking bread.

8

The morning after my encounter with Louise, I awoke with a surprising sense of energy and purpose. I had a sudden, palpable desire to create—what? Something brimming with beauty and authenticity that I alone was capable of making. What form this might take, I had no idea. Returning home with the groceries, on a whim, I stopped into the dusty *tiendita* near our house and bought a cheap spiral notebook. But Ida, amused by the cover art—a tacky photo of a wet cat climbing out of a cook pot—claimed it before I had even written my name inside.

Since the morning he left, Tom and I had been emailing several times a day. Without articulating the intention either to Tom or myself, I began to focus my creative energies into these notes. Mostly they were about things I'd seen on my walks to and from school that struck me as almost painfully beautiful. Stray dogs and gilded fountains. The clear sky, drained and pure. Rows of painted doors hiding lush courtyards smelling faintly of decay.

More soulless meetings, Tom wrote with characteristic brevity. *Cold already. Wish I was there.*

Incredible light today, I wrote back, playing at adopting his syntax. *Being here is like standing naked against a white wall.* I reread that line in satisfaction several times, though I vaguely suspected it wasn't mine. Maybe I'd read it in a novel, or was it something Louise had said? For a moment, I considered telling Tom about her, then decided not to. There wasn't really anything to tell, and in haste, I typed out a closing: *Miss you*, though I didn't much. I was content in the space our separation afforded, happy crafting and polishing these small compositions.

On Friday morning, we were late again. After Ida didn't appear for breakfast, I had found her at the bathroom mirror lifting her long blond hair above her ears and sticking bobby pins into it at random angles, a fierce expression on her face.

"Ida, it's time to leave for school."

"I can't. I need to make it so my hair looks short."

At first, I was gentle, patient. "I don't think that will work, darling."

"It will if you help me!" she yelled.

We went back and forth. At first, I tried to accommodate her demands, pinning her hair underneath so that it mimicked a bob. But no, she wanted it to look like Justin's, a boy from our block in Minneapolis with short, elaborately feathered hair. I guessed then what this was about. A few weeks before, as we were leaving the courtyard after school, a girl in Ida's grade had suddenly touched my shoulder, saying in heavily accented English that failed to conceal her ridicule, "Miss, is she a girl?"

I felt Ida stiffen beside me. The child's mother reddened, saying loudly, "What are you saying? Of course she is, don't be stupid."

"Then why doesn't she have earrings?" the girl retorted with feigned wonder, after which the mother, glancing anxiously at me and laughing to cover her embarrassment, whisked her away. For days afterward, I waited uneasily for Ida to ask to have her ears pierced. Now I thought: *Rather than belong, she's decided to wage war.* I was tempted to admire her ferocity, even though I knew it would only make trouble for her in the end.

In the mirror, Ida was still twisting her hair into strange shapes, turning her face critically to one side and then the other, and I said lightly, "It simply won't work, my angel. You'd need a haircut."

"Is there time for one this morning?"

"No."

"Why not?" she demanded.

I took a slow breath, trying to master my frustration. In moments like this, I was thankful to have Henry. I thought: *At least one of them won't grow up to despise me.*

Throughout this exchange, María had been passing back and forth along the hallway, carrying stacks of fresh sheets, pausing to comb Henry's unruly hair with her thick fingers, fetching a second white shirt from the laundry room because he'd slightly dirtied the first in the course of breakfast, now kneeling gingerly before him to lift his sweater over his head. "*Señor Haynree, ¿le puedo ayudar?*" Although she spoke no English, I had an irrational panic about being overheard. A preemptive embarrassment that I would have to explain, in my rudimentary Spanish, complex dynamics I felt helpless to define. In the mirror, Ida's mouth had congealed into an ugly scowl. I imagined grabbing her shoulders, shouting at her, *Enough, nobody gives a shit how you look!* In the sudden charge of the moment María's calm felt almost confrontational, her mothering of us all a thing I measured myself against and came up short.

"*¿Todo bien, señora?*"

"*Vamos tarde*," I told her in a tone that, despite my vague resentment, was an appeal—*Help me, do something!*—to which she merely sighed, "*Ay, sí, señora, es verdad*," smiling placidly.

Returning my attention to Ida, I crouched down to her eye level. "Please, we have to go," I begged.

"To get my hair cut?" she said.

With an effort that made my hands shake, I swallowed down my fury, the desperation that only one's children can provoke. I don't even remember how I finally cajoled her into the car, what I promised her in return for going to school. Only bottoming out in the *topes*, the huge bumps that are meant to slow traffic. And Henry, imploring me with a note almost of terror in his voice, "Hurry, Mommy! We're going to be locked out!" Ida looking out the window, saying loudly, "Good, I *want* to be." As we were crossing the narrow bridge, I saw the beat-up pickup truck belonging to Fabiola, the woman who had given us a ride that first day Tom was gone. Briefly our eyes met as we passed one another. Through the windshield I saw her laugh and shake her head, mouthing the work *fuck*.

Then parking badly. Kneeling in the courtyard, exhorting them—"Run! I'll see you soon! Try to have a good day!"—full of pity and love at seeing them scatter across the grass toward their separate classrooms. The headmaster's assistant was already coming in her cheap heels, her huge ring of keys jingling before her. It was as I was standing to leave that I heard the voice behind me.

"Here you are, at last."

Louise, smiling at me when I turned. I'd never seen her here in the morning and wondered, with a quiver of happy unease, if she had come only to find me. Embarrassed, I smoothed my disheveled hair. In the chaos of the morning, I'd not even pulled a comb through it.

"What a nice surprise," I said, stepping through the gate, the assistant closing the door behind me and then pausing as the latch caught, the key turned loudly. I laughed. "It's still incredible to me that in a country where lateness is practically a universal trait, they would lock you out of school. Can you imagine the uproar in the States?"

"Mexicans have an entirely different sense of justice."

"How do you mean?"

"They accept that it doesn't exist."

I laughed more genuinely, at ease now.

Louise was rummaging in her big black bag. "I have something for you," she said.

"But why, what is it?" I said, flustered. She was already handing it to me, wrapped in beautifully understated paper. Or, rather, it was wrapped, I saw, in brown paper that she'd decorated with black line drawings whose significance I quickly understood: two faces, one with eyes closed, the other with eyes open, adrift above a park bench; a peach; a cup and saucer; the irregular ring of the bracelet. It was the sort of thing I might have done for Tom in the early days of our courtship, or for my children, in part because no one had ever done anything like that for me.

"Open it," she said.

It was a plain black leather-bound notebook. Inside the cover, she'd written imperatively, in jagged script: *Get to work.*

I was touched, and not by anything so banal as her encouragement. Encouragement, after all, is cheap. Tom had encouraged me, saying I didn't need to work; I could do whatever made me happy. My mother had, too, if only because that is what mothers tell children, *You can grow up to be anything you want*, even as I trailed behind her like a tiny empty suitcase.

"Louise, I don't know what to say."

"It's nothing."

"No, really. I love it." We had turned and were walking mechanically in the direction of town. "I have the car this morning," I said, suddenly remembering. "I could give you that ride."

"Only I'm going to La Gruta." Seeing my blank expression, "Don't tell me you've never been to the hot springs? But you must, you have to come, I won't take no for an answer."

9

There was a scattering of cars in the dusty graveled lot. At a grayed wooden shack bordered by tall bamboo fencing, we paid and were given a paper ticket. Stepping through the gate was like that moment in *The Wizard of Oz* when the world turns from black-and-white to color. The grass was impossibly green, intersected by damp stone paths. The sound of water was everywhere. In a small shop inside the main entrance—more a stone hut than a shop, selling a few each of nose- and earplugs, plastic sandals, bottled water—I bought a bathing suit. They were not displayed, but sealed in clear plastic and stacked on a shelf, on the edge of which was written, in black lettering, MALE, FEMALE, YOUTH, all sewn from the same navy-blue fabric. The shopkeeper wearily drew down a bag, squinted at me, then replaced it with another. I wondered if she had made them herself.

"*Cincuenta pesos*," she said in a bored voice.

Outside, Louise pointed to an arched doorway with a hand-painted sign beside it that read VESTIDOR. "We'll change in there." The room had a smell of wet stone, a single long bench fashioned roughly out of mesquite wood. Leaning her cane against the wall, Louise asked if I would help her. Her legs got stiff, she explained; it was difficult to bend them.

"Yes, of course."

"The look on your face," Louise laughed.

I quickly lowered my gaze, uneasy, horribly curious. I'd rarely been naked in the presence of another woman. Even as a young girl, before she abandoned me, I had assiduously hidden myself from my mother. Her physical immodesty repelled me, the way she would use the toilet with the door open or walk through the house naked in the morning, her untrimmed pubic hair extending toward her thighs, her hideous birthmark exposed.

"Don't be so terrified, I already have my suit on." She'd undone the clasp and zipper of her slacks. "Just slip them down for me so I can step out."

I crouched beside her. Her hand gripped my shoulder tightly. I'd reflexively turned my face away, and as I slid the pants down, my hands read an unevenness that ought to have been smooth; an inelasticity about her skin that could only be scarring, with hard, raised cords of flesh. She stepped free, first one foot then the other.

"Thanks," she said.

Only as I stood did I see the full extent of the damage. One leg was noticeably shorter than the other, so that her hip bones jutted from her suit at uneven heights. There obviously had been some plastic surgery to repair the skin, now a patchwork intricately crisscrossed with scars.

"One bone came through here," said Louise, indicating a pale oval on her outer thigh several inches long. "And here"—she gestured below her knee. "Here, here"—motioning above her hips and pelvis, which were hidden within her swimsuit, a handsome burgundy one-piece, finally gesturing to her face, the asymmetry of her nose and the bones around her eyes, the scar that rose along her jaw. "I was cracked to bits." What kind of accident could have wrought all of this? I opened my mouth to ask.

"It's not something I like to speak of."

"No, of course," I said quickly. "I'm so sorry."

"What the hell are you doing?" In my nervousness, I had begun to fold Louise's pants. Flushing again hotly, I handed them to her. "Now *you*, slowpoke."

"Gosh, I hope it fits."

"Here, let me do it," she said impatiently, removing the suit from its plastic and then smoothing it against my clothed body, cupping it against my breasts with the disinterest of a seamstress. I tried to hold her gaze and, for a moment, did, saying in a high voice:

"What do you think?"

"It'll do."

We set our belongings on side-by-side lounge chairs near a small tiled pool. There seemed to be few people about. A man dozed across from us, a towel draped over his eyes. Mist rose off the surface of the water. I dipped my feet in. It wasn't as hot as I had anticipated. Louise waded in ahead of me, after perhaps six steps diving in a single swift motion, her head slick as a seal when she surfaced near the mouth of a narrow tunnel.

"Aren't you coming?"

I stroked forward tentatively, as through something slightly viscous. On my lips, a faint salt taste; the minerals, I supposed. Some air had trapped in my suit, making a bubble, and I reached back to release it. In the changing room, I had turned away primly, exposing only my back to her as I hurriedly pulled it on, although it was as much to keep my eyes from dwelling on the mess of Louise's legs. As I neared her now, she turned to face me. The water was over our heads, and I noticed a slight current. I kicked in jerky motions. Louise fluttered her arms and legs, staying afloat with little effort. The water made her more graceful than she could be on land. In the strong sun, the scars at her jaw and hairline were nearly invisible.

"Sally," she said a little scornfully. "No, that name doesn't suit you at all. It's obvious your mother didn't know the first thing about you."

A laugh escaped me. It was the most wonderful thing anyone could say to me.

"I'm glad you came," she said.

"Me, too."

A few beads of sweat clung above her lip like glass. She seemed to me again very beautiful, as she had at the café. For a serene moment, we continued to face one another, smiling, treading water. Then, without warning, she turned and dipped beneath the surface, stroking ahead into the darkened tunnel, and a second later, I followed.

The tunnel was maybe thirty feet long, and hotter than the pool, its whitewashed brick ceiling dripping with condensation. I stared fixedly ahead of me, swimming in mincing little dog strokes toward a small half circle of grayish light that seemed to hover in the darkness. I had only come halfway when Louise dove again and I heard her surface, splashing into the opening beyond the tunnel. A few seconds later, without warning, there was a deafening crash.

"What is that?" I called, unable to keep the panic from my voice. "Louise?"

"The *chorro*," her voice echoed back, blurred within the crashing noise that continued to build, as if an immense wave were funneling toward me. Resisting the urge to retreat, I dove for the first time, pulling myself forward until my hands described a step, another. Rising, my body briefly heavy out of the water, I stepped through an arched doorway, then descended, wading into a round room where small holes in the domed ceiling let in beams of light, filled with steam. Peering through them, I found the source of the noise: a thick gush of water, cascading from a two-foot-wide opening high up on the far, rounded wall. I began to make out figures in the steam; voices. One in particular, a man's voice, rose above the others. *It's Tom*, I thought nonsensically, seeing him stand up and move toward me, his broad chest, the comforting solidity of his features.

It was shallower in this room. Half swimming, half springing from my toes, I fell in line behind Louise and the six or so other people who were queued along the curving wall. There seemed to be an unspoken rule of silence. Taking turns, bathers swam the short distance from the wall to where the chorro battered the surface. People had their own style beneath it. A bald man rose into it from underwater, standing erect, his hands palm down and quaking slightly beneath the force. A squat man stood facing inward with his arms crossed before his chest, letting the chorro pummel him matter-of-factly, like a wearied boxer caught against the ropes. The oldest and seemingly frailest of the women braced her hand at the wall behind and lifted her leg. While the water struck her thigh, she allowed a snaking breast to slip briefly from her swimsuit, before calmly replacing it with the modesty of indifference.

It was as I was watching her that I felt someone brush against my back. I turned to discover the man I'd mistaken for Tom. He smiled guilelessly. I tilted my head; despite my annoyance, an almost shy gesture: *Can I help you?* He began speaking to me just above a whisper. I couldn't make any sense of the Spanish. Yes, he said now as a question, repeating it several times, "*¿Sí? ¿Sí?*" As I stared back my incomprehension, he took hold of my wrist beneath the water with casual authority. Even as I pulled back my wrist, I took care to keep my expression neutral—as if, though his touch disgusted me, I was unwilling to relinquish my attractiveness to him, make myself rude or brittle. He had a look on his face—mischievous and self-satisfied—that I'd seen on Henry when reaching to take a toy that didn't belong to him, gesturing with his chin as he said in thick English, "You come, under the chorro." Slowly he brought a hand to my face and lifted a strand of wet hair from my cheek.

I stiffened, even as a flurry of splashes startled me from my stupor. Louise had inserted herself between us, her hands on the man's chest. "Get away from her," she commanded in her blunt Spanish. "Want to find out what happens to boys like you?"

I waited tensely for him to lash out at her. But he was completely chastened, his face clouding with shame. "I'm sorry, *señora*," he stammered. "Please forgive me."

"*Veté*," she commanded him; go. To my amazement, he did. I watched his retreat, the heavy slap of his limbs and the brimming surface.

"I see I can't leave you alone for a second," Louise laughed. "You'd better stick close to me from now on! Come, it's our turn."

We swam side by side. When we reached the chorro, we stood facing one another, me with my back to the pounding water. The sound was too deafening to speak. With her eyes, Louise directed me to edge back. The force was tremendous; to keep myself from toppling forward, I had to take Louise's lifted hands, interlacing my fingers in hers, Louise leaning her weight into me, my own arms trembling slightly with the effort as, slowly, like a birth in reverse, my head was encased by warmth. Months later, when it had become a regular thing to go to La Gruta with Louise and sometimes with Tom and the children, I watched two young lovers do it the same way. The woman's face was obscured by the water fluting thickly around it. The man held his head slightly back, watching her.

10

These were the first of many things she showed me. The elegant, hidden café; the deafening chorro. In time, she would show me an entire other version of my new home. The orchid garden near my house that could only be reached on foot, winding along a maze of interlocking paths; the seller who arranged whole fish like iridescent sculptures in the back of his truck, having driven all night from the sea; the pop-up market in Independencia. She taught me the history of the region, which during the silver mining boom had been one of the wealthiest places on earth, and of San Miguel de Allende in particular: the Bellas Artes that had once been a convent; the Plaza Civica, which was the town's original center, constructed in 1555. From her, I learned to distinguish between the town's Indigenous people, the Otomí who sold things from baskets on the streets, and the Chichimecas who came to town to attend church. I saw the street where, when she first lived here, the Sanmiguelada, a running of the bulls similar to that in Pamplona, still took place.

It seemed to me then, and still does, that she was genuine in her role of guide and teacher. On those occasions, she devoted herself to me completely, as if she wanted to communicate in a few hours everything she'd learned over the course of a life. She would passionately interpret our surroundings, their import, their relevance to us and to art, gender, politics, social justice—not that she believed in this last notion. Through her, I came to regard even the places and people I already knew quite differently. La Parroquia, the town's most famous church, was an abomination, I saw now, its late-nineteenth-century neo-Gothic pink towers vulgar and entirely out of keeping with the town's austere beauty. Handsomer and more to our taste was the Templo de San Francisco, with its Spanish Baroque facade.

"If you're going to live in this country," she instructed me early on, "you have to know its history. You can't merely enjoy it, the way a child enjoys a candy that's been given to her."

Despite the harshness of that statement, or maybe because of it, I was gratified. I wanted her to see me as a serious person, well educated—even if I didn't always want to do the work to become that person, would rather sit passively beside her and be told.

That first day at the hot springs, perched on the edge of her lawn chair, Louise spoke in urgent tones about water that had been warmed by the earth's core. Wasn't it astonishing, to have bathed in liquid that had traveled nearly four thousand blind miles? She was animated and even gleeful about the man who'd grabbed my wrist. Had I noticed the boyish face, the smooth skin? He'd certainly never been a laborer, never learned a trade, and so lived with the disgrace of not knowing how to make anything with his hands. He was *incapable*; just look how easily she'd disposed of him. "Men are all like that in Catholic countries. Strutting cocks, making a show of their machismo. Deep down, they're cowards. It was exactly the same in Italy."

"You lived in Italy?"

"Yes, in Rome, after my husband died. My daughter and I," she clarified after a slight pause, as if she'd initially held back the fact to spare me; I had a pang of jealousy toward the girl who'd lived in Rome, surrounded by artists and writers. "I've lived a lot of places."

"Is that why you have that accent?"

She laughed warmly. "I have an accent?"

A man in an apron came traipsing over the grass, asking Louise did we lovely ladies require anything? A massage? Drinks? I grew fascinated watching the way they interacted, the man's flirtatiousness despite being thirty years her junior, Louise's complete indifference. "Have you ever had a michelada?" she asked me. Before I could answer or ask what it was, without redirecting her gaze, she said loudly, "We'll take two." It was a drink made with beer and spicy tomato juice, she explained as the man walked away.

"Beer," I said, "you're joking." It was barely ten thirty in the morning.

But when it arrived, I drank thirstily. It was surprisingly refreshing. A woman had claimed a lounge chair across from us, very elegant, fully made up, her chest strewn with gold chains. She began to speak on a cell phone. I caught only pieces of her Spanish. "Listen, I told him, no music," she said. "And then the mariachis, my God!" She gave a shrill laugh, shrieking incomprehensible words. "*¡Las trompetas!*" she cried, repeating it several times as she howled with laughter.

"Rich Mexicans are almost worse than rich Americans," Louise said.

I spread my sweater over my legs, stretching beneath the sun. The waiter returned with a fresh drink, replacing my empty glass. "Did I order this?" I said in English as he padded off, laughing a little sloppily. Maybe it worked that way, I thought; they kept bringing more until you told them to stop. Louise's drink was still half full. She had taken a black-and-silver camera from her bag, two differently sized lenses. She was going to hunt for images, she said.

"Sounds nice," I said drowsily, stretching my legs long, closing my eyes beneath the hot sun.

"You remind me of her. My daughter."

My eyes flickered open. "Do I?"

"You're tired."

"Not really." But I must have been. I fell asleep, only for a few minutes. When I awoke, Louise was smiling down at me curiously, the camera in her hands. "Are you a photographer, then?" I said, remembering her telling me she'd worked in fashion.

"I dabbled." She had begun taking pictures of me. "At the moment, I'm doing a bit of work at a gallery owned by an old friend of mine and Allan's."

I wondered what kind of job it was, but didn't ask. It was off-putting to speak to her through the barrier of her camera. I felt self-conscious, not knowing where to direct my eyes, how to hold my mouth.

"Your face is so clear, like a porcelain doll." It seemed an insult somehow. "You seem—don't take this the wrong way—like someone to whom nothing horrible has ever happened."

"Maybe you just need to get to know me better."

"So, then. Tell me something about yourself."

She was turning the long lens in her fingers—perhaps zooming in closer on my face?—and I leveled my stare at the camera for a moment, then laughed and hid my face in my hands in a playful, almost flirtatious way, as the desolation of my girlhood briefly assailed me.

In the early days with Tom, I had shared certain things about that time. The grief at being taken from my father; the poverty we lived in after the relationship my mother had fled to fell apart; that I'd lived as a young girl believing myself ugly and unwanted; then, as an adolescent, intoxicated by my newly discovered power over men, compulsively engaging in reckless sex. Lying in Tom's cramped bedroom, I was aware there was something calculating in these confessions, that I was using them to hasten in him the very things I'd been deprived of: protection, adoration, concern.

"Tell me a secret," Louise pressed.

"What, am I supposed to tell you about how I lost my virginity at thirteen or something?" I laughed. "Are we bonding now?"

"Really? I'm shocked there was anyone before your husband."

"Anyway, there's nothing to tell."

"So make something up. Love," she said, setting the camera into her lap and raising her voice as if she were about to quote some famous poem, "is one person saying to the other: Tell me a story."

Just like that, we were no longer talking about my story but ours, the burgeoning feeling between us, what were to be its terms. It was one of her great tricks; extracting information was another. Except on this occasion, I didn't give her any.

"I'm too tired to talk," I said.

"One secret and I'll let you sleep."

"Lay off, bitch," I said, immediately aghast at my coarseness. But she threw her head back and laughed with delight, as if my calling her that had announced to the world a new level of intimacy between us.

"So, it's like that," she said, and I laughed in my turn. It was easy again being with her; I didn't have to hide away all my rough edges.

A few minutes later, glancing at my watch lazily, I saw it was nearly time to get Henry.

11

With Henry clambering about in the back like a puppy, we drove her home, navigating the potholes on the Obraje road where I'd first seen her. Louise sat very erect beside me, lapsed into one of her extended silences.

"Why are we going this way?" Henry asked, resting his hand on my shoulder, then bunching my hair into his little fist as he sucked his other thumb.

"We're taking my friend home."

"That lady?"

"Yes, *Louise*."

The small sucking sounds as he considered. "Your hair's wet."

"Is it?" I said in a false voice, rushing to fill the silence as I tend to do when nervous. "Well, it's because I went to the most amazing place. You would love it so much, Henry. It has pools, but—you'll never guess—the water? It's warm like a bath! And there's a tunnel you can swim through, and a huge waterfall. I'll take you there sometime if you want."

"Daddy, too?"

Beside me, Louise made a noise, like she was clearing her throat.

"Of course Daddy will come!" I said in the same emphatic voice.

Some people were trudging along the side of the road. I recognized the young produce seller I frequented, walking beside two young women, his sisters perhaps. As our car overtook them for a moment, our eyes met. I had an urge to look away; probably he wouldn't recognize me anyway. But his face immediately brightened. He waved cheerfully, calling *buenas tardes*. I glanced sideways in gratification, as though I'd proven myself a good person; the vegetable seller knew me! But Louise hadn't even noticed. She was telling me about a restaurant she had owned outside of Rome; about her Italian, which was much better than her Spanish.

"There's my house on the right," she interrupted herself, "across from that empty field."

The building site. I reflexively looked for Tom, though he was, of course, out of town, and the site empty. I pulled onto the shoulder. The house was not nearly as rudimentary as she'd led me to believe. Two full stories, attractive save for the color, a pungent acid green. Beside it, almost touching Louise's, sat a squat house with only a single window and rebar sticking out the top, clearly awaiting the addition of a second floor. On its stoop, two barefoot children of about Henry's age were playing with Tazos, tossing the plastic disks you got out of chips bags.

"There used to be so many colorful houses when I lived here with Allan," Louise sighed. "Now it's all so *tactful*, so tastefully restrained. The whole town's been all but ruined by rich Americans. But isn't that always the problem?"

I made a sound of agreement, surreptitiously glancing across the road. The field was now mostly cleared, and a large fountain that had been built off-site had been installed. There were a few shells of a structures, the smaller units presumably. Other than that, little had changed since our arrival.

"Mommy, can we go to the market and get a *licuado*?"

"How about a nice glass of water at my house?" Louise said.

In the mirror, I caught Henry's expression of mingled irritation and disbelief, as if he had fallen prey to some sleight of hand.

The house was dark after the blinding sun, the rooms separated by wide Moorish archways. Laughter from a television show drifted in from the house next door. I followed Louise from the kitchen area, holding my glass of water. Henry had refused his, fleeing instead to Louise's back patio. He'd stripped off his navy plaid school sweater that was polyester and felt like recycled plastic. Even without it, he must have been unbearably hot; the patio was bald concrete, fully in sun.

"Thanks for the water," I said. "It's just what I needed. I think I'm still a little tipsy."

"Oh, please! I can't stand that I don't have anything else to offer you."

We had stepped into a large open room with a red-tiled floor, its monastic white walls decorated with African tribal masks, a woven basket resembling a hornet's nest, a few abstract paintings in a vivid palette. It had the look of certain ad campaigns you might see in *Vanity Fair*, in which dazed and very beautiful people sprawl over artfully disarranged furniture. In lieu of a couch, a twin bed was wedged into a corner, covered with a sheepskin rug and several embroidered Moroccan pillows. On the other side of the room, an old turntable sat on the floor, several records leaned against the wall beside it. Every surface held interesting objects: a dark green ceramic ashtray, a leather box embossed with faded lettering, a silver lighter. "It's a terrific house," I said, thinking it was the kind of house I wanted to have, the house of someone who's really lived.

"It's hardly the house of my dreams, but for the price I paid! Well, I can tell you, why not? It was seventy-five thousand dollars US. Of course now I don't have enough money for a telephone, much less a maid."

Through the tall doors at the back of the house, glass and wrought iron, I could see Henry playing with an amber-colored chicken. Somehow the vision enthralled me. Henry's brow furrowed in concentration, the top of his head ablaze in sunlight. Some cardboard boxes were arranged against a high wall as a coop, with arched doorways that mimicked the house's cut into their sides.

"I see he's found Bella," Louise said.

"Bella! What an absolutely perfect name; she's the most beautiful chicken I've ever seen. Not that I've seen many." I laughed.

"Smoke?" She had picked up a blue pack of cigarettes from a small octagonal table inlaid with what looked like mother-of-pearl.

"Mm, yes." Putting the cigarette to my lips, I said, "Tom doesn't approve of me smoking," then laughed to conceal my embarrassment.

Louise held the silver lighter forward. "Then it's a pleasure to corrupt you."

"Jesus Christ, that's good." I sighed through a thick cloud of smoke, taking a few steps deeper into the room so Henry wouldn't see me, stopping before an abstract painting hung on the wall. It was a series of stacked geometric shapes on a blue-black plane, although from the uppermost rectangular shape two rudimentary limbs sprouted, like the kind children will draw. "Is this your husband's?"

"Yes," she said, and in unison, we moved a bit closer. There was a signature in the lower right corner. *Pearlman*, it looked like, though the letters were loopy enough that it might have been *Nieman*.

"It's wonderful," I said before I'd really formed an opinion. "It's got an unexpected tenderness, the way this rectangle becomes almost figural? There's something so . . . fragile about it." Louise seemed pleased; I was encouraged. "Fragile, and yet persistent, you know? Even this tone of orange here. It's like the remnant of sun after it's finished setting."

"Ah! I adore the way you speak about his work." She lifted her finger, wiping at her eyes. "It's clear you've studied art."

"Well, my husband did, before he became an architect. He has a wonderful eye."

"*You* have a wonderful eye."

There was a knock at the front door, a woman's voice calling through the window, "*¿Hola, señora? ¿Está en casa?*"

Louise set her mouth in irritation. "My neighbor. Will you excuse me?"

As soon as she had gone, I began to look around, picking up objects and setting them back down: a clay sculpture of a dog; an octagonal leather box; a small paperback book set open on a wooden crate-cum-table, the text in French, its title partly worn away. I went over to the bed with the sheepskin thrown over it and ran my hand over it, letting the deep fibers sift between my fingers. The wall behind was of stacked stone, with a high square window I had assumed opened onto the courtyard, but now realized opened onto another, smaller room through a narrow archway.

I glanced cautiously toward the front door. I could hear the woman's voice, higher than Louise's, more nasal, saying, "Please, *señora*," and Louise answering in her colorless Spanish, "I told you last week I don't have the money. I'll tell you when I do."

They continued this way back and forth, bored and aloof, like students reading out of a book. I quietly stepped inside the hidden room. It wasn't much larger than a walk-in pantry, the bulk of the space taken up by a wooden desk strewn with black-and-white photographs. Street scenes of San Miguel mainly: people lingering in cafés, strolling through the square. I assumed they were old, perhaps from the time Louise first lived here. Lifting one, I was surprised to discover they were contemporary. I picked up another. There was something strange in discovering the familiar stage with all its players, frozen between my hands. The shoeshine man, the toy vendor. One photo, of the Jardín crowded with people, caught my attention for no reason I could discern. I held it closer, examining it. A boy and his dog. Some pigeons. In the upper right corner, a couple was about to step out of the frame. My eye caught on them with that faintly queasy, groping sensation of struggling to awaken after a heavy sleep. The two were holding hands, their backs to the camera, the woman's face turned slightly toward the man. It was nothing about either one of them, but something between them; the angle at which their shoulders leaned together, the blank space between their hips. It was me and Tom.

I dropped the photo as if burned. At the front door, Louise's voice had grown louder. "*Tal vez en el futuro*," she was saying. Then the would-be maid's downtrodden voice, "*Sí, señora. Tenga buen día*," and the door being loudly shut.

I hurried back to the living room, Louise calling ahead to me, "Mexicans! They refuse to believe an American can be poor." She drew up short when she saw me. "What's wrong? You're all flushed."

"Am I? It must be all the sun."

She made as though to put her hand on my forehead. I could see Henry behind her, chasing Bella along the low concrete ledge. Suddenly the bird fluttered upward, Henry falling onto the pavement, beginning to wail. In an instant, I was at the door. There was a moment of confusion, trying to open it.

"These damned Mexican latches," Louise said calmly, limping up behind me. "I can never remember, do I push or pull?"

At last, the door swung open with a whine and I rushed forward, scooping Henry into my arms, blowing on his skinned knee.

As his tears subsided, Henry asked in his little voice, "Does she make eggs?"

I hadn't fully tracked, so it was Louise who answered him, "Not yet, but she will soon. You'll have to come back and hunt for one, you and your sister. If you find her first egg, you can taste it. Would you like that, Henry? To taste an egg right from its shell?"

"Yes." His voice was so trusting and eager that my eyes filled with tears.

"He's tired," I said, turning. "I should get him home."

If Louise noticed my upset, she didn't show it. She followed me to the door, calling happily as we climbed into the car, "There's a big celebration in town tonight. You should take the kids."

12

How reckless the attraction is between people; how fatal. Even now, despite everything she took from me, the Louise who calls to me out of the past, whom I dream of, is still the one who stood in the doorway that afternoon, waving through the sunlight pouring into my car. The Louise holding the bunch of flowers, her handsome smile, her flashing teeth; exhorting me, *Promise you'll come back soon!* And still I catch myself calling back to her, *I will!*

For as soon as I'd reached the car, I'd begun to calm down, telling myself, so what if Louise took our picture? She probably didn't even realize it. It was only a coincidence, another strange point of connection in a town small enough that people inevitably collided. I became magnanimous. I took Henry to the market for his *licuado*. When we picked up Ida and she asked for a treat like Henry had, I said, "How would you like to get *fresas con crema* in the square?" Sensing my generosity, my uncharacteristic decisiveness, Henry asked, "Can we get toys, too?"

Yes! They could have toys! They could have and do whatever they wanted!

They cheered, unable to believe their luck, the three of us hurrying along the narrow sidewalks, gaily jostling into people, laughing. I remember it for its sweetness, the perfect harmony between us. The fact they were still young in that particular way, simple to delight and take delight in. One of those perfect days about which everything retains its vividness. The swept gray cobbled streets closed to traffic, the square packed full with people. The silent, towering scaffolding of fireworks to be lit in celebration of El Grito.

At dusk, I sat on a bench surrounded by the assorted remains of our food—half-drunk apple sodas, roasted corn on wooden sticks, slender *salchichas* with grilled onions and melted orange cheese—while Henry and Ida played with a pack of other children. It pleased me beyond anything to see them in their school uniforms, bouncing the rubber balls with mylar tails I had bought them high into the air. When it was dark, I bought a glass of wine at El Rincón, watching the dueling mariachi bands make their slow circle, occasionally losing sight of the children and then finding them again like a passive game of hide-and-seek, suffused by contentment, a feeling of having been blessed by this place, as if nothing bad could ever happen to us here.

Finally, near midnight, the crowd gathered tightly for the lighting of the *castillo*. There was a noise as it began to catch, a series of sharp reports. An older woman gestured to me, handing me several sheets of a newspaper. "Here, take this," she shouted over the clatter, "like this," showing me how to hold it spread over our heads.

"I'm scared!" Henry screamed with crazed joy as the hot sparks rained down.

"It's like falling stars!" Ida hollered, the sparks thudding the newsprint over our heads.

13

I awoke the next morning to a telephone ringing, María calling to me from the upstairs landing. I must have slept very late. She had already mopped, the house full of the scent of lavender soap.

"*Teléfono, señora.*"

"*Está bien, estoy despierta*," I called back. In my underwear, I hurried down the winding hallway that followed the drop and curve of the hillside to the room Tom used as an office, the old rotary-dial phone. "Hello?" I was slightly out of breath.

"Sally?"

"Tom!" It was only seconds before I realized: It was Saturday, the day of his return. "Oh my God, Tom—"

"I can't believe you forgot."

"No, I—I just overslept." I laughed nervously. "We stayed up late to see the fireworks."

"Oh." He sounded crestfallen, in addition to everything else; Henry was still young enough that he had never seen them before. "Did Henry like it?"

"God, he *loved* it. It was wild, a woman next to us actually caught on fire. Well, her newspaper did, and some men threw beer on it, and they stomped it. Everyone was laughing."

There was a brief silence.

"Tom, I'm so sorry, truly! I could come and get you now—"

"No. It doesn't make sense. I'll get a cab."

"I'll be waiting! I love you!"

I hoped he would say something, but there was only a click; then the phone went dead. I sat for a minute in the cold room, getting my bearings. I could still taste yesterday's cigarette in my mouth, stale and filmy. I brushed my teeth and washed my face. I dressed and went upstairs. María was straightening the living room while Henry and Ida watched cartoons. Seeing me, she paused and asked did I want coffee. I thanked her, saying that Tom would be home in an hour.

Her face lit. "*Qué bueno*," she said, it was good the *señor* was returning home. Shyly, averting my gaze because I had again not brought home groceries the night before, I asked if she could make enchiladas suizas, Tom's favorite meal. "*Sí, señora, claro*, we only need chicken and tomatillos. I can watch the children."

"Thank you," I told her, kissing her on the cheek in relief.

I grabbed my bag, my car keys. In town, I hurried through the few errands I had neglected in Tom's absence. First La Conexión, the service that carried our mail across the border because the Mexican postal service was notoriously slow and corrupt. Despite the thickness of the stack the girl handed me, there was little of interest: a few magazines, some bills that had already been automatically deducted. A postcard from Henry's friend Etta took me a moment to decipher:

I am aksitd for wen you com hom will you spek spanesh?

Her mother, with whom I'd walked along the sidewalk before we left, had written the Texas mailing address Tom and I used, with an ironic cactus in the place of the *T*. I put it into my pocket, thinking I would save it to give to Henry at some moment when he was particularly happy here.

Next I bought the homemade yogurt Tom liked at the *tienda* on Mesones, the chicken from the harshly lit *pollería*. In the covered market, passing the counter where Henry and I had eaten, a wave of nostalgia swept through me—as if those pleasures, those small adventures, were ending with Tom's return. At the produce stand, I chatted briefly with the young seller whom I'd passed on the way to Louise's. "It's a pleasure to see you on the weekend," he said in his urbane way. He really was extremely handsome. I wanted to respond in kind, perhaps inquire about his father, but before I could formulate the sentence, he had turned and picked up something from his stand that looked a little like an artichoke. "A small gift for your son," he said. "It's called *cherimoya*."

The moment was only briefly sullied when, putting the fruit into my bag, my hand brushed the blue bathing suit, still stuffed in my purse and wrapped in sodden paper towels. I didn't want Tom to see it; or María, from whom I could hide nothing. All morning, a vague resentment had been building, a wariness toward Louise. Wasn't it she who had suggested I take the children to the square? If not for her, I wouldn't have forgotten Tom, neglected to bring groceries to María.

Touching the wet suit, I thought, *I can't see her anymore*. It wasn't a considered response. It was an impulse of self-preservation, as if her misfortunes—the crippled leg, the dead husband—had become contagious, a sickness capable of infecting anyone foolish enough to get close to her. There was a large trash bin outside the public restrooms. I walked to it quickly. With my back to the entrance, I disposed of the suit, pressing it deeper with the flat of my palm, burying it.

Stepping from the market moments later, I felt lighter, cleansed. As I made my way back to the car, I practiced the name of the fruit, fixing it in my memory. *Cherimoya, una cherimoya, las cherimoyas*. My lips lifted and fell above the hushed sibilance. In such moments, I felt what I imagined the faithful feel when reciting a prayer.

14

For several weeks, I succeeded in avoiding her, by which I mean we weren't in one another's presence. In other ways, she continued to insinuate herself, sometimes forcefully. One occasion in particular recalls itself. It was a few days after Tom's return. He had finished work early, and we'd gone together to get Ida, leaving Henry at home with María. Because we were enjoying one another's company, rather than wait in the courtyard, we had stopped on the bridge that spans the arroyo, holding hands and chatting. Some younger boys from Henry's class, still in their uniforms, were playing unsupervised along the littered banks. The water was filled at that time with slender red snakes, and the boys were poking sticks into the filthy water in the hopes of impaling one. Tom and I began musing about the savagery of little boys and the indulgence of Mexican parents; how different it was from our milieu at home, where playing at violence, and especially using a toy weapon of any kind, was not widely permitted. They were serious topics, but we were being lighthearted, caught up in the ease of being together, the shorthand way we could speak to one another. Tom had just begun an anecdote meant to illustrate the absurdity of extreme political correctness, something he'd read in the *New York Times*, when I saw Louise walking toward us on the pedestrian path beside the arroyo that led from the shops and galleries at the Fábrica Aurora.

My first reaction was panic, as though a dark secret of mine were about to come out. *She's looking for me*, I thought, my heart quickening. Just as quickly, I tried to dissuade myself. *She said she works in a gallery; she's only heading home from work*. I had instinctively moved behind Tom, reaching my arms around him in a hug from which I peered, tilting my head slightly, still watching Louise.

"Someone's very cuddly today," Tom said with a laugh.

It was then I noticed the man in the pale linen suit following her. He might have created the gentle impression of rumpled dignity but for the fact his fists were clenched and the determined way he stared at the back of Louise's head, his jaw set in anger. With a sudden lunging step, he grabbed her arm and roughly jerked it back. She teetered. Her cane swung up, still gripped in her hand. For a moment, I stood dumbstruck as she spun to face him. They were a similar height, so I was unable to see her expression or his, only the back of her head, the sleek silver hair. In my alarm, I had disengaged from Tom and stepped forward, about to yell. Somehow no one else seemed to notice or be concerned—women carrying their young children, couples, shopkeepers heading home for comida, even Tom. I could tell they were arguing now, and the reason for people's indifference was the familiarity between them. There was an unmistakable intimacy to the way they fought, grabbing one another's shoulders, gesticulating. As if that realization had punctured the deadlock between them, to my astonishment, they began to kiss. Not the chaste kiss of two old people. Louise clasped his hair in her fist while the man gripped her wrist roughly as if to tug it away or thrust it deeper. His other hand cupped her ass, pulling her tightly against him.

Adding to my shock, almost at the same moment, one of the boys withdrew his stick with a shriek of triumph, and I saw pierced on the sharp end a slender red snake. He jerked it at the other boys, who shoved and punched one another in that way boys express both solidarity and ridicule, the delicate creature writhing in anguish.

The bell had finally rung, the usual pandemonium erupting. The mother of the boy with the snake called to him, "*¡Fernando! Ven acá.*" I was struck by the mildness with which she spoke, showing no care for the animal or her son's cruelty, repeating her entreaty with the same gentle indifference, "*Ven, mi amor.*"

The other boys began to clamor at once—"Give it to me!" "No, me!" "Fernando!"—as, with a malicious grin, the boy casually flung the stick, still piercing the snake, into the filthy water.

They weren't kissing any longer. Louise wore a strange smile, the bracelet catching the light as she lifted her hand to wipe her lips. I didn't wait for her to spot me, but hurried to the school courtyard and, seeing Ida—alone as always—motioned impatiently for her to come.

"We're in a hurry," I called in Spanish to the teacher's aide whose job it was to wait with them, smiling to mitigate what would surely be perceived as rudeness, saying, "*Discúlpeme, perdón.*" I'd left Tom on the bridge, and as Ida and I neared, I nodded to him tensely, *Let's go.*

"What is it?" he said, scanning my face.

"Nothing. I don't feel well."

He made a quizzical face, drawing his eyebrows together. "And this just came on?"

"Obviously."

"Mommy, walk slower," Ida said. "My books are heavy."

"Hand them to me," I snapped.

"Why are you being like this?" she demanded.

"Like what?" I laughed in an attempt to make light of my impatience.

Yet even in the car, as Tom chatted with her, as we neared our beautiful house where our beautiful meal was waiting, I couldn't shake my agitation. My reaction was strange. I didn't feel embarrassment at the sight of two old people arguing and then kissing passionately on a public path, but repulsion, even rage, as though the whole disgusting spectacle had been orchestrated to ruin my time with Tom. A memory dislodged itself. I must have been about Henry's age. My mother had taken me to a small cabin, somewhere far from our apartment. A man answered the door, much younger than she was. He seemed embarrassed by my presence, my small hand touching my mother's leg, but she offered no acknowledgment of his discomfort or mine. She didn't alter the smile she had fixed in the car mirror moments before, fluffing her hair with her fingertips. "She's very good at amusing herself," she told the man as she pushed my hand away, saying, "Look, Sally! There are books over there." Then I was alone in a room with books with no pictures in them. My coat still on. A rug covered in cat hair but no cat. There was a small instrument with metal tines you could pluck with your thumbs. Loud sounds had begun behind the door, low moans. Another child that age would have been frightened, but I knew by then what adults did; that even though it sounded as if she was in pain, my mother would be smiling when she opened the door. And so I sat mutely holding the instrument and occasionally plucking it as the cabin filled with the animal smell of their acts.

In the car, Tom was wondering aloud what María had made for comida. Ida was staring out the window. As we neared the top of the hill, I suddenly laughed. It was an unpleasant sound, unnatural.

"What is it?" Tom said.

"Oh, nothing," I said. "Just, women are such cunts."

I had delivered the sentence with forced lightness, as though making a joke. Tom shot me a disapproving look, nodded tersely at Ida, though she was still staring fixedly out the window and appeared not to have heard. "That's a pretty messed-up thing to say," he said.

"Oh, and you're so perfect?" I shot back. "You're so fucking beyond reproach?"

"Jesus, Sally, do you even hear yourself?"

"I'm sorry," I said, my voice catching, my throat filling with a kind of horror. It was as if someone had jerked back the veil covering my life.

"Sorry, Tom," I repeated. And I kept saying it, "I'm sorry, I'm sorry," like someone frantically rubbing a pencil back and forth to cover the obscene word they'd written, tearing at the paper beneath.

All the while, in the back of my mind, the belief persisted. I'd carried it with me as long as I could remember, in my chest, my slender limbs, my fingertips when they caressed my husband: the cuntishness of women. Not men who kill defenseless animals, who assault women on paths and fuck them in front of their children, but women. Women who entice, allow; who smile at their power when it's done.

15

After my lapse in the car, I redoubled my efforts to be a perfect wife and mother. I asked María to prepare all Tom's favorite meals: enchiladas suizas, chicken with mole sauce. Every evening, I read stories to the children, talking with them about what we read without impatience. I made sure they were tucked in bed on time so that Tom and I could share a drink on the couch watching soccer, or on the terrace while I listened attentively to his concerns about the project, reassuring him. I still had an amorphous desire to create something—especially now we were no longer exchanging daily emails—but I kept it to myself. I didn't explore that desire with Tom, as I would have when we were first together, when we would stay up all night discovering one another, when sharing ideas and aspirations was an act of seduction, a prelude to sex. Instead, I offered an emptied version of myself, as marriage and then motherhood had taught me to do. I made myself a well into which he tossed the coins of his own thoughts and desires, first tentatively and then more confidently, hearing the echo of his voice as I receded, smiling my encouragement while silently resenting him.

Still, I wanted to feel close to him. One day, when Tom had been back a little over two weeks, I convinced him to skip work to have a special date with me while the children were at school. He was resistant at first. In his overly methodical mind, dates were things that occurred in the evening;

plus, we only had a few hours before Henry finished school, and with María milling about, there were constraints on our intimacy at home. But I was determined to make it special. I had gotten it into my head to take him to the hidden café Louise had shown me. Surely I'd be able to find it if we went by foot from the Jardín. Then we would stumble upon it as if by chance.

As soon as I returned from dropping the children, I ran downstairs and carefully did my makeup, my hair, put on perfume. I chose a dress I knew Tom liked—a vintage wrap in a green-and-white print—even though the morning was much too cold for it.

"You look pretty," he said when I appeared in the living room.

"Really?" I said, smiling with feigned surprise, greedy for him to say more. I was stunning; I was fascinating. Instead, after a longish pause, he said:

"You know what would look great with that dress? The silver bracelet."

"Which bracelet?" I said, pretending not to understand.

"The one we got at the market. I love that bracelet. Haven't seen you wear it in a while."

"Oh, that. You'll never believe it, but I misplaced it somehow, and now I have no idea where it is."

"When?" he said, a look of concern knitting up his eyebrows.

"I don't know, a week ago maybe?" I let my eyes trail away as if I was trying to remember.

"But you've looked for it," he said, adding in an undertone, "You don't think Antonio . . . ?"

"God, Tom—no!" Antonio was María's brother. Twice a month, he served as gardener to the many potted plants scattered around our courtyard. "How could you think that?"

"You're right, you're right," he said, chastened. I had crossed the room, my back to him. As I stood surveying the town, first south and then, like a slow panning shot, to the north toward Montes de Loreto, I suddenly heard myself say:

"I met someone interesting when you were gone." In the window's reflection, I saw Tom glance up sharply. "A woman," I added, as if to diminish any significance the person might have in my life now or in the future—*it's only a woman.* Sensing him relax, I added, "She's a bit older than us, around sixty."

"A bit!" He laughed. "And you met her how?"

"Just sitting in the main plaza. I'd noticed her before, though, at the school."

"She's Mexican, then?"

"No, American. You may have seen her, too, I think. She's tall, with swept-back silver hair, and she wears these oversized men's oxford shirts." He shook his head. For some reason, I became defensive. "She's super beautiful, actually. She looks like that Italian actress."

He creased his face into an ugly mask of bafflement. "Who? Doesn't sound like anyone I remember seeing?"

"Well, she remembers *you.* She said we seemed in love."

"What a weird thing to say."

"Only if it weren't true."

"And she's lived here how long?"

"A few months. But she lived here before, I guess, when she was younger, with her husband."

"And you say she just approached you in the Jardín? Seems odd."

"Everything's odd to you, Tom. It's frankly a little boring."

"Yeah, but why did she just come up to you out of the blue?" he persisted, ignoring my insult.

"It could be a million things," I said, finally losing patience altogether. "She liked the look of me, I don't know! She thought we could be friends. Tell me, Tom, enlighten me, why did *you* first talk to me?"

He smiled at me tolerantly. He always did that, became ever calmer as I lost control, which was its own form of punishment. "Speaking of which . . ." He glanced exaggeratedly at his watch.

Stepping from the house a few moments later, I thought furiously that this was how he engaged with the world, with niggling questions and facts, steadily wringing all the mystery out of life. Of course, by the time we reached the square, it was too late to find the secret café. So we made do with El Rincón, the large restaurant on the north corner that Louise had said was only for tourists. The same waiter was there, in his shiny pointed shoes. We sat outside overlooking the Jardín, everything exactly as it had been the morning I met Louise: the shoeshine man, the newspaperman. Seeing the scrawny kids with their box of Chiclets surround a woman toting groceries, I laughed.

"What?"

"No, nothing."

Tom looked at me expectantly, but I didn't elaborate. "Well," he finally said, "it's nice to be back."

"I know; the children are so happy."

It was nasty of me, an invitation to fight. True to our pattern, he maintained his good manners, and I took it as a slight: He was instructing me, with paternalistic detachment, in the proper way to behave. We exchanged a few more remarks. How quickly the day was warming, the things we needed to buy in the market. Mostly we ate the mediocre food in silence, biding our time before leaving to pick up Henry. The whole while I kept looking expectantly across the street at the park bench, thinking I might see Louise there.

16

It's true: I hoped to find her. I hoped for proof of our connection, that my longing would compel her to appear, secured at the end of my glance, even if I turned away, remaining at the table with my husband. That afternoon of looking for her in the park seems to me now a fulcrum. One of those nearly imperceptible turning points, on the other side of which were formless days in her company, mornings scribbling in the black notebook, arguing with her, joking with her, lying on the bed in the living room sharing secrets, or hiding them. For, the very next day when I came to pick up Ida, dashing through the gate because the bell had already rung, there she was, standing in front of the stone bench where several mothers still sat waiting for their children.

"Louise? What are you doing here?"

"Nice to see you, too," she said with a smoky laugh, as if there was never a question that eventually everything would resume between us. She looked me up and down. "I love those jeans, by the way. The cut of them. You look terribly chic."

Mindlessly I returned the compliment. She was wearing one of her tailored shirts with a pair of high-waisted menswear slacks, her hair gelled wetly back. I couldn't stop myself glancing around to see if people were noticing my speaking to her, certain we were breaking some sort of rule by Louise being inside the gate.

"The look on your face," she laughed. "Don't worry. I'm not here for your lovely self."

I ejected a little snort, *As if I would think such a thing*, at the same time doubting her; what else would she be here for? But a few seconds later, Adriana, the daughter of Fabiola, who had given us the ride, came sauntering up to Louise. Since then, I'd bumped into Fabiola once or twice, in the morning. She always greeted me by name, the only mother to do so, kissing me on the cheek. It pleased me, even though I sensed she was looked down on by the others, a single parent who worked.

Louise was speaking briskly to the little girl: Did she have everything? Was this her only bag? The girl nodding, saying, "*Sí, sí, es todo.*" I was amused by the way the two of them interacted—in this context especially, where most of the mothers doted on their children as though they were prized dolls, shiny emblems of their wealth and success. Between Louise and Adriana, it was more like haggling over a price at the market, the way the girl announced in Spanish, "We'll go now," and Louise countered, "Two more minutes," Adriana responding that she was hungry and Louise saying briskly that was too bad, she didn't have any food. "But where are your manners, Adriana? Say hello to my friend."

"*Hola, señora,*" she said in a defeated way. To children, adults are either an impediment or a tool for the attainment of their wants and needs. I glanced into Louise's face, turned toward the tiled corridor where children were still streaming from the classrooms. I still didn't understand what she wanted, why she'd insisted on lingering, beyond the obvious of asserting the upper hand with the girl. Certainly she could be petty like that.

I got my answer a moment later. She lifted up her chin, her face rearranging in recognition. Following her gaze, I saw Ida striding slowly toward us, something majestic and apart about her, like a cat stepping slowly through a field of pigeons.

"Ida, how lovely to see you," Louise said to my surprise, as if they'd already met, she'd known my daughter all her life.

To my even greater surprise, Ida accepted the intimacy. Ida, who was so contained, so deliberate, smiling, saying, "It's very nice to see you as well."

The two of them regarded each other steadily.

Mostly to break the strange charge of the moment, I said to Louise, "I didn't realize you and Fabiola knew each other."

Louise nodded; they worked together at the Fábrica Aurora. Of course, I thought, remembering how Fabiola had said she was curious about me, wondering if Louise had mentioned me to her? But no, that was impossible. Louise and I hadn't yet met. "Actually," Louise said, still looking at Ida, "we're heading back there now; would you like to come?"

Immediately Ida began to beg me. "Please, Mommy, can I go with them?" Not, I noted, *Can I play with Adriana?* Clearly it had nothing to do with the girl, who was looking around impatiently and kicking her brown school shoe at the ground.

"I don't know, my love. Louise has work."

"Nonsense, I'd be happy to take her. Why don't you come, too? Oh, but your husband must be back in town," she said with an air of regret, adding, "How is it I've not met him?"

"You'll have to come to comida someday."

"That would be marvelous. When?"

Thus, I found myself proposing dates, going back and forth a few times before settling on the Saturday after next. "In the meantime," Louise said, "you have to come to my house for drinks. I'm having a few friends over this Friday." Seeing my hesitation, she added, "Bring Tom, if you like." I made a show of being uncertain we were free, although we had no plans. "I'll be terribly upset if you don't come. Eight o'clock?"

Ida wanted to come, too, Louise saying yes at the very moment I said no, it wasn't really for kids. Fixing Ida in her gaze, Louise mockingly repeated that moniker. "*Kids*," she scoffed, Ida beaming back at her.

17

On Friday, after I'd gotten the children to bed, I showered and carefully dried my hair. I tried on various outfits, a dress, jeans. I put my hair up, took it down, messed it with my fingers so that it wouldn't look like I was trying too hard. When I finally went upstairs, Tom, seeing me dressed, said, "What's all this?"

"It's just, there's this party tonight. A woman from school invited me. I thought I might go. I don't know."

"No, you *should*," he said definitively, refocusing his attention on the television, where the last minutes of a soccer game were playing out.

"I wish I'd remembered earlier and we'd gotten a babysitter so you could come, too."

"No, I think it's great you're making friends," he said.

I was strangely nervous as I pulled up, seeing the cars parked on the verge, the house illuminated. For several minutes, I stood on the stoop beneath the dome of stars, filling my lungs with cold air and considering turning back. I could hear the sounds of voices, music, raucous laughter. At last, I knocked. The door opened. She was standing before me.

"You made it!"

"Yes. Hello."

"But look at you." She held me at arm's length, assessing me. A small gray dog was yelping and circling around us. "I just adore what you're wearing."

"Oh, come on!" I said, smiling. I had on jeans and one of Tom's oxford shirts with the sleeves rolled up, the buttons opened low to reveal several thin gold chains of varying lengths, one with a charm of a crown that I'd found it in a junk shop in Back Bay the last time I visited my father, but always said had belonged to my grandmother.

Louise lifted it in her fingers and let it fall back. "You're perfect. My perfect Mia."

I made a show of my confusion at the name, like someone who has longed to be proposed to performing her surprise when it comes to pass.

"Suits you so much better, don't you think? Come then, my lovely Mia—come meet everyone."

As we made our way into the room, progressing slowly because of her cane, I had that feeling of making a good entrance. I was aware of people turning to see me, smiling. Flamenco music played from the turntable, a woman's voice singing roughly. The dog was still frenetically yipping at our feet, and Louise kept commanding it to be still, to hush, which had no effect whatsoever. I noticed a small, motionless form on the bed-cum-sofa. Adriana, sleeping peacefully in that way only children can, briefly inured to the commotion around them. It took me a moment to locate Fabiola. She was huddled in a corner of the dining area, caught in a tense exchange with a beautiful woman.

"A lovers' spat," said Louise. She had begun introducing me around in Spanish. Hector, her boss; Hector's son, Pedro; a painter with a sullen look and bangs that hung over her eyes. "Pleased to meet you," I said in Spanish over and over, sounding demure and faintly apologetic, as I always did when speaking a foreign language. I kept lifting and lowering my eyes, laughing at hearing myself called Mia. Louise asked Pedro if he could take my coat and he came behind me and drew it slowly from my shoulders, letting his hand trail clear down to my wrists. He looked to be about my age, maybe a little younger. Handsome in a sort of grizzled way, very different from Tom. The beautiful woman had come over, inducing a fresh round of barks and circles from the dog, as Louise introduced us in English: "Carmen, this is Mia. Mia knows Fabiola from school."

My gaze darted to Fabiola, smoking on the bald patio where Henry had fallen. "Yes, she was kind enough to give us a ride one morning when we were running late."

Carmen stared at me frostily. "Oh?"

"Wine?" Louise asked. "Red, white?"

"Red, please."

As she hobbled away, I bent down to pet the little dog. Its fur was inexpertly cut, pink skin showing through in patches. I stroked its small head, aware of not wanting to do anything to ruin the good impression I'd made, taking refuge in the little animal the way I often did in my children or the telegraphing of attraction between Tom and me. At the periphery of my vision, I could see Pedro smiling as he stared. I offered my hand for the dog to lick, trying to coax it closer, observing myself as if I were someone else: the leanness of my arm and wrist, the flowery scent of my perfume.

"*¡Este perro!*" Carmen said.

"*¿Es tuyo?*" I asked. Is it yours?

"Please!" she said, switching back to English. "I hate dogs, they're filthy. It's Louise's." She cast her a black look. Louise was arriving with the wine, an enormous bowl-shaped goblet filled nearly to the rim.

"I didn't know you had a dog," I said, taking a sip to keep from spilling it.

"I only found him this morning, shivering in the field across the street. He must have been clipped by a car, his hair was all matted and covered in blood, look." She pointed to a red line on his side, about two inches long. "But isn't he handsome after the haircut I gave him? And the best thing, he fits into my bag. It's how I carried him home."

"*Su bolsa*, my God," Carmen exclaimed in a scandalized voice. "Mexican dogs are filthy, you know this! They live on the streets *como las ratas*."

"But rats are utterly marvelous," Louise said, launching into a meandering story about a society of rats that lived in the walls of the gallery she once owned in Italy. When the walls had to be opened to repair some old wiring, they had discovered a trove of jewelry. It was the rats', amassed during the previous decade when the space was a pawnshop. "Mind you, this wasn't just some haphazard jumble but a curated collection." Louise lifted her fine chin, glancing slowly from me to Carmen. "They were terribly discerning, these rats. They had an eye for the best pieces."

I stared at her. I couldn't tell if she was joking. Pedro had stepped beside me, making the rounds with the bottles, one in each hand. "More wine?" I reached out my glass.

Louise was still extolling the Italian rats; somehow the tale had become a disquisition on fascism and socialism, Louise favorably comparing the societies of rats to humans. But my attention kept wandering to Hector. I found him terribly attractive, even more than his son. His intensity drew me, and the calm way he returned my gaze. Suddenly noticing we were looking at one another, Louise interrupted herself, saying to Hector, "She's not just beautiful, you know."

"Oh?" He smiled at me expectantly, stepping closer, as Louise related my remarks about Allen's paintings, how I'd spoken about them with so much eloquence and insight, she'd actually cried. She pulled her face into a cartoon of sorrow now, bawled exaggeratedly so that everyone near us laughed, after which she said, "She really should do the notes for our next show, though. Simply marvelous writer."

"Truly—a writer?" Hector shot me another expectant look, stirring me with a sudden anxiety. But just then Louise called out gaily, Fabiola was going to sing. I turned to see Fabiola standing inside the patio, her thick hair a bit disheveled. "No, please, I can't," she said, frowning and tilting her head in a show of modesty. Louise began to clap, the slow heavy claps that are meant to coax people, everyone joining her. "All right, all right," Fabiola finally relented. I felt a preemptive embarrassment for her, watching her step to the far wall. Pedro had gone to turn off the record player as Fabiola turned to us, closing her eyes in preparation.

There was an excruciating moment of silence. Then, at last, she began a meandering melody that, after my initial tense fear, I realized was rendered with real artistry, throatily and with a kind of private passion, as though we were watching someone undress without self-consciousness. It was arresting and painfully beautiful, and everyone seemed to find it so; all of us listened beyond mere politeness, with the rapt attention of people being given something vitally important. When she finished, we erupted in wild applause. Instinctively I looked to Adriana, worried that the noise might have awakened her. But she remained heavily asleep, ignorant of her mother's triumph.

"That was amazing," I said to Hector. "I hadn't ever heard her sing."

"Yes, she sings with great honesty, *y con pasión*." He smiled to himself. "It's been said artists are people with burning questions of the world. So tell me, Mia, what are yours?"

The question was so pretentious, I almost laughed. And I had the sudden impulse to puncture the lie I'd been caught within; tell him my name wasn't Mia, that this was all a joke Louise had concocted. But to my surprise, I began telling him a story about an American girl on vacation in Mexico and the daughter of the gardener where she stays. Alone in the walled garden, surrounded by drab everyday poverty, each night, the girls share their deepest secrets and fall in love. The story arrived without effort, stark sentences stacking easily, one on top of another. I drew from my own life, Louise and Nuria, the Navarro prints when I described a scene in which the girls sneak past a row of Federales standing with rifles at the edge of a field, and later kiss, hidden among the tall grass. In the climactic scene, the Mexican girl whispers into the dark whorl of the other's ear the words she has unknowingly longed for: *Forget where you came from. Love is two people telling each other a story.*

By the time I'd finished, I was flushed, hot with joy. Somehow I had managed to become quite drunk. Across the room, Louise was speaking with Pedro and Carmen about the building site, "some crass US developer erecting another monument to capitalism. Meanwhile, every night, local couples go there to find something of true value, these poor Catholics stealing a hasty fuck. I've named it the Ardor Sanctuary."

I looked at Hector conspiratorially—*Louise, what a character!* He nodded and took my hand with formality, saying he'd very much like to see my story; would I send him a copy? I muttered something about it being in its infancy. "Whenever you're ready. I know a great many publishers."

"Oh," I said stupidly. "I mean, thank you, that's so kind. Would you excuse me?"

I hurried upstairs. In the bathroom, I rummaged through the cabinet, opening a lipstick and dabbing some onto my lips with my finger, liking the color. I looked at the brand. It was only a cheap drugstore brand, which somehow made it better. I found my coat in a heap on top of Louise's bed. For a few minutes, I lay on top of it and closed my eyes, hearing the swells of laughter from downstairs, thinking vaguely that I should go home.

"You can't leave," Louise loudly asserted when I came downstairs in my coat. A staggered chorus went up, echoing that I should stay; they were gathering blankets and flashlights, about to go across the street to the "Ardor Sanctuary." A palpably different energy had come into the room, one of reckless interrogation, as if they were about to thrust a torch into the deep recesses of a forgotten cave. Only Carmen seemed to have remained cool. "By all means, come," she said, sealing her mouth into a tight, thin line.

Putting his arm around me, Pedro said, "Shall we share a blanket?"

"Stop harassing her," Fabiola said, laughing hoarsely, shooing him away. Bending to my ear, she whispered, "So, you're Mia now? It suits you. I saw that photo of you, you know. It was amazing." She drew away, smiling and bunching her lips together. "Very, very sexy."

I laughed sloppily. "I don't know what you're talking about. It wasn't me."

"Yes, you, definitely. Your mother showed it to me."

My mother? I was too stunned to respond—or was it the shock of being confronted with my own complicity, my longing? In the moment, I merely stared at her, her mouth from which the song had emanated, allowing awareness to overtake me slowly in a strange mixture of horror and pleasure: *They all think that; they take me for Louise's daughter.*

When Fabiola turned away, saying something in rapid Spanish to which everyone erupted in laughter, I slipped out the door.

18

That was the night I was awakened by a horrifying wail, almost inhuman. Ida or Henry, I thought frantically; which one? My mind conjured bones jutting from skin, pools of blood. Another shattering cry: "Mommy!" Not Henry. Ida, calling to me from the hallway. I'd pulled the covers off, heart thudding, cold floor against my feet.

"Mommy, help!"

"What's happening?" Tom murmured, surfacing.

"It's Ida." She had gone silent; I called hoarsely to her, "I'm coming; stay where you are." I found her frozen at the foot of three shallow steps, halfway to her bedroom. Crouching, I began running my hands over her. There didn't seem to be any blood, but she was shivering. "It's okay," I soothed, "you're all right."

Very slowly, she shook her head, no. Pointing, "Look."

I stiffened. On the step behind me, the one I had just walked on with my bare feet, was a small white scorpion, its tail lifted. "Ida, stay still."

She nodded, her eyes white orbs of panic.

"It didn't sting you, did it?"

She began to cry again, to scream in fury, "No! You're the mother! Do something!"

"Don't speak to her that way," came Tom's disembodied voice from the bedroom.

"What will happen to me?" Ida panted, ignoring him.

"Nothing. We just need to stay calm."

"But what if it stings me?" she demanded. "Will I die?"

"You'll be fine," I told her.

"Don't lie to me!"

"I would never lie to you; come, come, my angel, put your arms around me."

She whimpered but did as I said, and I struggled up to my feet, clutching her tightly as I turned toward my room. To calm myself, I continued to speak into her ear, "We're fine, it won't get us, we're safe," dumbly lifting a bare foot onto the first step, the second, like a person just thawed from ice, awkward and bewildered, Ida's ungainly limbs overspilling my arms as I shuffled ahead, her sharp chin pressing my shoulder, her cold hard feet little muscled fish striking my knees. At the bedroom door, I barked, "Tom, get up."

"What is it?"

"There's a scorpion on the hall steps. The bottom one," I said, clipped, making clear what I wanted him to do. Clumsily I lowered her onto the jumbled covers, climbed beside her. Tom had picked up one of his shoes, carrying it into the tunneled darkness. We heard the first quick strike, the second.

"What if it's still alive?"

"It's not. Daddy made sure." I pulled her stiffened body to me. I was still a bit drunk; I had a drunkard's self-indulgence, thinking, *When did she get so tall? She isn't even mine anymore.* As if children ever are, Ida especially.

"It's dead," Tom said, dropping heavily back into the bed.

"You see, darling? You're okay," I cooed at her. "We're together, safe."

"Mommy's right, Ida," Tom said, rolling onto his side to reach across me, stroking Ida's cheek. "*Estás bien.*"

"No Spanish!" Ida shrieked, jerking away from his hand. I turned my back to him, making my body a wall between him and Ida, curling against her. Having divided us, Ida calmed. Through the dimness, I saw a look of uncanny wisdom and otherworldliness pass onto her face; it was the expression that I had associated with her from the very first moment she appeared, only her head yet born, her eyes black wells. At length, she said in her clear, determined voice:

"Do you know what I feel like when I hear Spanish, and I understand, but I can't say anything back? I feel like I'm this very, very small person, and the world is very, very large, and no one can hear me. I'm like the song of a tiny bird."

The phrase astonished me. Her face was still wet with tears. Tentatively, bracing for a harsh lift of her arm, I touched her cheek. For once, she allowed the small affection.

"I used to think it would be fun," she said. "I thought it would be easy to speak another language." For moments, she seemed lost in her musings, her eyes squinting in concentration. "It isn't." A few more tears escaped her, stoic, hot as bathwater beneath my fingers. Then, at last, she rolled onto her side and slept.

19

The next morning, there was a note from Tom on the bedside table: *Meeting Bill this afternoon. Won't be home for comida. Love, me.* The house was quiet, Ida no longer in bed next to me. María was mopping the living room floor. Seeing me come up the stairs, she stopped and went to fix my coffee. I carried my computer onto the balcony and opened my email, surprised at finding a note from Louise—I didn't even remember giving her my address. She asked if I'd meet her later that morning. Also, could I send her a copy of the story about the two girls in Mexico? I read that sentence several times, unsettled at my lie, the viral way it continued blossoming without my consent. I typed hurriedly that it was still too rough to share, but I would send it when it was more polished; held down the delete button, watching my response disappear until there was nothing. I replaced the renewed blankness with a promise that I would come to her house at eleven. She'd attached a file, and after hitting send, I opened it, my screen suddenly filled with my own face staring back at me.

It was one of the pictures she'd taken that first day at the hot springs. She'd sent only one, although she must have taken forty or more. I guessed it was taken in the moment right before I covered my eyes, after she said I seemed like someone to whom nothing bad had ever happened. In the photo, I stared at the camera, not smiling. Face and shoulders naked but for the thick straps of the navy suit. My lips were slightly parted, one wet-dark strand of hair dropping near to my right eye. It was jarring to see myself without the usual filter of self-critique and presentation of looking in the mirror. I thought, I'm beautiful like that? Not the pretty, careless beauty I consciously projected walking along the Cuesta in my strappy sandals, holding my children's hands or Tom's. It was intense, even a little brooding, the look of someone who has things to say but might not share them. In my eyes, I read hunger. But also—harder to recognize, because as long as I could remember I'd endeavored to banish it in myself—hopefulness. It was what I'd seen in Henry's face when Louise asked would he like to taste an egg from the shell.

It wasn't much longer before the children, who'd been playing beneath me in the courtyard, began to argue and cry. Ida had hit Henry; Henry was ruining everything. I blamed myself, I'd been absorbed in my own thoughts, they were bored, they were hungry. I closed the laptop, steeling myself for a morning, like countless others with young children, spent arbitrating, redirecting, playing boring games sitting on the floor hunched into uncomfortable positions.

But it never came to pass: María took care of everything. She gave them a task involving a stack of old bricks and cut sprigs of bougainvillea. "*Sí, está bien. Las flores están muy bonitas*," she encouraged them as they pushed the flowers that would soon be wilted into the cracks of the brick tower they'd erected. A little later, when they wanted something to eat, they went to her. They watched her mop move back and forth over the stone floor, sitting on the sofa with their legs tucked beneath them. She spoke to them in Spanish as she worked, and they listened with wide-eyed expressions as though drugged. In this way, I spent the morning undisturbed, writing in the notebook Louise had given me, trying to re-create the story I'd told Hector.

At the party, I had been elated, transported as in a dream, where all the constraints, the choices you've made—work, husband, children—lift like starting gates and you are galloping with all of it still ahead of you, free. Here, even with Henry and Ida occupied, the urgent, simple sentences never arrived. Instead, they were labored, pretentious. After an hour, I ripped the pages out and threw them into the trash. At eleven, I loaded the kids into the car and drove to Louise's.

20

As the days passed, the landscape grew more and more arid, covered with dust. The earth cracked and turned gray. Each day, the dusk gilded everything: the dirty streets and emaciated dogs, the littered riverbed on the cusp of running dry. At dusk, the townspeople poured into the streets. Parents carrying children; men pursuing love; girls with linked arms; musicians toting their instruments without cases, their mariachi suits straining, their buttons iridescent. Bella, meanwhile, still hadn't laid her first egg.

"It's because she needs more protein," Louise said one afternoon, and we dutifully fanned into the empty building site to hunt for bugs. I can still see Henry and Ida darting among the chalk-white, half-built structures. Their bleached hair, their darkly tanned faces. Ida trying to catch a butterfly. Henry squatting, intent; then, with a triumphant cry, lifting his cupped hands, in which he'd trapped a cricket.

He cried when Louise killed it, refusing to watch. Ida watched. As always, she was an eager student, keen to understand the world as it actually is, in all its cruelty, her intelligent face very still.

"Now we'll be able to drink an egg right from the shell," Henry said to console himself.

"But doesn't she need a rooster?" Ida asked.

"No." Louise laughed. "That's the beauty of it."

Whereupon Ida laughed, too. She adored Louise and listened to her the way a dog listens to its master, cocking its head this way and that, happy. She was struggling at school, at war with the other girls in her class. She'd recently renewed her demand to cut her hair short. She had begun to express dislike of the school uniform that she'd at first been excited to wear, scowling into the mirror as María braided her shoulder-length blond hair before school. Around this time, she bought a chintzy crucifix at a stall outside the town's most famous church that she declared beautiful and wore on a piece of ribbon around her neck, imploring me to take several pictures of her wearing it over her school sweater, standing on our terrace against the white wall of our house. I'd never seen her take so much overt pleasure in her appearance. And yet there was a strange intentionality, an inscrutable solemnity, as if she'd been cast as the Catholic schoolgirl in the play of her own life.

Of course the same might have been said for me, playing a rich housewife, a writer, Louise's Mia. One morning when I was working on a story I'd begun—I still had no idea what it was about—the school secretary called to say that Ida had a headache and was refusing to return to class. When I arrived, the woman drew me aside and explained with a smile, as though reciting some accepted fact of life, "The other girls are teasing her."

Ida said nothing during the ride home. She stared out the window in the back seat, eyes welled with tears she would not let fall.

"I'm sorry about the girls in your class, sweetheart," I said.

"Why?" she said sharply, as if my sympathy were an insult, catching my eye in the mirror with a look of challenge. "I like them. They're my friends."

What was I supposed to say? *No, they aren't?*

Those were the times I was most grateful for Louise. I would run to her the following morning, pleased to make coffee or sweep her floors or tidy her things, engaging in the domestic work that I no longer enacted in my own home, relieved to feel that particular happiness of a straightforward job done well. Sometimes I would see men working in the building site across the way as I arrived. Every so often, I saw Tom there, a head taller than everyone around him, his sandy hair bleached almost white, come to monitor their progress. I had gotten into the habit of parking my car around the corner, out of sight. I watched him through Louise's window as though regarding a statue of a handsome stranger.

21

It was Friday, one of the many local holidays when the children didn't have school. Louise had summoned me by email. She was excited to show me something. "Trust me" was all she said as she got into the car beside me. With Ida and Henry tussling in the "wayback" and Louise cagily giving directions, we drove west of town to a nondescript neighborhood with squat gray buildings and littered streets. "Park here," she instructed, indicating a spot beneath a gnarled jacaranda tree. When I opened the trunk door, the children bounded out like freed dogs. Henry found a stick on the ground, dragging it behind him as he chased after Ida, who was laughing.

"When will I finally get to see this story of yours?" Louise asked.

"It's not ready."

"You're too concerned with perfection." Henry had begun to make low howling noises, still dragging his stick, and she called sharply, "Stop making that horrible noise," adding to me in a patronizing tone, "They have to learn to fit into the adult world, the way Mexican children do."

I stared at her, furious. *How dare you talk to my son that way.* I felt the words in my throat. *How dare you tell me how to parent*. But as I was about to speak, I saw in amazement that Henry wasn't upset. He was going along in happy silence, dragging his stick against the ground, allowing Ida to drift far ahead of him in a reversal of their usual roles. And so,

I calmed myself. My emotions changed; I was only a little nervous for Ida, now several blocks ahead of us. That, too, I quelled, worried about seeming out of place if I raised my voice to call her back, or racist for worrying about her safety. Instead, I glanced to Louise, as if she alone could decide to call Ida back. Louise said approvingly:

"Look at Ida, so far ahead of us! It's like she knows the way."

It was several more minutes before we arrived at a tiny concrete square—in reality not a square but an empty triangle, its boundaries three crumbling walls. At one corner, several stray dogs nosed lazily at an old Styrofoam container beneath a makeshift shrine.

Settling onto a dusty segment of wall, I said, "I see why you took us here, it's charming."

"Just wait," she said, tilting up her chin haughtily.

I laughed, stretched my legs ahead of me. The children made a game of searching for things on the ground. "Artifacts," Ida called them. A twenty-centavo piece, a shard of blue-and-white pottery, a plastic fork. Louise sat in apparent distaste, erect in the fierce midday heat, holding her huge black leather handbag over her head as a parasol.

"Disgusting," she sniffed when Ida showed her the white fork. Again I watched anxiously for Ida to become upset by Louise's harshness, and was surprised when she took it in stride. She was creating an altar to dead fairies, she told Louise.

"Well, all right then," Louise allowed, pursing her lips.

Some more minutes passed before a battered van pulled up. Almost immediately, women appeared in doorways along the sidewalk. Three men had come out of the van and were wielding metal poles, a tall frayed broom. "*Buenos días, buenos días*," they called cheerily, turning all around like masters of ceremony. Pointing to them, Louise said in a whisper:

"Watch carefully, Mia."

It was like fast-forwarding through a well-edited film. In seamless movements, the men erected a tent, tying a blue tarp to the ends of the poles, around the broom handle, pushing the broom against the base of a streetlamp. A sound began, like a shovel rhythmically scraping against ice, as a boy who couldn't have been more than twelve expertly threw plastic crates from the back of the truck, each coming to rest in the exact center of the tent. As quickly as they came to rest, they were overturned, arranged into steps, tables spread with white cloths. An old-fashioned scale was carried out, a roll of clear plastic bags. Last the goods were brought out, with the same efficiency and understated ceremony. Produce of every imaginable type and color, nuts and dried fruits and beans, gleaming jars of honey. A smell of earth rose, overtaking the pavement smells of dust and dog waste. The last to appear were gaping heads of lettuce. The boy who had thrown the crates stood in a far corner stripping them of their outer leaves, a mound of gargantuan red-veined petals at his feet.

Taking in the completed composition, I noticed the vibrant yellow of the building that formed the backdrop to the red fountains of mounded ripe strawberries, the various hues and textures of green. I saw the swath of blue of the tent, punctuating the yellow. Above everything, the cloudless sky. It was like sitting before a magnificent abstract painting. But in the next moment, the oldest of the men raised a roll of plastic bags, then set them prominently onto a central pedestal, and on cue, dozens of women rushed forward from where they'd stood waiting in doorways, in small groups at the periphery of the square, from nowhere, it seemed.

"Go," Louise said, pushing my back.

I drifted ahead, engulfed in a current of bodies. Almost without thought, I took bags and filled them. Small green squashes, their skins slightly prickly, their orange blossoms not yet wilted; tiny white potatoes, some no bigger than marbles. I plunged my fingers into a bin of beans, cool and hard as pebbles. My hands could scarcely keep pace with my eyes. A woman's huge forearm brushed my breast, her musky odor meeting me when she reached to retrieve a handful of velvet gray mushrooms that had suddenly appeared. Henry ran up, asking for strawberries, the English words jarring.

"*Señora, señora, mire*," one of the men was calling. "*Muy rica, muy sabrosa*." Smiling with pride, he held up a huge papaya, turning it slowly for me to inspect. Several women edged closer, awaiting my decision. I didn't even like papaya, but I took it. The man nodded his approval, "*Sí, llévela. Está muy buena*," and the women rushed forward, sighing ruefully as they searched the wooden crate in vain for a papaya as wonderful as mine.

"*¿Qué más, señora?*" the man behind the scale was calling to me.

Dazedly shaking my head, I began to hand the bags to him one by one to be weighed and tallied. I anxiously counted the bills in my wallet, cowering at the thought of coming up short. It suddenly seemed impossible I had enough to pay for all of this. He was calling out the sum to me, *noventa y cinco*. Not even ten dollars. I handed him the single pink bill, waving off the change. Bags at my wrists, dangling from my fingers, I stumbled away toward Louise and the children, flushed hotly, my face dewy with sweat. The whole ride back to Louise's, my mood persisted, like the residue of salt and sun on your skin after a day at the beach. A pleasant spaciness. In the back, the children lay curled against one another. Maybe they'd fallen asleep, I thought. As we pulled onto the verge beside Louise's house, I called quietly, "Ida? Henry?"

Whispers. An eruption of laugher.

"It's like they're stoned," Louise said.

"I think I'm stoned! That was wild. But, God, my Spanish—"

"It will come. Once you've been here a few years—"

"If only! I wish we never had to leave."

"Then don't. You and the children belong here."

We had arrived at Louise's house, and as the car idled, I gazed out over the street, lost to the dream, jarred back by the chiming of Louise's opened door.

"See you tomorrow," she said. I must have shown my confusion. "Didn't you remember? I'm coming to your house for comida. I'm finally meeting Tom."

The thought sent a spasm of panic through me. "Oh, of course," I said quickly, "I've been looking forward to it."

I offered a few more platitudes—it would be fun, Tom would enjoy meeting her—smiling to hide my unease, the fact I had forgotten.

22

The cold dread that had burst in me persisted on the drive home. It prickled my skin, seeped through my pores, like the feeling right before you become sick. The car full of groceries, the children whispering in back. As we were turning into the driveway, Henry asked, "Why does she call you Mia?"

"It's a nickname," Ida answered for me.

"It's ugly," Henry said, Ida refuting him:

"It's nice. It's a term of endearment."

Where had she learned that phrase? I wondered, at the same time thinking desperately: *It has to be perfect when Louise comes, the house, the food, everything.* As luck would have it, María was still at home, long past the time she usually left. I found her standing on the kitchen countertop, the dishes stacked around her, dusting the topmost shelves. These depths of cleanliness any normal person would never think to execute. Quietly setting my bags down, I addressed her, eager to speak with her about tomorrow's comida.

"*Ay, señora,*" she laughed, starting and clutching her chest. "*Me sorprendiste.*" She seemed unusually happy to see me, almost girlishly embarrassed as she climbed down, wiping her hands over the shapeless dress she always wore. At her warmth, I was overcome by an urge to fall into her arms, hide my face in the warm folds of her neck, and cry.

It caught me completely off guard. I bit my cheek, swallowing back my tears, deriding myself for being weak. *I'll give her an extra big tip this week*, I thought. Each week, we left an envelope of bills on the kitchen table for her to distribute as she saw fit between herself; her daughter Rocío, who helped with the cleaning; and her brother Antonio, who occasionally tended the plants.

As I was thinking all of this, before I could speak to her about Louise coming for comida, she began to tell me about an event "in the future." "*Es un bautismo*," she said several times; it took a while longer before I understood that the baptism was for her grandson Kevin, Rocío's son. Rocío had brought the baby to the house with her once, allowing Ida and Henry to take turns holding and touching him before setting him to sleep in the laundry room as she finished her work. María repeated his name now to make sure I had understood, pronouncing it in rounded syllables, *Kay-veen*. She gave the date: "*El segundo domingo de diciembre.*" There was to be a church service, followed by a big party at her home.

"It's a lot of work for you," I said, adding that it wasn't necessary for her to clean our house that week if she needed the time; we would still pay her as always.

No, no, she shook her head, she wanted to work for us, it was her life. "*Quiero que sean mis invitados*," she said, searching my face.

Only then did I realize she was inviting us. I again felt I might cry, and to cover my emotion began to speak all in a rush: Of course we would come, *claro que sí*, she was so kind to invite us.

"*Está bien, señora.*" Smiling, she lifted the bags of produce onto the counter. Though it was over an hour past the time she usually left, she began to wash everything with great care, using the special drops to purify the water. I wanted to tell her no, don't bother; she should get home to her family. But it comforted me deeply, and so I stood there in silence allowing her to. When she drew out the papaya, she held it up as the man had, praising it as though it were an infant: "*Qué bonita está, señora.*"

I told her to take it. "*Es un regalito*," I insisted, a little gift.

Shyly she took it in her hand and left to get her coat. I lingered in the kitchen, a momentary peace engulfing me at the sight of everything I'd bought gleamingly clean and neatly laid out. Bowl after bowl of the most beautiful produce you've ever seen.

But when Tom arrived a half an hour later, my panic returned stronger than before, spiraling off in all directions. Louise would disapprove of the house, in some obscure way its beauty. She would criticize our neighborhood's pretentiousness, or bring up her own, referencing the hated building project that I'd never mentioned Tom was overseeing. And what if she wore the bracelet, which she did nearly every day? Or called me Mia? What would I say to Tom? Beneath these articulable fears lay something more amorphous and pervasive. A fear that our closeness was an illusion; that, in the course of her being here, I would be exposed to Tom or—worse—myself, and so lose her.

Night arrived. I tried to console myself with routine. I bathed Ida and Henry, sat on the floor between their beds reading aloud from a chapter book. I grew impatient turning the pages. Sweat pricked the back of my neck. I kept checking my watch. As soon as I left their room, I ran upstairs, thinking there might be an email from Louise. There was nothing, and so I distracted myself by looking at pictures of movie stars with hair I liked and houses for sale in Minneapolis in higher and higher price ranges that we could never afford because none appealed to me; even the million-dollar homes were tasteless and crass. Only after a half hour did I remember that I had agreed to a "date" with Tom, to have a glass of wine and make love. Idiot!

I ran my hands through my hair, hurried down the stairs to our bedroom. He was propped against a pillow, his shirt off, an opened bottle of wine on the bedside table.

"What kept you so long?"

"Was I long?"

He cocked his head, seeming to stare straight through me. "I was starting to think you forgot."

"No, no, not at all! It's just, there was an email from Jessica." Jessica was the neighbor whose daughter had sent Henry the postcard, about whom I'd often complained to Tom that she was needy, always demanding reassurance, whining when too much time had elapsed between communications. "Actually, I'm thinking of changing my email," I said.

"Seems a bit drastic."

I didn't answer. I had sat down onto the edge of the bed.

Mechanically he began to reach under my shirt, unfasten my bra. He leaned forward speaking my name into my ear, the wash of his breath repellent to me. I flinched. "Do you need a glass of wine?" he asked, and I noted the verb with irritation, as if I was so cold, so damaged, that I had to be drunk to have sex with my husband. He was continuing with a kind of doggedness, lifting my shirt over my head, caressing my arms, murmuring things. I leaned back against the pillows in a posture of submission. I smiled to him. But when he lowered his mouth to kiss me, I averted my face, sighing impatiently as if to say, *Let's go, stop panting over me*; guilty as he awkwardly entered me, humiliated by my dryness, telling myself to breathe, to relax, don't be such a fucking bitch.

There is no one but you, Tom, I silently recited—absurd, melodramatic thought—telling myself, *You lied about an email, so what? The truth isn't even worth mentioning.*

I took a breath, exhaling deeply. I closed my eyes. I reached between my legs, tracing the place where we met, trying to rise to the challenge of pleasure, to arrive into it, because to feel nothing seemed a second betrayal. But I could see on his face, grimacing slightly, there wasn't time. And so I said the words instead, "There's no one but you," knowing it would hasten the end. "Tom, oh, Tom, there's no one but you," I said, grimly satisfied when he shuddered against me, his heavy weight slackened and gone still.

In the expanding silence, I told myself I would make it up to both of us; we would have the true sex later. Once he'd rested. Then I would kiss him without reservation—his mouth and fingers, his manhood that had already been inside me, patiently and slowly, tasting and taking him everywhere. And when we were finally spent, we would lie awake like we used to before marriage and kids. I would confess everything to him. My failed attempts at writing; my restless dissatisfaction, teetering on self-loathing; how at the market I had felt like a woman in a new way, and afterward wanted to cry in María's arms, to accept love as I never permitted myself to.

He had begun sweeping his hands beneath the bedcovers. I knew he was searching for his underwear, without which he couldn't sleep peacefully. When, moments later, he curled away, for minutes, I stared with a sense of rejection and umbrage at his broad shoulders, damp with sweat; the base of his skull; his blond hair shorn short. "Tom?"

"Hmm?"

"No, nothing."

23

Louise stood in the center of the living room, taking it all in. The live-edge coffee table and lounge chairs and built-in banquette that Bill had designed himself, vintage now; the Turkish rugs and polished stone floors; the gleaming walls of glass. The view, particularly stunning that day. Not a cloud, not a wisp of white. "Well, this is really something," she said at last.

"Really, you like it?"

"No wonder she's kept me away," she said to Tom in that way she had, where she might equally be paying a compliment or expressing disdain. "It's almost too perfect."

Tom chuckled. "I guess we *are* a bit Cinderella at the ball," he said affably.

"Come midnight, back to Minneapolis, and dragging this one behind you."

"I'm sure she won't mind."

She had leaned her head back imperiously. "Won't she?"

Tom laughed, thinking it a joke. At that moment, María stepped to the top of the three broad steps that lead up to the dining area. "*Listo, señora*," she said, indicating the meal had been laid out. As we began toward the table, the children rushing ahead, Louise lurching as she gripped her cane, I hung back clasping Tom's hand in a preemptively conciliatory gesture. *Love you*, I mouthed, and he smiled back at me, inclining his head toward Louise with bemusement, touching my hand to his lips. We began to take our seats, the kids already peeking inside all the little covered pots and dishes. María came in carrying a magnificent majolica platter on which the sea bass I had bought that morning was arranged over a bed of edible flowers. There was a strange expression on Louise's face, and in a flurry of panic, I said, "It's *filete de róbalo*, I hope that's okay?"

"Why wouldn't it be?"

"Oh, thank God."

"Crisis averted," Tom said, elaborately rolling his *r*'s in the Scottish accent that always made Henry laugh, shooting me a puzzled glance. "Good things come to those who bait."

"Jesus, Tom," I moaned. To Louise, I added, "He's always ready with a bad pun."

"Duly warned," Tom said, still with the accent.

A few more awkward moments. As usual, I had to remind Henry not to sit on his knees; the dining chairs were too fragile. They were mid-century classics, cantilevered cane and chrome.

"Where's his pillow?" Tom asked. It was something we'd bickered about, my insistence on tidying the pillow away whereas Tom thought it should be left there permanently—as though life was about maximizing efficiency, I'd jeered, rather than creating beauty. "Obviously if it were our house, we'd have different chairs," Tom said to Louise.

"Nonsense, they're perfect. The whole house, down to the very last detail." She said it like *lahst*. "Do you know," she went on after a pause, "I don't think a single thing's changed. That might even be the same maid."

I stared. "I'm sorry, the same—?"

"You've been here before?" Tom said.

"To Bill's?" Louise threw her head back and laughed. "Oh, please, don't get me started. Bill Barnes and my husband, Allan. Well, that's a long and very sordid tale."

"I love a sordid tale," Tom said, reaching toward her plate with a portion of fish, Louise smiling her acceptance, declining to elaborate.

The usual sounds of spoons against dishes, water being poured, pots and platters passed. I was groping my way backward, trying to remember if I'd mentioned Bill or the house. No, I was certain I hadn't. If anything, I'd taken care to avoid the topic. María shuffled in and out, carrying little bundles of warmed tortillas in her hands, a small glazed bowl of sliced limes. Henry sat sucking his thumb, not eating. Tom asked if he'd looked in all the bowls, and Henry said he had and there was nothing he liked. He'd liked María's fish last time, Tom said, Henry countering that it was fried then. All the while, a pressure was building in my chest. Catching Henry's eye, I pantomimed removing my own thumb, then smiled encouragingly. Ignoring me, Henry patted his father's leg with his free hand, considering.

"I want ketchup," he finally decided.

"*Catsup, María, por favor,*" Tom called toward the kitchen.

From the small opening in the wall, María's gentle voice: "*Ay, sí, para Señor Haynree.*"

"*Como siempre, ¿verdad?*" Tom called back cheerfully, making a show of their rapport, how happy we all were together. In the momentary silence, while we waited for it to be brought, Louise seemed to me mortally offended, whether because of the request for ketchup or the fact we weren't getting it ourselves, I couldn't decide. Tom, oblivious, was ceremoniously opening the bottle of Chardonnay that I had paid a small fortune for in the new wine shop off the Jardín. "May I?" he said, extending the bottle toward her glass.

"Oh, please, absolutely."

"Welcome to our home," he said as he poured. "Or, I guess I should say, welcome back." He twisted the bottle as he righted it to catch a drip. "I'm curious how you came to be in San Miguel in the first place. Assuming you can tell us *that*." He had settled back into his chair, turned slightly sideways to accommodate his long legs, which he'd crossed urbanely, and I thought, as I often did, how handsome he was. *Dashing* was the specific word that came to mind. Tanned, his white oxford shirt cuffed and open at the neck. His discarded cashmere scarf draped on the back of his chair like an affectionate cat.

"To really tell the story," Louise was saying, "I'd have to start quite far back."

"We've got all afternoon."

"I might need another glass of wine," she said wryly.

Tom lifted the bottle and began to fill her glass clear to the brim, Louise laughing gamely.

"How marvelous, we'll all be drunk by four o'clock. But I'm sure the children will take care of themselves nicely, won't you?" Halting her laughter, she gave a menacing lift of her eyebrows.

"Wine makes you forget," Henry said.

"I forget nothing," Louise deadpanned, to a fresh wave of laughter, continuing, "I remember being poor and hunting for our food, just in those hills over there, not far from my house in Montes."

"Really, Montes? That's funny—"

"Well, funny. It's certainly a far cry from this, I'll grant you. Bill's is a very grown-up house," she said, making it seem a terrible insult.

"I like your house much better," Ida said.

Seeing Tom's surprise that Ida had been there, I said nervously, "You'd like it, Tom, it's got sort of a Moroccan vibe." Turning to Louise, "Tom has always wanted to go to Morocco."

"Yes, Morocco's wonderful," Louise said. "I lived there for a time, on the invitation of Paul Bowles. Oh, forever ago; my daughter was very young, younger than Henry. Well, I was practically a child myself. I had lost my husband, and Paul . . ."

On and on it went. The meals they had eaten; Paul's wife, Jane, who was "crippled by illness." Louise conjuring Tangier for him now, its heat and headiness; the Grand Socco and the Avenue Pasteur. I watched Tom become interested. He had often professed to love fiction above all other art forms. The only thing he had insisted on bringing to Mexico was a box of his favorite novels, *The Sheltering Sky* among them.

"And what about you, Tom?" Louise suddenly said, as if she'd only just remembered he was there. "How did you come to be in San Miguel?"

I looked quickly from Tom to Louise. The sun had shifted, hitting Louise full in the face. It reminded me of a scene in an old movie I once saw, where the witness was interrogated before a glare of sunlight. Only it was Tom about to confess.

"I'm surprised Sally didn't tell you. I'm an architect overseeing a new housing development."

"Are you indeed?"

"It's one of Bill's designs. Actually, funny coincidence, it's in Montes. That vacant field on the Obraje road?"

"My God." For a moment, my breath caught, before she said, "It really is astonishing how unobstructed you are up here. But that sun! It's gotten so hot. Would you mind, darling?"

At Louise's gesture, I rose and went behind her, easing her sweater up over her head and then folding it neatly and laying it across the back of Henry's vacated chair. I was unable to meet Tom's look—surprised, no doubt, at my subservience toward this woman whom he didn't know, whom I'd told him nothing about. But in the next moment, I understood that it was something else. He had noticed the bracelet, revealed when I'd removed the sweater.

"That's a lovely bracelet," he said, looking at me rather than Louise.

"There's an interesting story about that," I began. I was still standing behind Louise, and as I searched for what next to say, she very slowly lifted first the braceleted hand and then the other, fluttering them above her shoulders for me to clasp, which I did, shamefaced.

"We have a remarkable bond, your wife and I."

There was a silence, in which I was unable to meet Tom's eyes. "So, what's the story?" he finally said. He was addressing me, but it was Louise who answered:

"It turns out we're the same person, separated by a few decades."

I glanced toward Tom, who was gazing steadily at me, a crooked smile lifting the corner of his mouth. Ida had come back into the room, Louise saying to her, "How would you like to come over tomorrow? I have some special art supplies, and a beautiful old easel. They once belonged to a very famous artist. Would you like that, to paint with an easel? You could do a portrait of Bella."

"Bella?" Tom said, patting Ida's shoulder in a way I could see she didn't like. "Who's Bella, biscuit?"

Ida drew quiet, seeming to stiffen away from Tom.

"Biscuit?" Louise said.

Reviving the Scottish accent, "Aye, it's what I called her when she was a wee babe. My little wee bairn. My wee bairn biscuit."

"I hate those names," Ida said evenly.

Tom had been waving his arms as he spoke, merrily tapping the table to the rhythm of his words, and now he stopped, the smile draining from his face.

"I didn't know," he said at last.

24

Tom sat in bed, following me with probing eyes as I moved about the room. For the last hour, I'd been avoiding him, waiting to enter the bathroom until he'd finished rather than brush my teeth next to him as usual, now turning from him as I changed into the tee shirt and underwear that I slept in.

As I climbed into bed, he ejected a short laugh. "Well, she's quite something."

"Louise? I thought you'd find her amusing."

"Sure, she's amusing, in a cunning sort of way."

I could hear the edginess in my voice. "What do you mean, cunning?"

"Bowles, Kerouac, Burroughs, Mailer, Dylan . . ." He was counting them off on his fingers. "Is it even chronologically possible? I'd have to look at a timeline. And that weird, like, pan-European accent she puts on," Tom said with a snort.

"I'm sure some of it's true. She knew Bill."

"But it's the way she always has to go one better," he went on. "Every famous person you mention, she doesn't just know him, she attended the birth of his child or gave him a tattoo or something."

I laughed.

"Just be careful, Sally."

"Of what?"

He was looking at me closely. Taking my hand, he said, "Why did you lie to me about the bracelet?"

"What do you mean?"

"Sally, come on, you can tell me. Did you give it to her?"

"It's a coincidence. They sell them at the market."

There was a silence before he said, "Is this about your mother?"

"Please, I barely remember her."

"You know what I mean. It's only natural, given who your mother was, that you'd want that—"

I snorted out a laugh. "Whatever, Tom. I'm a grown woman, I don't need a mother."

He put his hands on my shoulders and I shook them off, enraged by his look of pity. It was so much worse than being despised. I had an urge to provoke him, tell him he was stupid, he knew nothing about me. I wanted him to yell at me, call me a lying bitch. I knew how to make him lose control.

Instead, I lay on my side, swallowing it all down, trembling within the expanding silence. When, at length, he rubbed my back, I began to cry. I couldn't stop the tears spilling out, hot and loathed, furious with myself for being weak, ashamed that I continued to let him touch me when I could have taken a butcher's knife and chopped his hand clean off.

25

I couldn't sleep. I was agitated, incensed by Tom's peaceful presence beside me and the regularity of his breathing, his scent that gathered fog-like in the dark bedroom as he slept. I sat up, staring at his unruly eyebrows, his mouth gaping open as if he were a corpse. I went upstairs, walking in bare feet through the crypt-like cold with reckless disregard for scorpions. How dare he suggest that I would crave a mother? I, who had surgically removed her presence from my life. If anything, I told myself furiously, huddled on the living room couch, she was a harmless shadow, a discarded photo negative, the inverse of all I was and had made. I had scrupulously banished in myself all the qualities I detested in her: the physical coldness and withholding; the inability to access joy; the refusal to ever apologize; her mutability, adopting a different persona with each new lover—the cop who gave her a speeding ticket, her boss, the husband of a friend. Perhaps more than any of these qualities, though, I abhorred her inability to react decisively to protect herself and me. Her bewildered smile, her feigned naivete putting me on a Greyhound bus alone to Boston every other weekend beginning when I was Ida's age. Often my father wasn't there when I arrived. I would sit at the terminal among prostitutes and homeless people and addicts asleep in their own piss, trembling like an abandoned dog.

Equally troubling to me, and more vehemently repressed, were the moments of shared happiness. The summer afternoon spent at the Central Park Zoo, watching the seals. We had moved in with a man named Damian, a doctor who'd recently left his wife for her, to a beautiful house on a lake an hour outside of the city. I was nine and already felt too old for zoos. Still, we stood watching the seals the whole morning, laughing at the sounds they made to cajole one another, as though an innocence we'd so long ago lost had unexpectedly been returned to us.

When we returned home, the lake was quiet; no one else was outside. By some unspoken agreement, we pretended to be seals. We had gone in without our swimsuits—something I never did, intent on guarding whatever remained of my innocence. But this day, to be a seal with her seal mother, for once, I swam naked, the two of us venturing into the middle of the lake, barking and diving and cresting up out of the water. We swam like that for hours, cleansed of the physical awkwardness between us, the dirtiness we'd witnessed in one another.

I'd been reticent toward Damian at the start of their relationship, disapproving of his being married with a young daughter. Patiently, slowly, he'd won me over, bringing gifts that hinted at a respectability I'd never encountered. A set of grosgrain-ribbon headbands; a small leather coin purse holding three silver dollars; a photo book wrapped in shiny red paper of "Old New York," places he would show me one day, he promised. He began to spend weekends with us, cooking elaborate meals, driving us to New York for concerts at Lincoln Center. And then the beautiful house beside the lake. He and his wife had not been good together, he confided to me as we were unpacking one of his many boxes of records and books. They hadn't ever felt like a family, not like us. On Valentine's Day, he gave me a gift along with my mother: a small garnet-studded heart on a chain that I wore every day to school. I wondered only fleetingly if he had given one to the other girl, too, a few years younger than me, whose picture he had shown me, whom his wife would not allow to visit.

When he decided that spring to reconcile with his wife and his real daughter, I suffered the betrayal personally. But I reserved the bulk of my rage for my mother, for having been unable to keep him.

For her part, she obsessed about winning him back. "I want you to write him a note saying you're not upset," she instructed. "He's worried you're angry with him. You have to tell him you miss him, and everything will be fine between the two of you if he comes back."

I wouldn't do it. As long as I could remember, words had been a private refuge—children's books, song lyrics, the stories I made up lying sleepless in my bed or on the long rides to and from my father's—a way of comprehending my reality or else escaping it. More than that, though, it was the fact that I had allowed myself to love him that kept me from doing what she wished.

For days, we were locked in a stalemate. She sat at the side of my bed imploring or berating me; she invited me for breakfast before the start of school in order to resume her crusade, gripped by a desire to get him back that eclipsed everything else. "We have to look ahead," she would say. "We have to imagine the reality we eventually want." We were living in a small house then, near Albany—Damian must have arranged it. One evening, she arrived home flushed and excited. She had been with him. He was close to coming back. I watched her pace in the kitchen like an animal enflamed by scent, gaunt, her hair disheveled, the sharp report of her heels striking the worn linoleum floor as she strode to a cabinet, took out a sheet of paper, a pen. Better than her face, which I grope toward in dreams, I remember her body with its lean limbs, her way of moving when she was agitated, all efficiency and strike.

"Here," she said, setting the paper and pen onto the kitchen table where I was sitting, the car keys she'd been gripping, smiling tensely. "Here you are; write to him."

"No."

Her smile quivered. She sat down beside me, announcing with forced cheer, "I'll start with you. There, see? See how easy it is?" She had given me the pen and, taking hold of my hand, moved it jerkily over the page, intoning the syllables, *Dear Day-Mee-Unn*, that bore no relation to the jagged shapes we were producing. Tears pooled in her eyes, her lip trembled, her hair falling over her face. I resisted. I pressed my lips together as if to hold in the words she was bent on extracting, my heart beating frantically. I bore down on the pen, ripping a line through the paper. As a girl, I was like Ida. Unyielding, opinionated in a way that sprang not from my thoughts but from a more unassailable source, the summative self that precedes and outlives us. Did I recognize that here was the principal battle of our lives? The war that had been waged between us since my infancy, in which she endeavored not to make me lie, but to make me become the lie, the story she'd invented on my behalf.

Her face had tightened into ugliness, her mouth. "Goddamn it! Just do it! Say you love him!"

"I don't," I replied with icy calm.

With a jerking motion, she pushed her chair back, snatching up her car keys as if to abandon me. Halfway to the door, she halted and, without warning, turned and threw them at my face. I remember closing my eyes and willing them to strike me; a second later, the sound of them clattering against the floor behind me.

"Life is funny," she said breezily several months later, when, in a moment of calculated cruelty, I'd recalled to her the hurling of the keys. We were driving to the bus station. Summer break had just begun. I was going to see my father. "I really ought to thank you for not writing that note. I've met someone so much more wonderful. He's going to take me on a marvelous trip to the beach." There was a note of triumph in her voice.

I didn't respond. I held my gaze out the window, scrupulously keeping myself from her, my shoulders folded into my chest, my breath shallow. I hadn't yet learned to lose my temper, to throw things as she did, to rant and cry. I only knew to swallow, to withhold, to spitefully make myself into nothing.

The rest of my things arrived at my father's a week later. Two smallish cardboard boxes, securely taped shut. I never met the wonderful new man. I never saw my mother again.

26

The night after Louise came to comida, I had the old dream from my childhood. I hadn't had it in more than a year. It's always the same. I am hitting my mother, but the blows won't land. My fist rebounds without doing damage, as though she's made out of rubber. Her face, no longer fully remembered, is always a slightly different version of itself. But I know it's her, and I hit harder, aiming clear through her to the wall behind, hindered by air that is gummy and thick. In a frenzy of frustrated rage, I push her to the ground, tear at her clothes, kick her, claw at her stomach with its ugly purple birthmark, her chest and face.

What it is that's enraged me, I never know. Only that, when I can't hurt her with my body, I begin to rain down words. Every slur and condemnation I can think of, spit flying from my mouth: *Fucking cunt! Bitch! Selfish whore!*

Still, she smiles. That moony, self-satisfied smile, stubbornly asserting a reality in which she is blameless and even noble. Asserting an ownership that I can never free myself from. Because nothing, neither blows nor words, will ever break her surface.

27

I awoke early and exhausted, Tom asleep beside me. As always after those dreams, I felt exposed: I was incapable of being a good mother; I was vulgar, unworthy of love. *Stop*, I commanded myself. *Don't be pathetic. Don't let her reach her shadow into this house, this day.*

I took a long shower. I washed myself until my skin squeaked beneath my fingers. When the children awoke, I bathed and dressed them. I combed Henry's unruly hair and braided Ida's into two trim rows almost as neatly as María could. "Darlings, let me fix you breakfast." It was Sunday, María's day off. I served them pancakes with the maple syrup they loved that is mostly corn syrup, the only kind you could buy here. I kissed them as they ate, their sticky cheeks and lips. I inhaled their breath, Ida's a little fetid, Henry's milky sweet. I stood behind Henry on his wooden stool at the sink, caressingly rinsing his hands, like plump pink newborn animals.

Tom was still in bed, sheepishly reading. I bent to kiss him, saying I would take the children on an outing. "Really?" he said, pleased. Since having them, it was the greatest conceivable luxury, to be fully alone.

I took them to get pastries in town, to the playground at Parque Juárez, then to Louise's, as she had proposed, where they searched the terrace for eggs and took turns painting at the easel Allan had once used, perhaps Navarro, who knew? Louise said nothing about our previous day's lunch, and neither did I. Neither did I feel compelled to ask about her past life in San Miguel, how she knew Bill. I sharpened my gaze on the present: *Look at all this beauty! Look at what I've made of my life, what I'm giving my children!*

Toward evening, I called Tom. He sounded drowsily happy, having spent the day reading and doodling in his sketchbook. It was great to have a break from the kids, but he hoped it hadn't been too tiring for me, having them all day? I assured him it hadn't. In fact, why not continue to enjoy himself? He could stroll into town for dinner or a drink. The kids and I would fend for ourselves.

There was no food to speak of at Louise's. At seven, we walked to the neighborhood I'd driven through with Tom before we moved here, imagining how it might change when the building project was complete. A cluttered *tiendita*, a crumbling church, two metal benches set before a stone wall. Louise knew of a woman who sold tamales from her stoop. We brought them back in plastic containers and ate sitting on the living room floor, Louise with her bad leg extended before her. Afterward, I spread out a blanket for Ida and Henry, who lay close together, quietly conferring, as Louise and I sat on the sheepskin-covered bed.

"I love when they get along."

Ida was whispering intently in Henry's ear, her arm draped casually over his shoulder.

"I'll bet you were innocent like that."

"Right." I snorted. Making my voice into a crude imitation of Louise's, I said, "You don't know the *haahf*, darling."

"Bitch!" She laughed; it was the way things were between us now, the teasing intimacy, the sudden deep claims on one another. "You'd better be careful, pretending to be someone else."

"Or what?"

She took my hand, rubbing it along the palm. "I practice chiromancy. I see you don't know the word. I can expose your character with humiliating accuracy."

"With *what*?" I was laughing.

"Oh, it's just something Mark Twain said after visiting a famous palm reader."

"Don't tell me you knew him, too."

"Don't be daft. What do I look like, a hundred? Here, I'll recite a poem, see if you can guess what it means. 'When your hands go out, love, toward mine, what do they bring me flying? Why did they stop at my mouth—'" She lifted my hand to her lips, and I pulled it away, saying:

"I love how you do that."

"Hmm?"

"Recite poetry."

"Can't you?" Louise said, as though it were as common as tying your shoes, and I was momentarily chagrined, thinking, *I'll learn some.* "That poem was Neruda's, whom I *did* know. Well, met. A painter I knew introduced us in Italy."

"Come on, you're kidding me—Neruda?"

But even if I didn't strictly believe her stories, I sensed it would be stingy of me, an admission of my own smallness, to regard them as meaningless or devoid of emotional truth. Sometimes, now, she tempered her bluster with stories of degradation and loss. She had been a foster child. Her mother was a whore and an addict. "This fake indebtedness to people, blood is thicker than water, what nonsense! I made myself from nobody and nothing. When I stand at the podium accepting my award, I'll start by saying I have no one to thank."

When she finally read my palm, it revealed I was a fire person, very potent—although that formidable power, which might otherwise be turned to the creation of art, was frequently hobbled by a pervasive need to please.

"What the hell?" Laughing, pulling away my hand. "I thought you were supposed to tell my future."

"What, *You will live a long and prosperous life*?" She scoffed. "Anyway, only fools believe in these arbitrary distinctions, the future and the past. It's all just life. And life is character."

These sweeping statements; the assessing way she lifted her chin, steadily regarding me along the length of her handsomely reconstructed nose, the nose that once, I kept remembering, had shattered to bits along with the rest of her. These were the moments I felt closest to true affection for Louise, even love.

"Where were you?" Tom asked when we finally arrived back home.

"Only Louise's."

"Not the whole day?" He had a look of concern, disapproval.

But he was grateful, too, for the time alone. He'd been smoking a cigar on the upper terrace when we arrived, his skin cool as I kissed him hello. His clothes smelled like smoldering leaves—a smell you might catch from far away on a chilly fall night.

28

A routine had been established between us. The hot springs on Monday. The fish man on Thursday. The pop-up market on Friday. On evenings when I knew Tom would be occupied until late, I would ask María to return after I'd put the children to bed, then drive to Louise's. Sometimes the house would be filled with people—Fabiola, Hector, artists whom the gallery represented. We would banter in a dizzying mix of English and Spanish about chauvinism in Mexico, gun violence in the US, whether race was to North America what class was to South, whether monogamy was an antiquated idea. On a few of these nights, I took the children, insisting to Tom if Ida or Henry let slip where we'd been that it lent them sophistication to be around Louise's friends, as if I were taking them to gallery shows and lectures. Henry would kick a half-deflated soccer ball with the neighborhood children or run up the street with them to the *tiendita*, his fist damply wrapping coins with which to buy a *paleta*. If there were no other children about, he complained he was bored, he wanted his special blanket, he wanted to go home and take a bath with his toys. Ida, never. She kept close to Louise, who encouraged her to participate in discussions, to argue her opinion alongside everyone else. When there wasn't a party, Ida would sit for hours at Louise's small dining table, head bent studiously as she drew. Louise periodically offered praise, though never with the warmth or lavishness with which adults customarily praise children. She would push Ida to articulate her vision, saying bluntly, *It's impressionistic, is that the effect you wanted?* Or she would challenge her: *Maybe you should quit for the day, you're tired.* I'd feel the sting, the umbrage rising in me and in Ida. Then, invariably, I'd see, above Ida's trembling lip, a determined look come into her face, after which she would make something truly extraordinary that Louise would later show her friends with proprietary pride.

"Why not let me take her home from school a few afternoons a week?" Louise said one day, in Ida's hearing. "It would be good for you to have some time to yourself. You could write."

I took her suggestion as a veiled critique, not of my mothering but my writing. I'd recently shared a vignette with her about walking Ida and Henry to school, something similar to the word sketches I'd sent Tom when he was away. In other words, something preoccupied with its own prettiness, the cadence of its language, lacking any real emotional power.

Lowering her hand onto Ida's head, the bracelet gleaming on her wrist, she said, "You should return to the love story between the girls. Hector was so impressed." Meaning, *Take another stab at it. Maybe all your efforts won't be worthless.* "Anyway, Tom is providing you with a great opportunity. You should take full advantage."

That *anyway* annoyed me, as though she were referencing a complaint I had with Tom, that he was uninteresting, or only valuable for what I could extract from him. Her backhanded compliments. Her dubious generosity: I could write if she took Ida. *And what about Henry?* I thought but didn't say.

"Where's Ida?" Tom asked as we were sitting down to comida the first time without her.

"With Louise."

"Doing what?" he said sharply.

"I think she was taking her to the Fábrica; don't look at me like that, Tom."

"Why would you let her spend time alone with someone we barely know?"

I could feel the insistence of his stare and didn't lift my eyes to meet it. I had sensed a demand in his assertion that *we* barely knew her, an implicit mandate that I share his opinion of her.

"She wanted to."

"So? You'd let her eat cake for breakfast? Run around naked?" His voice had risen, less out of worry for Ida's well-being, I suspected, than exasperation at me; that I'd defied him by not acceding to his concern—a feeling that was confirmed when he added, "You're the adult, remember? You're the mother. Just so we're both clear who's in charge."

I glared at him, eyes brimming. In silence, we began to pass the dishes around.

But as quickly as it had risen, the tension between us began to ease. There was something undeniably pleasant about it being the three of us, the magnetic pull of Ida's thoughts and demands removed, no bickering between her and Henry to arbitrate. Pleased by our undivided attention, Henry kept up a steady patter all the way through the clearing of the table, agreeably relieving us of the need to speak.

29

I sat on a bench in the Plaza Civica. It was late October and quite cold. I'd just dropped the children at school. Pigeons littered the ground, cluttering the bronze statue of a man on a horse, cooing and shitting, huddling into their wings for warmth. In my lap, the blank notebook sat unopened. I drew my hands into the sleeves of my coat. Another few minutes, I told myself—until what, exactly, I hadn't articulated.

I was about to stand and go when a man at the bottom of the church steps, perhaps twenty feet from me, caught my attention. He was bent tying his shoe. I knew him from somewhere, although I couldn't place him. It must, I thought, be that I'd passed him a few times in the market, or on the street. He was unremarkable: a middle-aged man of average height and build, fair-complected, his hair graying at the temples. San Miguel was full of people like that, people who might have been Mexican or Canadian or Spanish or Italian. Yet I had the sense of a deeper connection, and as he rose and looked for a place to sit, I felt momentarily exposed, alone on the bench, for whatever reason hoping that he didn't sit beside me. It was only when he began to walk toward me that, with a start, I placed him: the man who had grabbed Louise and kissed her. I'd never asked Louise about him and had all but forgotten his existence—or, more accurately, I'd removed him, as if he were someone I'd once dreamed of instead of a person with agency.

He took a few steps closer and our eyes met. It was then something strange occurred. I read the shift in his face like weather: *He* had recognized *me*. In a gesture of self-protection, I dropped my hands to my notebook. At my signal, he jerked back, in that way some men will shrink into themselves as if suddenly ashamed of their physical power. It made me sorry for him. I had an impulse to smile an apology. But he had already turned and was hurriedly retreating, the pigeons flapping up noisily before him.

30

Aside from this incident and a few inconsequential spats with Tom or Ida or Louise, it was a time of overwhelming contentment. It seemed as though Fate was smiling on me; nothing bad could befall me. I had begun Spanish lessons two mornings a week in a beautiful old building on Mesones. I would save some small bit of shopping until after my lesson so that I could practice the things I'd learned with José Luis, with Enrique, the produce seller's handsome son, laughing, flirting, spinning tales of my life in various tenses. I took Henry to the *tiendas* or the covered market after picking him up at noon, chatting with the other housewives as they ruffled Henry's hair and offered him treats, asked him where he attended school.

¡Vasconcelos! ¡La mejor escuela de San Miguel! Has de ser muy inteligente.

Despite his excellent Spanish, Henry was shy when speaking with adults. Only with María did the children speak Spanish more freely—perhaps because María was so profoundly illiterate, unable even to copy down telephone numbers when someone called, much less their spoken message. In this and every imaginable way, she was an unintimidating presence, a wholly benign and loving force. Every day, she ironed their uniforms, made their beds, and tidied their room, nestling Ida's stuffed animals beside the pillows, arranging Henry's action figures with immaculate care, posing them in various states of battle. Some afternoons, in the empty hours before it was time to pick up Ida and have comida, Henry would play at a little fountain in our neighborhood, disused and overgrown. He liked to do this alone. It was an adventure for which María packed him a snack consisting entirely of sweets that she wrapped in a handkerchief and tied to the end of a long stick Henry had found on one of our romps through the botanical garden near our house. He liked to gallop with the stick straddled between his legs and pretend in was a horse. "*Eres muy guapo, Señor Haynree*," she called after him. "*Eres un vaquero.*"

"You're sure it's all right for him to go alone?" I asked, less out of concern for his safety than at being judged negligent, as I surely would have in the States.

"*Ay, sí, señora*," she sighed. "*Todos los niños lo hacen*—they are little men."

I laughed and nodded my agreement, somehow charmed by the chauvinistic sentiment and the sugared treats that had formerly been anathema, things to vigilantly defend my son against, just as I was charmed by the mothers in the school courtyard and the market who flashed their vividly colored nails, the air tinkling with their laughter and the loud ringtones of their phones. In the States, my interactions with other mothers had been characterized by a certain wariness; a shared sense that as mothers of young children our lives were on hold, but that one day a more remarkable existence might be resumed or invented. Whereas here people were not merely resigned to their immobility but content. It made sense to me, at last, that María didn't sit with us at mealtimes. There was a certain comfort in knowing who you were, where you belonged.

One morning, I expressed some of these views to Louise, declaring that the constant striving in the States produced only dissatisfaction. I was standing in her kitchen making coffee, warming the milk and the cinnamon. "It's nice to be somewhere where 'women's work' and the importance of family are still valued."

Louise was appalled. "The absolute stupidity! Women of your generation don't know how good you have it! As if all these freedoms you enjoy didn't have to be fought for, or couldn't still be lost."

It was difficult to take her seriously, not to smile derisively at Louise's diatribe while we stood in a beautiful room with music on the turntable, cups of coffee in our hands.

Her invective took on an entirely different meaning when she repeated it several days later. We were having a drink with Hector at the café in the Fábrica. They had spent the morning hanging a new show of a female artist from the DF, and using this as her starting point, Louise made a sneering reference to "Mia's nonsense about women's work the other day," after which she repeated almost word for word her speech about freedoms won through ongoing battles. Only this time, she prefaced it with a smile, a little laugh high in her throat, saying, "Women of my daughter's generation . . ."

It was clear in the way Hector regarded me, lifting his eyebrows in affectionate complicity about Louise's militancy, that he believed I was the daughter in question. What's more, I was certain it was an intentional miscue on Louise's part. She seemed to be assessing my reaction as she spoke, her gaze meeting mine in pleasure and slight curiosity, as if daring me to correct her.

"I'm proud to be a housewife, a mother," I parried back. "Why shouldn't I be? As work goes, it's as honorable as any other."

"Don't be a fool, Mia."

I caught Hector's eye across the table and smiled. I said lightly, "You're right. I'm really pretty stupid. Good thing I'm so attractive."

She stared for a long uninterrupted moment as if she were undressing me—the way a governess might undress her ward when she had tramped through mud, cold and controlled and disdaining, *You foolish girl, stop wasting so much of my time.*

Still, when the check came, Louise reached for it, then drew out her wallet, ostentatiously counting the bills and laying them one at a time onto the table in a show of ceremony, as though making a public declaration of her maternal care.

31

It's true. It pleased me to assume the role of Louise's daughter. Just as it pleased me, gratified something very deep inside of me, to call myself a housewife. My resentment toward my mother had long ago distilled into a generalized contempt for any woman not able to hold on to a man, too ugly or needy or foolish to keep him. Once abandoned to my father, I quickly learned to protect his ego and mine by being everything my mother had failed to be. I cooked elaborate meals, cleaned and rearranged the house. When he returned from work, we would sit in the spotless living room with its flowers in glass vases as I listened to him expound on whatever interested him—the variety of grapes used to make the wine he'd opened, the director of the movie he had chosen for us to watch later, the female colleague whom he despised—nodding eagerly, assuming his interests as my own, allowing the veneer of our shared lives to displace what had been before. And when a junior partner at his firm wanted to talk to me in a certain way, or the father of one of my friends, or one of my teachers, I knew how to respond. How to surprise them, saying coolly, yes, I knew how pretty I was; yes, let's.

I see now that I related to my life with Tom, and my new life in Mexico, in much the same way, attempting to pick and choose among its beauty and ugliness, hiding whatever was unacceptable in it or in me. In the scattering of cigarette butts and broken glass and used condoms beneath the chipped Madonna of the shrine near my house, I doggedly saw only battered elegance and civility. Not the shabbiness of the men who had stood there slowly becoming drunk; the couples who had hurriedly fucked with little pleasure, their desire fueled less by love than by anger and hopelessness, afterward finishing off the cheap bottle and letting it slip through cum-wet fingers with the same nonchalant malice with which the little boy had flung the dead snake over his shoulder.

I think of the woman I overheard as a young girl, being raped or giving birth in a bathroom stall in the Back Bay bus station as I waited for my father. The sounds she made told a story more efficiently and with more power than any words could have. How that night, my lonely father lay on top of my covers to warm me, and beneath his awkward weight and wine-scented breath, I became so still that I imagined I had made a part of myself disappear.

Yet I had not permitted myself to dwell on these moments, to write about them in the notebook Louise had given me. I refused to permit that part of creation that is ugly, that is covered in shit and blood and wails as it is born. I still wanted to be the author of only beautiful things: beautiful children; beautiful houses; a beautiful, youthful body striding in high-heeled sandals along the Cuesta, smiling at all I passed. As much as I denied the ugliness of my origins, I remained their victim, incapable of either owning or discarding what I was stupid enough to imagine I had turned to ash.

Louise said: *You should leave the children with María more often. You need to be writing. How about tomorrow? We'll drive to the country. I'll take my camera.*

Yes, I unfailingly answered her. And then I would ferry her around, writing nothing, cowed and largely silent as she spoke of what she saw, interpreting our surroundings for me. In these moments,

I saw myself for what I was: grasping and meek, careful to never displease her.

And yet the simple fact of the notebook, and the prints I stared at, had opened up a portal. In bed at night, after setting aside whatever book I was reading, after lovemaking, when Tom slept, long-repressed images descended like an arm, shoving, imploring. Words arrived with fevered urgency, strung together with the clipped rhythm of my childhood, the color of its landscape.

Certain scenes began to assert themselves so insistently that one night I got up out of bed and began to write. And though the content was ugly, the sentences poured out with the same abandon and joy as they had that night at Louise's. This time, it wasn't someone else's story. It was only mine. I wrote of the afternoon when the boy Leo showed his penis to a group of us walking home from school. The pink denuded look of it that appalled me. How, after he'd shown and we'd looked, he and all the other children ran back to their decrepit homes. Me, no. I walked to the edge of the ravine where he had stood gripping himself, then made myself lean beyond it, staring at the black crusts of snow, making an inventory of the trash scattered there. Broken appliances, soiled clothing and diapers, food wrappers. Eventually my gaze settled on a child's broken bicycle. It had no seat, only a rusted pole thrusting upward where a child would sit.

I showed this vignette to Louise. For days, I waited anxiously for her reply. When it finally came, we were sitting across from one another in the hidden café—that dark, elegant space where I was received warmly now, always by the name she had given me: *Bienvenida, Señorita Mia. ¿Qué desea tomar?*

"Bravo, Mia." Gesturing at the pages resting in her lap. "It's good."

I flushed with joy, and even welled with tears. "It is? Really?"

"Really, really good. You're becoming so much more than the pretty girl I first met. In these pages is the truth that we are all fundamentally alone. We all must fend for ourselves, make our own realities. Mommy will not make it all better."

At that phrase, *Mommy will not make it all better*, the tears overspilled hotly. She had uttered it sneeringly, in a way that seemed to locate blame not with the inadequate mother who cannot comfort her child, but with the child who, in a pitiful moment of weakness, allows herself to expect it.

32

In the days and weeks following this exchange, I began to look at the Navarro etchings almost compulsively, always clandestinely, the secrecy a part of their dark pleasure. If someone came close to discovering me looking, an exquisite thrill passed through me. A shiver of pleasure, seeing the monkey's libidinal abandon as María reached forward to take hold of the empty teacup beside my computer.

"*¿Quiere más té, señora?*"

"*Sí, María, gracias.*"

María's face, hovering above the screen's craven image when she handed me the tea, was as serenely beautiful as a portrait of the Virgin Mary.

There was one etching that particularly upset and allured me. It depicted two monkeys at the foot of a huge brass bed, fucking—really, it is the only word. A single bare bulb hung above them. Curtains were parted at either side of the image, as though they were performing the act on a crude stage. At the bottom of the page, the title: *As Apes Do*.

I don't know how many hours I spent furtively looking at that image, sensing in the foulness some vital meaning, some answer to a question from my past I couldn't yet articulate. But it also unnerved me. Sometimes I would grow excited and even touch myself. Then, for days afterward, I wouldn't look at it. I would distance myself from Louise, even make fun of her with Tom, aligning myself with him in a way that was false, not because he didn't deserve my allegiance but because it was motivated by a kind of self-disgust, a fear that there was some part of me that must of necessity be disavowed to be worthy of love.

One night, after I'd been staring at *As Apes Do* for nearly a half an hour, I went downstairs to discover Tom waiting up for me. I understood immediately that he was hoping to have sex. I picked up the novel folded open on my bedside table.

"Oh, are you going to read?" he said in a forlorn tone.

I relented. Without words, I acquiesced to him: *Yes, whatever you want.* As he eagerly reached to turn out the light, I caught his hand. "Can you leave the light on?"

He looked surprised. I usually preferred it be dark. I had arranged myself against the pillows, crossing my arms over my breasts, which were ruined from nursing, though Tom still found them unaccountably pleasing—or so he told me; maybe his pleasure in such things, not in themselves attractive, was that he found himself written into them. He began to stroke my arms, my shoulders. "What's wrong, sweetheart? You're all tense."

"It's nothing. Just keep the light on, okay?"

"If that's what you want." He gave a stiff smile, quickly stood taking off his clothes, leaving them in a pile beside the bed. Then awkwardly climbing on top of me, like some enormous animal outside of its natural habitat, attempting something too delicate for its girth. He took himself into his hand, nosing, searching with the tip. I lay inert, declining to help him. There arrived that shared moment of slight resistance; his held breath, the tick of his pulse between his legs. His eyes rolled up beneath fluttering lids.

"Don't close your eyes," I said.

"What?"

"Look at me."

"Sorry."

His meekness repelled me, his desire to avoid offense. I had a sharp urge to scold him, *Don't be sorry, don't say that.* Tentatively he began to move. A little faster now. I watched him struggle to keep his eyes open, his face contorting slightly. Mine remained composed, expressing neither happiness nor unhappiness. In the unadornment of this protracted stare dwelled something unflattering to us both. It was as if we had given birth to a third person, perched menacingly between us. A blackmailer. Tom had begun to thrust in swift jabs, agitatedly working toward an end. I was repulsed, humiliated.

And then, out of nowhere, pleasure overtook me. It lifted from my feet. I felt it like an impossible intake of breath, a dam that broke behind my eyes, releasing its store, gushing into and out of me. He seemed frightened by it. He could no longer hold my gaze. In the final seconds, he began to cry, big innocent tears, murmuring the name that now sounded almost foreign to me, "Sally, Sally."

Afterward, I lay on my back, depleted. He leaned on one elbow, his face above mine, waiting for me to say something, reassure him.

"I wish I didn't have to leave tomorrow," he sighed out at length. "You gave yourself to me so completely tonight," he said quietly, as though confiding a secret, a plea for it to be true, for me to agree, but all I said was:

"You won't be gone long."

After perhaps another minute, he reached across me turning out the light. I had curled onto my side. With almost excruciating care, he pressed the covers against me the way I liked.

"Just sleep," he whispered.

My silence added to my deception—like that moment in a dream when you suddenly realize you have committed a crime and now must commit another to cover the first.

33

November. At the hot springs, the pools were shrouded in steam. Draping the matching towels I'd bought us over our chairs, we made our way to the water. The grass silvered with frost, our breath streaming into the cold. By noon, it would be seventy degrees, the days capering from winter to summer to winter again.

"I had the sweetest exchange with José Luis," I said.

"Who's this?" she said, suddenly alert.

"My friend who manages the butcher shop." We had entered the tunnel, treading water as our eyes adjusted to the darkness. "The one who keeps the books on his desk and reads them to his wife over the phone."

"She's probably illiterate," Louise said grimly, stroking forward.

"I hardly think so. He taught literature at a university in Guanajuato. He's a very educated man." I was annoyed. "Anyway, I think it's sweet."

"Sweet! In some ways, Mia, men are all alike. They enjoy marrying beneath them."

"Is that why Allan married you?"

Slowly she turned to face me, bracing her hands on either side of the wall so that I was unable to swim ahead of her. "Don't be a fool, Mia. Your friend, please! He sees a hundred spoiled Americans pass in and out of this town every month."

"*North* Americans."

"You're correcting me now?"

"The correct term is *estadounidenses*—José Luis taught me that forever ago. It's offensive otherwise."

"Offensive! Listen to you! If you weren't a grown woman, I'd pull you out of this pool and spank you."

"I'd like to see you try," I said, my voice quiet with rage. I was stroking in tiny circles so as not to brush against her. For seconds more, we squared off, before I turned and swam back toward the chairs.

The rest of the afternoon was passed in shallow politeness. I offered her a glass of wine. She refused. I drank one, pretended to doze. In the last hour, we played a form of Scrabble using only the tiles. I yawningly lost round after round until it was time to get the children.

"I suppose I ought to be grateful for the ride," Louise sniffed, getting out of the car.

"No need," I said without turning, thinking: *Good, I was getting bored with her anyway.*

But after a day of not speaking to her, two, I became troubled at the thought of her angry with me. I imagined passing her on one of the city's narrow, shaded streets, the two of us saying nothing to each other. Or Louise becoming sick and not telling me; or Ida asking to spend an afternoon with her, and me not knowing what to say.

"Mommy, will you read to me?" Henry called one evening from the bottom of the stairs.

"Yes, angel, be there in a moment."

I'd opened my laptop to check. Nothing from Louise. It had been three days. I opened a blank email. *Sorry I was such a pill earlier*, I typed. My hands, I noticed, were shaking. *I don't know what came over me. Please forgive me.* I began to cry. I cursed myself. I detested that kind of weakness, the groveling. I deleted the hated sentence, retyped it, read it over several times. For moments, my fingers hovered above send.

"Mommy, are you coming?"

Quickly I typed out a closing: *Love you, M.* I stared at the initial that wasn't mine but the one she'd given me, my eyes brimming with rage and self-pity. I hit send.

In Henry's room, pressed tightly against him in his twin bed, I read *Little Bear*. It was a special book out of my childhood—a rare artifact of happiness. Henry was too old for it, really, but he seemed not to mind. He curled against me, his plump hand patting my thigh whenever I turned a page. My voice quavered. The tears kept threatening to fall. Once the lights were out, I lay waiting impatiently for him to fall asleep, listening to all the usual festive sounds drift up from the Jardín. The out-of-tune mariachis and the calls of street vendors. The drunken laughter and shouts. The night before, I'd had a nightmare—I only now remembered it—in which I was running through the building site in a long coat with nothing underneath, and it was full of monkeys screeching as I passed, threatening to dart under the coat and bite my genitals.

When I left Henry's room at half past nine, there was still no reply from Louise. I checked six or seven more times, vacillating between hopefulness and fury, before finally falling asleep near midnight.

It wasn't until the following Monday that an email arrived from Louise, written entirely in capital letters as always: *SOMETHING I MUST SHOW YOU; COME AT ELEVEN.*

I went, nervously, as summoned. In the car, driving to whatever it was she wanted to share with me, it was as if nothing had happened. Louise spoke of a gallery opening she'd attended over the weekend. "The absolute *naivete*," she scoffed. "The egotism. *Look at me! I slapped a little paint on a canvas, now I'm a painter!*" She snorted. "Do us all a favor: Go plant a tree instead." There had been a dinner party, too, she said, at which she'd been forced to sit next to Hector's fiancée, such a drag! "Not one even halfway intelligent thought in her pretty head. Not like you, Mia; I wish you'd been there."

A few minutes later, several miles from the outskirts of Dolores Hidalgo, we arrived at our destination: a tiny, ancient-looking stone church at the side of the road. As I parked, she pushed back my hair, asking solicitously, "Did you enjoy your weekend with Tom?"

As usual, I sensed, in her tone, in the quality of the silence that followed her question, an implicit critique. Also as usual, I did nothing to correct her, giving a generic answer: It was fine.

In the church, women bent praying. I was envious of their faith and wanted to join them. But I was too self-conscious and lit a candle instead.

We lingered another quarter of an hour and then drove home in silence. It wasn't until we were nearly to her house that she said, "If you're serious about staying here, if you truly want to live here and not just be a tourist, you ought to live in one of the farther colonias."

"Like Montes?"

"Yes, exactly."

I stifled back a laugh. Of course she would say that; I was surprised she didn't suggest I live in her spare bedroom.

"Then again, maybe farther out would be even better. San Luis Rey or—" She fell silent.

"What?"

"Only, I'm not sure Tom feels the way you do."

I let that pass, smiling at her transparency, thinking how quickly moments with her turned this way, like pages of a book caught in the wind, flashing from romance to disillusionment. I was suddenly sick of her, her old age, her bitchy knowingness. I thought, viciously, *What could she possibly know about marriage? Her husband is a corpse.*

She still had not gotten out of the car. At last, she pushed the door open, slowly extracting herself in her shuffling way, shifting her weight above her bad leg as she stood, then paused, saying, "You like La Cieneguita, yes?"

I nodded. It was the town nearest the hot springs, beautiful and lush. In fact, I'd fantasized about living there.

"I have a friend who lives there. You ought to visit him; he'd enjoy meeting you."

I didn't respond. I was eager to get going, to be out of her company, and she said, a little brusquely:

"You have to decide what you really want."

"Oh?" I said, affecting boredom. "Really, do I?"

A beat of silence. The familiar wry expression, the narrowing of her eyes. Reflexively I opened my mouth to apologize. But before I could find the right words, she went limping and clattering over the gravel to her door, where the dog was barking to raise holy hell.

34

In truth, I didn't need to decide what I wanted. I wanted everything. I wanted the silver bracelet on my wrist and the obscene print on my wall. I wanted the house in La Cieneguita, with chickens roaming the backyard and neat rows of rubber boots lined up along a tiled entryway. The purity of morning, fragrant and cool. Solitude and unfettered sex and the joy of work that I loved. Mostly I wanted never to go back.

Sometimes Louise seemed like the key, murmuring the answers to questions I hadn't fully formed, as if we were speaking in that shared code I'd perceived from the first morning in the café, when she told me she was going to kill someone and I thought, *She could*, and the thought pleased me and attracted me to her. At other times, she grated on me. Her unspoken demands for pity; her overweening authority; her petty jabs at Tom, at marriage itself.

One morning around this time, we were sitting in the hidden café, at the table near the entrance where I'd once observed the young woman reading her book. Louise was facing in, haloed by sunlight. Through the window over her shoulder, I could see rows of painted doors, women passing with their brightly colored plastic shopping bags.

"That first time you came to my house," Louise began, "when you were talking about Allan's painting. I never told you this: He made it when I was pregnant. You were speaking about the shape, with the tiny legs. *Tenuous*, I think you called it, or was it *fragile*? It touched me, your describing it that way. It was as if you knew." She searched my eyes. "I lost the baby."

"Oh, Louise, I'm so sorry!" A horse was passing in the street, I'd heard the clop of hooves and now saw at the periphery of my vision the absurdity of the rider's sombrero, like an actor portraying a Mexican at a theme park. In the silence, something nagged at me. "Your daughter—"

"Yes, finally we did have a baby. Only Allan never saw her. He died a month before she was born." She shrugged her shoulders and laughed, that peculiar laugh she had—*Oh well, that's life*. "That first pregnancy, we were living in Italy. We had a small farmhouse in Umbria, about an hour north of Rome. We had these two wonderful chickens, similar to Bella. Allan would be painting, and the chickens would come into my bedroom and nestle, one against each hand. After a few minutes—but you won't believe me."

"No, what?"

"The chickens would nestle in my hands, cooing, until two eggs dropped into my palms. Did you know they're soft until they come out? The eggs. If you touch them before they're out, the shells are warm and soft as water balloons. But then the instant they're out, they're perfectly shaped and hard."

"You're joking," I said, laughing lightly. It was true; I didn't believe her. Not just about the eggs. "I thought you told me that Allan died here, in San Miguel."

"Yes," Louise answered without hesitation. "We moved back after I miscarried. A change of scene. And then, after I lost Allan, my Italian friends helped me get back to Italy and open my gallery. I don't know how I ever got through it." She glanced at me. "The point is, sometimes true family is not given but found." She reached across the table, solemnly taking my hand. After a pause, she surprised me by saying, "There's a favor I have to ask you."

"Of course," I reflexively answered.

"I have an old friend, from when I lived here before. He's a marvelous artist, I very much want you to meet him, only—"

"What is it?"

"I want it to be at your house."

"Why not yours?"

She made a dismissive gesture. "My house isn't suitable for entertaining."

"But you entertain all the time."

"This is different."

We went back and forth a while longer, Louise saying that her house wasn't beautiful enough, she had no view, her furniture wasn't amenable to a seated meal with more than two or three people. I countered half-heartedly. My main hesitation, unvoiced, of course, was how I would present such an odd request to Tom. But as usual, she wore me down and I said yes. We settled up. A few minutes later, as I was flagging down a taxi, I asked if I could drop her somewhere.

"Oh, I couldn't possibly."

The usual rigmarole. The back-and-forth. Then speeding away along the narrow street lined with parked cars, banda music blaring from the radio. Louise had turned sideways, peering out the window. I looked at the faint lines around her eye and the trace of scar along her jawline and the slight, irreverent lift of her bottom lip. Those small details that I seemed to have known forever.

35

The development had finally begun to take shape. One could now see outlines of buildings, curving paths, brown swaths where grassy lawns would be. I marked the progress from Louise's with a detachment remarkable even to myself. "Isn't it loathsome?" she would remark, standing at the window after putting on a record, and I would nod and sip my wine as though it had nothing whatever to do with me. Occasionally I would remind her that Tom himself disliked the project. If it had been up to Tom, it would be entirely different, something of actual value, in meaningful dialogue with the colonial architecture that surrounded it, the landscape. Louise let such statements pass unchallenged, saying only that love had triumphed despite the construction; couples were still making nightly use of the field. She often spied them entering, holding hands.

One Sunday afternoon coming home, there was a terrible traffic jam. Only Henry was with me; I'd gone to Louise's on a whim, after taking him to get a new pair of school shoes in town. Now, with cars at a standstill, I became agitated. Tom and I had planned a family outing to the botanical gardens near our house; now I'd have to explain everything to him, and to Ida, who would be upset that we'd gone to Louise's without her. I decided to bypass the Cuesta and use the alternate route

Tom had once shown me. But all the one-way streets confused me. Soon nothing was familiar.

"Are we lost?" Henry asked.

I answered in a quick high voice, "Not at all! But can you not talk for a moment, darling?"

The windows were up and sweat prickled the back of my neck. Taking the next turn, without hope, like a miracle I spied María walking along the sidewalk. I could ask her for directions! She was moving away from me, but the pendulum of her thick braid, her bandy-legged tread, was unmistakable. Only as I neared, I had a tremor of doubt. She was wearing a dress I'd never seen and sandals with a slight heel. She held a girl's hand, the girl maybe a year or two older than Ida. Presently she bent on her knee, saying something to the little girl, whose face, I saw, was round and shiny like buffed clay, a small replica of María's. I slowed, watching, rapt, as María lifted her finger to her own mouth and then pressed it over the girl's eyebrow to smooth it, the girl impassive in the same way María so often was, allowing her mother to groom her, María brusquer with her than she was with my own children.

It suddenly occurred to me that I didn't know María's last name. For perhaps the first time, I wondered about her life without us. What did her house look like? Were the rooms empty; did they smell of lavender as ours did? Was she taking her daughter to church or a relative's, a sister's maybe?

Into these imaginings, Henry suddenly shouted, "María!"

I started and blushed, as though I'd been caught trespassing. Since I'd asked him not to speak, he'd been sprawled over the back seat, paging through a book Louise had given him.

"She's over there!" he shouted, his hands and face pressed at the window, almost desperate now. "Mommy, you're going to pass her!"

The moment of decision. I was drawing ahead, about to pull over, when Henry suddenly drew back from the window, his mood shifting. "Why is she holding that girl's hand?" he said, as though it were incomprehensible that she could hold the hand of a child he'd never seen, be absorbed in her needs, her appearance, rather than his and Ida's.

"Where was she going?" he asked a little later. We had turned onto a broader avenue, funneling toward Centro.

"Home," I told him. Then, realizing he still hadn't understood: "Her own house."

36

The day Bella laid her first egg was a national holiday, Día de la Revolución. Henry found it, running into the house shouting and holding it aloft.

"Stop yelling, Henry," Ida commanded like a miniature Louise. "Don't hold it like that, you'll drop it!"

He pivoted, darting past her, and she lunged at him so that I thought he really would drop it. But I grabbed her shoulder, holding her back, as Louise said calmly:

"Here, give it to me." She had gotten a knitting needle from somewhere. We went back out onto the patio, still bare except the arrangement of boxes. Carefully she pierced the shell with the needle. "We'll take turns," she said. "It's tradition."

Tradition for whom, I wondered, from where? I seemed to remember once seeing a girl do it in a movie set in the South of France. Ida and Henry were bickering about who would taste it first. "I found it," Henry kept exclaiming. Which was correct. I wanted Henry to be the first, but I was nervous about Ida's reaction to having to go second; she could behave as though Henry was contagious, recoiling from things he'd touched or eaten. As I was parsing all of this—the ways I cowered before Ida, the ways I so often privileged Henry over her—Louise broke in:

"Mia will taste it. Your mother goes first."

When she put it in my hand, still warm, I shuddered involuntarily. It wasn't like an egg from the grocery store. It seemed textured, one side marked with a yellowish smear of shit. But it was clean and smooth at its tip where she had pierced it, and with an effort to master my repulsion, I put it to my lips, thrilled as the warm viscous liquid filled my mouth.

"Now *me*!"

With care, I passed it to Henry, his eyes wide with wonder. I worried he would drop it, he would gag, he would be crushed by disappointment at the taste. He took his sip with gusto, Ida screeching, "Not so much!" Immediately after he swallowed, he cried out in triumph, "It's good; I like it!" Probably it was largely face-saving, but what did it matter? He would remember this moment forever, I thought. I sensed the current of Ida's impatience, almost aggression.

"Now Ida," Louise instructed.

Compliantly, Henry passed the egg with great solemnity. Ida took it from him as if he were a thief and she'd only just managed to wrest from him what was rightfully hers. Then she steadied herself as an actor does when about to step onto the stage. She audibly exhaled. When she lifted it to her lips, it was with her eyes closed and a little smile on her face, making a show of piety like she was being admitted into a divine secret. She kept her eyes shut for several seconds after she swallowed and, when she opened them, said nothing despite Henry's pleas, as if her experience alone was untranslatable.

Lastly Louise drank. She tilted her head all the way back, her slender throat moving with her swallows like an egret's gulping down a fish. You can tell a lot about people merely by observing them. If Louise taught me anything, it's that people give themselves away all the time. The only question is, are you able to see deeply enough? And are you prepared to accept what you find?

Henry was talking loudly about what would happen next. "It's finished," said Ida mockingly. "We ate it."

"But what about the shell," he whined, appealing to Louise when he asked, could he have it? Could he take it back to his house? Ida crossing her arms at the foolishness of that suggestion.

"Come. I'll show you what to do."

The pronouncement, the way it was delivered, made me want to hide Henry in my arms, somehow preserve the magic of what we'd experienced, keep her from showing him what the world really is. Ida was smiling smugly as we followed out the front door and across the street, where a half dozen men were busy at work. Louise as ever a solitary, irreverent figure, hobbling and lurching ahead of us. We went all the way to the farthest edge, where nothing had been cleared. Sunlight beat down without warmth. We stopped. When Louise lifted her arm ceremoniously, I was seized by the same desperate urge to stave off the moment, to scream, *Don't do it! Just give him the fucking shell! For once in your life, be yielding!* Her arm was extended rigidly, the shell tucked in her hand. In a few quick, pulsing motions, she had crushed it to powder and begun scattering it onto the cracked arid earth. Then Henry did scream at her, too late, "No! Please!"

She half squatted beside him, bending just on one knee, her damaged leg thrust stiffly forward. In a rare moment of tenderness, she rested her hands on his small shoulders. "It's okay; this is good, Henry."

"No!" he cried again, though with less conviction.

Patiently, she began a recitation on the cycle of life, that the shell would feed the earth, the earth would feed the bugs, the bugs would feed Bella so that Bella could make more eggs; the next one, she would let him keep.

"I can keep the next one only for me?"

"Yes."

"Can I have one?" Ida wanted to know.

"Of course! The very next one after Henry's," Louise said, and with the same intensity with which I had wanted to scream, stop her at any cost, I now wanted to fall on her in gratitude.

Back in her living room, she put on music and we all danced. Later they ran outside to play and Louise and I smoked, laughing as we blew rings into the air. Even after the cigarette and the two or maybe three glasses of wine, I could still taste it. I could still feel the viscous warmth of it in my throat.

37

"I don't like Ida spending so much time with her." It was the last Friday in November. Tom and Henry and I were finishing comida, Louise having picked Ida up from school.

I smiled equably. "What do you mean, 'so much'?"—making quotes with my fingers. I hadn't told him about many of the times they'd been together.

He made an impatient gesture, a glance to Henry that told me he felt constrained by his presence from giving full vent to his criticisms of Louise. The day of the egg, when the kids came home full of excited stories of their triumph, he had played along with them, but that night with me, he had reiterated his mistrust of her, his concern, me countering that she was giving them experiences they never could have had at home.

"I'm just saying, we should be encouraging Ida to make friends her own age, maybe setting up playdates with other kids in her class."

"She doesn't like the kids at school. With Louise, she can be herself; she can have Louise's undivided attention."

"But don't you think it's weird for her to spend time with someone so much older?"

"I think it's good for her," I said, and began to reiterate things I'd said before, that children benefited from knowing different kinds of people; that loving them meant preparing them to separate from you. I believed that, but I was invoking it fatuously. It was mostly complacency that had led me to permit Ida to spend time with her, while I wiled away the hours with Henry, walking the botanical gardens or huddling together under blankets in the feeble late-autumn sun, telling him stories.

"I'm going to get her," Tom said. "What's there for her to do over there? I want to see her. I have the afternoon off."

"No, I'll get her," I said decisively. "Just relax, read a magazine or whatever, you've already worked. I'll be home soon."

As I approached Louise's, reflexively I began looking for her and Ida in the field, imagining they might be out hunting for bugs, maybe sketching. The construction had stalled again; there was no one. The neighbor boy was sitting on the stoop. Beside him sat another boy I didn't recognize, paler and more finely made. The two appeared to be "drawing" on the concrete slab with sticks, or maybe they were ancient crayons. As I rose out of the parked car, suddenly, in that way that things transform before your eyes—the man becomes a coat hung on a stand, the stooping child in a red jacket a fire hydrant—the unfamiliar boy became Ida. Ida, who now turned to me, smiling, her neck paler than the rest of her, impossibly slender. She was beautiful and handsome, herself and not herself. I was stunned.

"Hello," she said without addressing me, as though we were meeting for the first time. She didn't stand, didn't run up to kiss me or embrace me.

"Ida, oh my God," I said. "You cut your hair."

"Louise did it."

"Oh? Did she?" I was struggling to modulate my voice, my heart thrashing in my chest. "How did that happen, my love?"

"What do you mean?" she said, her tone faintly mocking, as though I were an idiot. It happened with scissors—what did I think?

"I mean, how did it come about?" I said, fighting myself back, trembling slightly.

"In the field."

"But when? Whose idea was this?"

A little satisfied smile. "We both wanted to."

I got into the car and turned it on. "We need to go," I called shortly through the window, a rigid smile pasted on my face.

"Why?" she said, still mocking me. But she walked over to the front passenger seat, springing from her toes, her head very erect. I pulled back over the gravel without saying anything to Louise, who must have been inside the house now that the deed was accomplished—doing what, exactly? Smoking, paging through some outdated communist tome, I thought furiously. A surge of panic: What would Tom do when he saw Ida? When it came out that Louise had done it? I imagined him seething with rage, ranting that she had altered our daughter without our consent, violated our trust. Certainly that was how he would see it: We'd been violated, he and I. Meanwhile, Ida maintained a defiant silence. As we came to the top of the hill, unable to contain myself and against my better judgment—Ida always leapt at any opening like a hunter—I said, "Ida, you're so quiet; is everything all right?"

"Why wouldn't it be? I finally got my hair cut, and it's exactly how I wanted it."

Meaning: I hadn't done it for her; I had failed to please her. Impetuously I nearly struck back, *Daddy and Henry will certainly be surprised. I don't think they'll like it.* But I managed to check myself. We had rounded the final curve and were descending the steep driveway, Ida staring ahead through the window, her face set in a particular way. Catching sight of her from the corner of my eye—the way her mouth lifted, her eyes narrowed over her private thoughts—an unpleasant sensation passed through me. Her expression was so eerily like Louise's.

Tom was on the patio relaxing when we stepped up into the main living area. Without greeting him, Ida ran to play in the lower courtyard. In the kitchen, I filled two glasses with ice and then lime, tequila, a little grapefruit soda.

"Drink?" I said, handing him one as I stepped outside.

"Where's Ida?" he asked in surprise.

I told him she was downstairs, and let a minute or so pass before saying, "I forgot to mention, I took Ida earlier to get her hair cut." I hadn't planned to lie, not fully anyway. Something in his face when he'd asked for Ida made me understand in a different way the finality of what had happened. What it might mean for Louise and me.

"When was this?" he said, as always stuck on the details, the logistical facts.

"Right after school, just before I dropped her at Louise's." I'd added a second lie on top of the first; Louise had been the one to pick her up. He made a questioning sound in response, and I went on, "I just want you to prepare yourself, it's a big change. It's a lot shorter. But she really loves it. She's very proud of it," I added, conveying with my tone a warning to let it be her thing, preserve her happiness.

"All right," he said with a small sigh, like he was resigning himself, being the bigger man. "So, let's see this haircut." Lifting his voice, "Ida! Come up, I want to see you!"

"Can't we just enjoy our moment alone?" I said, smiling, reaching a hand to his shoulder and bending forward to kiss him. He acquiesced, and for a while, we drank, speaking only a little and superficially about the weather and the beauty of the view as I tried to tamp down my worry. After ten minutes or so, hearing Ida speaking below, Tom went to the edge of the balcony and called down to her. When she called back, presumably stepping into view for the first time, his face went dark. It was unbearable. I stood and began toward the glass doors, saying over my shoulder, "Should I refresh our drinks?" I glanced back inquiringly. He was staring at me, his face contorted. "Be nice," I whispered to him. "She likes it." Then I went dashing off into the house, busying myself with this and that, like a naughty child attempting to hide.

I had anticipated Tom's anger with Louise, and also with me. What I hadn't fully anticipated was the force of his anger at the haircut itself.

"It's so ugly," he pronounced as soon as we were alone that night, sitting stiffly on the edge of our bed. Climbing beside him, I tried to temper his reaction: Ida had such a beautiful face, now you could really see it, lots of beautiful girls and women had pixie cuts.

"She looks like a fucking dyke."

"Jesus Christ, Tom! Do you hear yourself?"

We'd always allowed each other to vent about our children, to be coarse if we needed to blow off steam: *Henry's being such an asshole*. But there was something so brutal in his reaction that I was unable to let it go, furiously telling him that I had only facilitated what Ida herself wanted, she loved it, she was happy; wasn't that the point, not whether we liked it? "Anyway, I think it's pretty."

"It's not. It's hideous."

"Keep your voice down."

"What, I can't be upset about my child, my little girl—"

"Don't call her that."

"Why?" He had contorted his face into a mask of obliviousness. "Please, enlighten me: Why can't I call our daughter my little girl?"

"Because she doesn't belong to us like that." My voice had risen. "She's not some doll for us to tote around and show off—*look what we own, look how pretty she is, look how clever.*" As I gave that last attribute, I could already hear him protesting in his fastidious way, *What does cleverness have to do with it?* But he didn't comment. It was as though he hadn't even heard me.

"You know what it really is?" he finally said out of the silence. "It's that she looks like *her* now. That fucking woman. That liar."

38

The photographs arrived in my inbox the next afternoon. She'd attached them to a blank email. Why? Was she somehow upset with *me*, offended that I'd taken Ida without saying goodbye to her? As soon as I opened the photos, any umbrage I felt was silenced. Here was Ida in her essence, staring calmly into the camera, hair shorn, eyes wells of black, like the seconds when only her head was born and for that brief span between contractions she remained indefinable, neither boy nor girl.

While most of the images Louise had sent were of Ida alone, the one I looked at the longest was of the two of them. They sat slightly left of center on a low wall that I recognized as being in the little churchyard near her house. Louise's face was aimed squarely at the camera, Ida's turned to regard her, each an echo of the other, like a meditation on time and age. Even the litter of cigarette butts in the foreground was poignant, the way the two conjoined shadows extended toward them. For days, I habitually reopened it, always confronted anew by that sense of tenuousness and erasure; how little our lives belong to us, and how limited our belonging to one another, even our own flesh and blood.

I knew my admiration for the photograph—my ability to see it as a work of art, and as such extraordinary—would have infuriated Tom. I heard his objections without his even speaking them—how could something born from a violation of trust and power be beautiful; how could I ever admire something "wrong"?—as when, of late, I would speak about sexual encounters I'd had as a child, or the violence I'd experienced, almost with nostalgia, a certain gratitude for what they had taught me. *I don't like you to act as if any of it is okay*, he would admonish me in these moments. Then I would rebut him: It was my life; what did he want, for me to pretend otherwise? Sometimes I would become philosophical: Brutality was intrinsic to nature; lift up any rock in the woods, and you'll find violence and annihilation.

For all these philosophical wonderings, and as long as I studied the photograph, there was one question I never thought to ask myself. Namely, who had taken it? Whose eyes had gazed at the two of them, the field and the sky, composing it all within the camera lens, struck like me by the echo in the way their heads leaned sideways, their fierce determination, even in repose. The love between them. Those things that at once moved and frightened me.

39

One Friday, Louise again brought up the favor she'd asked: Could she host a guest at our house for comida? Although I'd said yes, I'd been vague when she pressed me about specific dates, redirecting, equivocating. I'd hoped something would come up with Tom's work—an afternoon meeting or another trip—so that we could have the meal without his knowing. Now Louise was pressing me to do it Friday; would that work? Say 2:30?

"Tom hasn't been in a great mood lately. He's been very busy with work."

"What's it got to do with him?"

I chuckled to myself. Really, she was incredible. "It's just that he's not in the mood for company these days," I said.

She leveled her gaze on me, narrowing her eyes in that way that she shared with Ida. "What's really going on?"

"What do you mean?"

"Are you embarrassed of me in front of Tom for some reason?"

"Of course not."

"I'm too shabby, the poor relation? Is that it?"

"Of course not."

"Oh, but you like to play the wealthy young housewife at the school. Trust me, Fabiola tells me all about it."

"You're being ridiculous, this is all absurd."

"Yes, it's absurd, because it's beneath you. Kissing cheeks, exchanging meaningless niceties, how's the weather. I'm trying to introduce you to people who are interesting, who can enrich you."

"Interesting," I said, laughing.

She looked at me severely. But after several beats, her expression dissolved into something almost soft. "No," she said, "you're absolutely right. I should never have asked you. I'm sorry. Why don't I just come alone? I'll bring the bottle of wine this time. You'll tell me what Tom likes."

Of course I relented. On the day, I decided to play it off to Tom as though it had happened spur-of-the-moment. Coming through the door with Ida in tow, I called out cheerily:

"Tom, you'll never guess who's here, and she's brought wine!"

Reluctantly, seeming a bit put out, he stood from the couch where he'd been reading to Henry and extended his hand in greeting.

"I'll just open this up," Louise said. As she left to the kitchen, I explained in whispers that we'd run into her walking to the car, and Ida had invited her to comida. It had been awkward; I didn't know how to get out of it.

"Christ, Ida," Tom said.

"I know; I'm so sorry."

He hesitated before saying, a little reluctantly, "What could you do?" and I smiled, telling myself I would make it up to him.

Louise returned, accompanied by María carrying a tray with the filled glasses. We stood, holding our glasses by the stems, smiling stiffly. There was an odd formality to the moment, the fact no one had sat. Ida ran to her room to get a picture she had drawn the day before. Louise only glanced at it, with none of her usual focused attention. She kept checking a watch I'd never seen her wear before, with a large round white face and Roman numerals. Since arriving she had been uncharacteristically tense, fussing with her clothes, her hair, tapping her watch as if it had become stuck. Abruptly she announced that she wanted to get some air; would I come with her?

As she stepped toward the balcony, she seemed to gain a new degree of control over herself, standing more upright, walking more steadily on her damaged legs as if through sheer force of will. At the door, she leaned her cane against the glass wall and, with her hand tightly gripping my arm, came the rest of the way outside without it.

I said something encouraging—*Wow, you're walking so well today*—to which she made no response. She didn't even look at me. We reached the railing, standing side by side in the magnificent afternoon light, looking out over the tiled rooftops to the city beneath us, hearing all the now familiar sounds that unfailingly filled me with joy: roosters, music and brash laughter, cars grinding gears as they climbed. I was gazing dreamily into the blue blank span of sky where Tom and I had once watched the rainstorm moving. But I soon became aware that Louise was staring intently only at the spot where the steps emptied onto the Cuesta. Her whole body was taut beside me, the way a dog will quiver and tense seeing an animal it wants to chase.

"What are you looking at?"

"Nothing," she said, not shifting her gaze from that single four-foot strip of sidewalk visible from the balcony, where occasionally someone passed, coming into frame for a few seconds before exiting. She had carried out her glass of wine, her forearms leaned on the balcony railing. There was a stiff breeze, riffling her hair and pricking the skin on her arms.

"Should we go back inside?" I suggested.

"No."

A few more minutes passed before a man entered the strip of sidewalk that had come to seem like a tiny stage. He stopped and, as though there was an invisible string attaching the two of them, looked up to Louise. It was the man she'd kissed on the path, whom I'd seen in the Plaza Civica. As they held one another's stare, Louise slowly inclined her head toward me. His gaze transferred, a look I couldn't read altering his face as he looked at me. Entreating, maybe.

It lasted barely a second. Louise cleared her throat loudly, drawing back his attention. Thrusting her arm forward, she opened her hand and let go of the wineglass. There was something horrifying in the brief pause of silence. At the sound of glass exploding against stone, splitting the still air, I started violently. Louise didn't flinch. With her stare still fixed on the man, she put her arm around my shoulder and drew me closer—a gesture that brought a murderous look into the man's eyes. His mouth hinged open. I braced myself for the stream of obscenities I knew would be next. But he remained silent, neutered by some unseen force. He only gripped his hair in his fists and swayed on his legs like a little boy trying to master his emotions, a desperate gesture that made me pity him as I had in the park. A second later, he turned and disappeared behind the ocher-colored wall in the direction from which he'd come.

I was deeply shaken. Her arm was still around me; I wanted it off but made no motion to move. "What the hell was all that?" I said, aiming at lightness.

She just stood beside me without turning, completely impassive.

"Was that the man you wanted to invite to our house? The man I saw you with on the arroyo path?"

She took her arm away, saying tersely, "Saw me when?"

"What the hell is going on, Louise?"

Without realizing it, I'd raised my voice, and now I saw that Tom had noticed, María had, the children. When I looked back to Louise, her eyes were shining with tears. *Perfect*, I thought. I was on the brink of laughing, my face burning with rage. *Now the selfish bitch is going to cry.*

"Is everything all right out there?" Tom called. "I heard glass breaking."

I called back: "Sorry, I dropped a glass." I don't know why I did it, what mistaken impulse made me want to protect Louise. Only that I had a terrible feeling that I'd ceded something vital to my autonomy and happiness, and when we turned from the balcony and Louise put her arm through my arm, a sensation close to terror passed cleanly along my spine.

"We really should try and clean it up," Tom said.

"Of course," I said, cheeks flaming, hurrying down the stairs and out the door. I remember searching on my hands and knees for the shards, hoping one would cut me so Tom might say, full of concern, *Are you okay?* But they were too tiny even to lift. The glass had practically shattered back to sand.

Later, when we were sitting at the sunny table passing dishes around, the children laughing about something and Louise speaking easily to Tom about how the project was coming along, what I wanted more than anything was to be in the kitchen with María. To watch her eat and be silent in the way we had been at first, when I couldn't speak to her or understand her, and her face was a still quiet pool.

40

Days fell one on top of another. María building fires in the morning, ironing the children's uniforms. Louise calling me along a narrow alleyway, from the end of a watery tunnel. Tom's eyes fluttering as he moved above me, my head resting on the pillow, my legs draped open. In these moments, it seems to me, I didn't have a single desire that originated in myself. And yet I was happy. We were becoming a part of Mexico in a way that was thrilling to me. Ensconced in the cloistered cold of the town in winter, I crossed myself before the makeshift shrines, as I saw others do. I exchanged kisses hello and goodbye with the other mothers at school, chatting loudly as we waited for the children to be brought out. Henry was often invited to play at friends' houses—elaborate new constructions outside of town with live-in maids and cooks and groundskeepers, or Spanish colonial homes in Centro that had been continuously in the family, their towering front doors made to accommodate a horse and carriage.

"I overheard the boys playing," the mothers would tell me over plates of cookies or *tres leches* cake or *pay de queso* and cups of tea when I came to pick him up. "Henry understands everything, and his accent! *¡Está perfecto!*"

These women, too, knew me as Mia, a name that was easier to pronounce and prettier than Sally.

"Mia, you can't go back to the States," they implored me. "The children are adjusting so well!"

I soon let it be known—to them, the head of the kids' school, Enrique and José Luis—that we had decided to move here and were searching for a house; I might even enjoy living in the *campo*. After all, I confided, I'd lived in the countryside as a girl, my mother having given up her career as a dancer to devote herself to her family.

They nodded their approval, cheered my decision to stay. "Mexico is so much better for children!"

I reveled in these exchanges. The hyperbole, natural to me now, the warmth and jocularity, the absolute privilege of family over everything. Winter break was approaching, and Tom and I had decided to take the children to a small fishing village called Huasquitico, with no hotels or shops, no restaurants to speak of, nothing but a few cabanas scattered along a pristine stretch of beach.

When I finally told Louise, she met the news with sarcasm.

"Eleven days without you and the kids! What will I do with myself?"

We were at the hot springs, huddled into lawn chairs. It was the Friday before we were to leave. "It's going to be so blissful for me," I parried back, not in the mood for her acerbity. "Ten days without internet or cell service, only us and the sun and sand!"

"And you heard of this place how?"

"From José Luis."

"Oh, well then. Butchers always know the best vacation spots."

"Yes. It will be so great to have time with Tom! All those nights . . ."

Louise set her mouth into a sardonic smile. "I've invited Fabiola, by the way."

This caught me up. "What do you mean—now?"

She laughed lightly. "You know she and Carmen broke up, yes? It will be good for her to be with someone young and beautiful."

I opened my mouth to object, perhaps announce that I had things to do in order to get ready and was about to leave. But just then, as if on cue, Fabiola's husky voice came drifting over the grass. "*Oigan, chicas, ¿qué tal?*" I turned to see her waving hello.

After kissing me on both cheeks, rather than take the nearest empty chair, she perched onto mine, bending her knees and stretching her sweater over her bare legs. "It's *un poco frío*, no?"

"Get closer to Mia for warmth," Louise said.

"Can I at least have some of the coat, please?" Fabiola said, leaning beside me, wriggling her body close to mine.

Taking out her camera, "Look how adorable the two of you are."

"Don't, Louise, I look a mess."

Fabiola rolled her eyes, saying to Louise in Spanish, "As if she ever could," the two exchanging knowing glances. A waiter was passing, and lifting her hand, Louise called in her leaden Spanish: "*Dos micheladas, por favor.*" Then, to Fabiola, "She's leaving us, did you know?"

Fabiola stared at me in shock. "Not back to the States?"

"Only to the beach," I laughed, flattered at Fabiola's reaction.

"Where?"

"Huasquitico."

With an entreating glance, Louise said primly, "She's looking forward to being away from us."

"She should be! It's amazing there, completely unspoiled."

I smiled and pressed my body closer to Fabiola, taking a petty delight in seeing Louise shut down, the two of us sinking lower, laughing as we tried to stretch the coat between us.

"Now my leg is out!" Fabiola protested, curling her face against my neck. I could hear the muffled thundering of the chorro, the clicking of Louise's camera as she snapped away. When the micheladas arrived, Fabiola lifted her glass, sitting at the foot of the chair and locking eyes with me. "To beach getaways! On the count of three: one, two . . ." We began to chug the drinks. At the last moment, I broke into laughter, spraying red everywhere, Fabiola lowering her drained glass in triumph.

"And now we swim," she said. "I haven't been under the chorro *en muchisimo tiempo.*"

"You two go ahead," Louise said, as if we'd invited her.

"Yes, come, the two of us," Fabiola said, making me screech as she tugged the coat away, reaching her hand back as she leapt ahead above the cold turf. She went into the pool quickly, diving under the steaming water and when she resurfaced, smoothing back her glossy hair with her hands, then pulling herself in broad arcs to the mouth of the tunnel. I followed with smaller strokes, keeping my face above water. Halfway in, she turned and began to close the distance between us. "Stay where you are."

"If you say so," I laughed, amused by her bossiness, how unlike other Mexican women she was.

"Yes, I do." She had reached me, her voice low, her breath coming in short, sharp sips. For seconds, we treaded water as Louise and I had once done, our feet and hands now and then striking like muscled fish, retreating, her aggressive proximity making me drift backward toward the wall. "Hold still."

"What is it?"

"You have tomato juice on your face." Her mouth was nearly touching mine, the hot wash of her breath joining with the dampness. Slowly she braced her hands against the wall on either side of me. "Here, let me fix you." She extended her tongue and licked my cheek with slow deliberation. I had kept my eyes open and felt something deep within my body uncomfortably rending and giving way. In the next moment, we were kissing. Not gently, girlishly, but frantically, Fabiola tugging at my hair, biting my lips as I met her lips and tongue with pants and moans. If not for the appearance of an old man at the mouth of the tunnel, I don't know what we would have done. As it was, we parted hurriedly, falling primly into single file, taking turns in silence beneath the gushing water.

Louise wore a smirk as we fell back into our seat, saying to Fabiola, "Well? Was it everything you'd hoped for?"

I pulled incrementally into myself, as if to deny I'd given anything away, holding the rigid inch or so of distance between us, relieved when she said in a neutral tone only that the water had been relaxing, she was happy to have been invited, relegating our indiscretion to the realm of daydreams. The rest of the morning passed uneventfully.

41

That night was the big holiday party for Tom's firm. We had been held up by a search for Henry's favorite stuffed toy. By the time we arrived, the small space—an art gallery two blocks off the Jardín—was already packed with people laughing and talking in front of overscaled abstract paintings. I anxiously scanned the crowd. Tom's arm was around my shoulder. "Can I get you a drink? Champagne?"

"Please, yes," I said, relieved that for the next few minutes if someone greeted me as Mia, or asked about my mother, it wouldn't be in Tom's hearing. He had already begun to pick his way through the crowd, smiling broadly, now and then stopping to tell someone hello, brimming with the certainty of his charm. Watching him, I was overwhelmed by tenderness and pity, the sharp conviction I was not worthy of him; I was tainted and disloyal. I refocused my attention on the paintings, broad swaths of beige and gray and black, above which a gritty texture had been haphazardly applied, as if a bucket of sand had been hurled at the canvas when it was still wet.

"Deep in contemplation, I see."

I turned to find Bill Barnes smiling at me quizzically out of his big black eyeglass frames. His manner competent, assured, his handsome sweep of gray hair and square jaw. The sort of wealthy person you might bump into at the opera as easily as at the hardware store.

"It's so lovely to see you!" We kissed hello. My warmth was genuine. Of all Tom's colleagues, I liked him the best.

"How have you and the kids been getting on?" He'd grown up in Maine and retained a trace of that accent. "The house is acceptable, I hope?"

"Acceptable! It's like living in a work of art."

"Please, you'll make me blush." He took my hand. "A house needs someone beautiful to bring it to life. I'm too old and ugly for it now, but you . . ." He lowered his eyes, looking faintly abashed. "So, what do you make of them?" he asked, indicating the paintings.

"They're pretty atrocious."

"Aren't they, though?" He laughed, as if the fact delighted him. "There's a great deal of bad art in this town these days. Not so when I first came here in the '60s. In those days, you would be at a party and Allen Ginsberg might show up, or Burroughs."

"Yes, I have a friend who was here then. You know her, I think. Louise Nieman?"

"Nieman, hmm. I can't say it rings a bell." He'd pronounced it with that faint Brahmin accent, *caahnt*, the way Louise would have.

"Her husband, Allan, was a painter," I went on. "Abstract, geometric shapes, with these little limbs, a bit like Paul Klee?"

"You don't mean Allan Pearlman's girl?"

"Yes, Allan Pearlman," I said, nodding eagerly. "I know his wife, Louise."

"Is that what she's going by now?" He shook his head. "Oh, yes, I remember *her*. It was later, though, she was here, in the '70s. Astounding she would have come back after what happened, and all the tomfoolery she got up to with that Spaniard—her name escapes me. Fernando Navarro's girl."

"Nuria."

"The four of them doing things you ought by rights to be hanged for, Catholic country like this! Not that I'm a prude. Still, that night, she and the Spaniard put on quite a show. It was humiliating, the way they were draped against each other, sucking each other's fingers, laughing at him. We all thought Allan should break it off, but he was out of his mind over that girl." His face had darkened. "Of course he always claimed it was an accident."

At that moment, he turned, nodding a greeting to someone passing. I was queasy, my hands and throat clammy with sweat. At the periphery of my sight, I could see Tom making his way through the crowd, two champagne glasses held aloft.

"Do you know, because the party was at my house, they wanted me as a witness?"

"What do you mean—?"

"Surely you knew? He threw her off the balcony. Gone completely around the bend. We all thought he'd killed her." He fell silent several beats. "I'll never forget the sound when she hit. And the blood! I couldn't stand to look out over the balcony after that. I had to pay for them to dig the rocks out. That's when the stairs were built to the Cuesta."

I should have been horror-struck, angry at having been deceived. Instead, I felt strangely emptied, numb.

"A pity, though, for Allan," Bill continued, shaking his head again. "He had so much promise. I wonder what ever became of him?"

"He died," I heard myself say.

"Moved to Italy is what I heard."

Just then Tom reached us. "Sorry it took so long." Handing me my drink, "The bar is absolutely mobbed. Hello, Bill."

"Tom." They shook hands.

"You both seem a bit somber. I hope you haven't been telling her anything gruesome?"

"Funny you should say that," Bill said, catching my eye. "No, your wife and I were having a rather interesting exchange. Seems we know someone in common, although we can't agree on her name."

"Speaking of people in common, a certain disgruntled investor just spotted you."

"Shit and damn," Bill said, both of them laughing. "You'll forgive me if I make myself scarce?"

As we watched him disappear into the dense crowd, Tom explained about the investor, things at work—anecdotes full of jocular deprecations, mock self-pity. "Considering the tap dancing I had to do in Minneapolis," I heard him say, and laughed on cue.

The whole while, the same thought kept intruding: *How far did she go to make him hurt her?*

42

I knew that if I told Tom what I'd learned, he would insist I feel betrayed. He would interrogate me over how she'd approached me in the park, the bracelet, the fact of the accident occurring in our house, and conclude that it had all been a manipulation, and need to know why, to what end? In short, he would demand I never see her again—not because he forbade me to, but because that was the only reasonable course of action.

And so I said nothing. I steadied myself. I held his hand on the drive home. After we'd paid María and sent her home in our cab, at Tom's suggestion, we went onto the balcony for a nightcap.

"To us," he said merrily, clinking his glass against mine, kissing me. Turning toward the view, his face opened into a boyish grin. "I still can't quite believe it." He rested his arms against the railing, leaning out over the black emptiness into which she'd been thrown, and I imagined her sailing backward, her face opened in amazement, her hair streaming crazily.

"Cold?"

I had shivered. "No. A bit, maybe."

He took off his jacket, gallantly draped it over my shoulders. "You look so beautiful tonight." Lightly he trailed his fingers over my breasts, kissing me again, filling me with shame.

That night, when we made love, I was as if nothing, a mote of dust. Afterward, I went upstairs to look at the Navarro prints, smoke a cigarette. I checked on the children sleeping innocently in their beds. I felt I was now on the other side of something I could not recross, where I would have to carry Louise's fictions, the pathetic myth of her storied love, of which I had somehow become a part.

As my initial shock subsided, what lingered was not the brutality or tawdriness, not even the creeping fear that I was being used. No, what bothered me most was that she had become a woman like countless others. A woman like my mother, willing to do anything for a man, debase herself, be hurled into thin air and broken open, and still hang his paintings on her walls and spin burnished tales of his greatness, this marvelous man, this important artist, her husband. Just as I had allowed myself to become hers, to become Mia.

43

The next day, I packed and tied up loose ends in town. We were leaving the following morning at dawn. Glad to be putting some distance between Louise and me, I resolved not to resume our routines after the long break, perhaps let the relationship naturally drift apart. I'd still have to see her, of course, when we got back. I'd arranged for her to pick up our mail while we were gone, and it would be awkward now to undo it. But I knew how to end things.

In the late afternoon, though, I became agitated without fully knowing why. I decided to walk into town, telling Tom I wanted to buy some sunblock, that I was sure they wouldn't have any where we were going. The familiarity of the steep walk calmed me. The men drinking beer on stoops. Outside the market, the blind couple dancing for coins, the legless beggar in the wheelchair. All the shops were decorated for Christmas. In the square, a massive tree had been erected, bedecked in a garland of red flowers.

On my way home, I stopped in at the *carnicería* to tell José Luis I'd be gone for ten days at the beach. We were leaving tomorrow; I was looking forward to being warm again.

"*¡El futuro subjuntivo, qué bien!*" he said, complimenting my use of tenses. "Truly, your Spanish is getting very good. Soon you'll be able to read one of my novels."

"You do know they were written in English," I teased.

"*No, Es-sal-lee.*" He wagged his finger at me. "*Este libro es en ruso.* Anna Karenina. *Y tiene más de mil páginas*," he added, shaking his head dramatically, saying it might kill him.

I laughed. I had nothing more to add, but I paused on the threshold, not wanting to leave. An irrational fear had come over me, that as soon as we drove away, everything I'd come to know and love would be irreparably lost. At the beach, I would be forgotten, the town sealing above me like a pond above a tossed stone.

44

"I still don't understand why you need to see to her." It was the night before our trip. Tom and I on the landing, surrounded by packed suitcases waiting to be loaded into the car in the morning, the leather handbag of cash we had withdrawn because there were no ATMs where we were going and no one used credit cards. He glanced skeptically at his watch. "It's already nine. Can't we just go to bed?"

"It's just that I'm worried I forgot to give her our account number at La Conexión," I explained, "and she won't be able to get the mail."

"Call her, then."

"She doesn't have a phone."

He rolled his eyes. "Of course she doesn't."

The simplest solution would have been to email. The truth was, I felt a compulsion to be in her physical presence once more before we left, if only to confirm to myself her diminished stature after what Bill had told me, my ability to dismiss her. Still, I had a tremor of nerves waiting, unannounced, for her to answer the door.

She greeted me as always. Unsurprised, happy, presumptuously turning back into the house for me to follow. As I stepped inside, the first thing I noticed was Allan's painting. It struck me as suddenly smaller, both in size and achievement, than our conversations had made it. This, and Louise's old, limping body, put me at ease. She had lit a fire in the living room, and there were two dirty wineglasses on the little inlaid table. Seeing me notice them, she tilted up her chin defiantly, signaling that she wouldn't explain herself, then went over to the record player on which the flamenco record was playing, repugnantly swaying her hips above her damaged legs with her back to me. After a minute or so, she came hobbling back to the bed-cum-sofa, fishing up the pack of cigarettes from between the pillows.

"Smoke?"

She held the lighter forward, my hand lingering briefly on hers as I inhaled. Smiling, she carried the used glasses away. I sat, closing my eyes. I could hear her moving about in the kitchen. It was like waiting for a lover with whom you know you're going to end things, the strange jumble of longing and anger roiling below the surface. I let the music wash into me, wondering vaguely how long I would stay; what, if anything, I would say before I left.

"Shall we try something new tonight?"

I opened my eyes to discover Louise holding a clear, unlabeled bottle of what looked like water.

"What is it?"

She poured some into a glass and handed it to me, motioning that I should drink it in one shot. It was incredibly strong and made me cough. Laughing, she refilled the glass, and I took another long, gulping swallow. It had a smoky flavor I liked very much.

"I first had it with Nuria. Allan and I were living in a half-finished place behind the church down the road. Two concrete rooms with one window. This was May and stifling hot. She gave me my first shower under a garden hose. 'Just take off your shirt and lean your head back,' she said. Once I tried it, I couldn't stop. We would do it standing in a washtub, shrieking, our nipples standing out to here."

I let go a short, derisive laugh. "Nuria sounds like quite something."

"Yes. She was so completely up front. I remember she said it straight out, practically the first time we ever met: 'Have you ever slept with a woman? We could do it all together the first time,' she said. Allan and Fernando, too. She wanted to know what that would be like."

"Was this the night of Bill's party?" I couldn't help it.

Louise arched her eyebrows imperturbably. "What are you talking about?"

"Why don't you just tell the truth?"

"The truth! How sweet you are." She reached forward, lifting my hair from my shoulder, letting it fall back with a faint slap.

I finished what was left in my glass, as the burn bloomed in my chest, thinking I shouldn't have; I was already tipsy. Louise had begun humming tunelessly to the music, her face very close to mine. "You have a terrible voice," I said. "You sound like my fucking mother."

Louise laughed, shoving my shoulder in mock umbrage. "The woman who gave you that atrocious name?"

She smiled smugly as she tipped the bottle, filling my glass, and as though accepting a challenge, I again drained it, not taking my eyes from hers, which were leveled on me. I had the sudden suspicion that she was attempting to read in my face how much I had discovered about her, that the second I broke the deadlock of our stare, she would know. At the *critch, critch* of the needle reaching the end of the record, simultaneously we released each other's gaze, Louise pouring more of the liquor into my glass, then into a second glass that seemed to materialize from nowhere. My head was spinning. Time seemed to be moving discontinuously. As if awakening from a sleep, I discovered myself staring intently at the record, circling and circling, the lift and fall of the needle a tiny boat riding above swells. "I'm not keeping you up, am I?" I said, in an unfamiliar voice. "It's just, I like the music. Can we hear the other side?"

"Only if you dance for me."

"Dance!" I snorted, the sound I made ugly. "I do like talking to you, though, Louise. That's the thing. You're a crazy bitch, but I like you."

"Imagination's first duty is transgression."

"You see? What the fuck does that even mean?" I had closed my eyes, letting my head loll back against the pillows as the room tilted and jogged sideways, not tracking when she said:

"You know what used to be in that field your husband is desecrating? Gnarled orange trees more than a hundred years old. Their fruit would become fermented in the sun, and all the raccoons got drunk."

"Did they behave badly?"

"*Mapache* is the word in Spanish."

"For drunkard?"

"Raccoon. And there were tarantulas"—she was playfully crawling her fingers up my arm, as I used to do with Ida and Henry—"and scorpions, and all manner of burrowing things that could crawl inside you and make a home. We built a bonfire to keep them away, even though it was terribly hot that night. The night Nuria introduced me to La Niña de los Peines, oh, other things . . ."

My eyes were still half closed. I heard her pouring more liquor. Propping myself shakily on my elbows, I tried to focus on the glass swimming before me. Somehow I couldn't figure out what to do about the fact that I didn't want it. Open my fist and let it fall? *Like Louise fell*, I thought, saying aloud, "Who was here earlier?" I took a few big sips, only to make it go away. "I bet it was the man from the Cuesta. That was so fucked."

"You mean on your balcony? That was nothing."

"But I saw you with him before, fighting on the arroyo path."

"Fighting!" She tossed back her head, laughing to show it wasn't anything. "My sweet Mia! You must never allow a man to think he has a hold over you."

"Me?" I made a sneering smile. "I know about you. I know what happened at Bill's party."

"You don't know anything, Allan and I, and Nuria and Navarro—"

"That reminds me. I've been looking at some Navarro prints. Actually, I'm thinking of buying one."

"You!" Suddenly she was angry. "If anyone should own a Navarro, it should be me."

I laughed at her. "Own a Navarro, you don't even own a phone."

"So I'm just a poor eccentric old woman, limping around with her cane, is that it? And you're the rich lady who's taken an interest in me, and now Navarro. The rich housewife chatting with all the vapid mommies at school. Oh, Fabiola tells me."

"If you say so." I tried to stand then, but it didn't rise beyond a thought.

"You think you're quite special, don't you?" Louise spat. "Quite something. *Me, me, me.* Do you know what my foster mother used to say? 'Half the world doesn't know you exist, and the other half doesn't care.'" She was staring in such fury that I involuntarily pulled my arm up to cover my face, and she grasped my wrists, saying roughly, "Stop that! What are you doing?"

"I don't know; I'm so drunk. I need to get home."

"Yes, by all means, hurry home to Tom! Ever the loyal housewife. You," she said, letting go of my wrists, her tone suddenly confiding, "were made for more important things."

I tried to stand again. When I couldn't, I laughed, saying stupidly, "And you're going to help me because I mean so much to you?"

"All I've ever done is help you! I love you, Mia." Leaning closer, she repeated it several times, "I love you, I love you." I managed to hold still through my revulsion while she wetly kissed my mouth.

Then I was leaning against my car, shivering slightly, every star visible. Louise's downstairs had gone dark. For moments, I tried to understand, with mounting panic, why I was here outside; had I done something terrible? *You think you're quite special*, Louise's words echoed. *And you're nobody*, mine echoed back, distilled by hatred. *You're a bitter, broke old woman, you could never own a Navarro! But I could.* It was the last thing I remember of that evening.

45

I was still drunk when Tom woke me the next morning. Dark outside, the house frigid. As Tom loaded the bags into the car, I wandered to the bathroom in a haze, unnerved that I couldn't remember driving home or what I'd done when I arrived. Tom called that he was about to carry the kids out, and I hurried ahead of him in my underwear, making a nest with several pillows so they would be comfortable and fall back asleep. After that, I dressed hurriedly. My ankle was stiff and swollen; I noticed a cut on the bottom of one foot as I pulled on my shoe. When I came back to the landing, Tom had already settled Ida into the car and had Henry in his arms. I passed him into the cold darkness, Tom locking the door behind us. For a minute, we sat with the engine idling and the heat on, Tom checking all the mirrors, looking over the maps and printed directions, being the competent husband. "You okay?" he asked, putting the car into gear.

"I'm just a bit tired."

He shook his head, emitting a short laugh as we began up the driveway and away. It was strange to reach the Cuesta and turn away from town. At the point where the road flattened out, running beside the botanical garden and then the very last of the grandiose houses and finally nothing but scrub grass, I began to see the shadowy figures of men moving along the side of the road. Some carried small brown sacks. Some smoked, or else it was their breath streaming.

"Who are they, Dad?" Ida asked. I'd thought she was asleep.

"Men going to work."

I would have had more to say about it, but Ida never asked such questions of me. Tom was the last authority for all of us, including myself—although, in this case, it seemed to me the answer was far more complex and intersected our own lives, for I had begun to think about the men who would soon be riding in the back of a pickup truck to the field across from Louise's. And then—maybe I'd dreamed it—for a few moments, I recalled the field at night; I was running wildly, hearing animal sounds around me, moans of pleasure. To push the memory aside, I said, "Maybe they're going to build the houses you and Bill designed."

"Yeah, maybe." He looked at me questioningly. But I didn't share more of my thoughts or my recollections, unsure in both cases what meaning to attach to them. Instead, I rested my aching head into my hands, and for a time dozed.

The sun was just rising as we reached the first tollbooth outside Guanajuato. Henry had awakened. I'd gotten a movie playing on the cheap DVD players we'd bought at Office Depot for the drive from Minneapolis, he and Ida listening on headphones. I counted out the money from Tom's wallet. When he handed me the receipt, I tossed it down at my feet. The task helped me sober up. Every forty-five minutes or so, we came to another toll. I kept the little pile of receipts in the pocket of the door, his wallet wedged beneath my thigh, while through drooping lids, I watched the landscape change. We drove past rows of agave, with their beautiful bluish tint; through deep tunnels cut into massive outcroppings of rock. We came upon pleated mossy-looking mountains that looked like topiaries of reposing wrinkled giants. As we neared them, Tom said, "Who would have said that the earth, with its ancient skin, would change so much?"

"Ancient skin, that's such a perfect description."

"Too bad it's not mine."

"Who said it?"

"Can't you guess?"

Somehow it stung me, his rhetorical tone, the fact I had no idea.

"It's Pablo Neruda," Tom announced, and after a brief silence began to recite it in a loud, slow voice, "'In the course of a day we shall meet one another . . .'"

He gave the whole poem that way, line after line, while I petulantly noted to myself his bombastic tone of voice, the staleness of his breath. I had propped my feet up on the dashboard, leaning against the window away from him. I stayed that way even after my hip grew numb. I felt terrible. My head was throbbing, the muscles around my eyes like twine pulled too tight. When we passed into a second, longer tunnel, in the darkness, the images of the field swam back. I was running, ears full of the filthy noises; my shoe had come off; I felt a jabbing pain in my heel. Then, driving wildly, in our bedroom searching into the top dresser drawer and removing Tom's wallet. When we passed into the sunlight, suddenly the Navarro lithograph *As Apes Do* was vividly before me, filling my computer screen. Then my hand holding Tom's credit card; the exhilaration as my fingers struck the keys, the terrible cresting joy, like the moment of losing control in an argument.

"Are you going to tell me what happened last night?"

I stared at him in terror. I could feel a cold bead of sweat wending its way down between my breasts. "Tom, I really don't feel well."

"Listen, forget it. It happens."

"What does?" I said quickly.

"You really don't remember?" He glanced into the rearview mirror, making sure the kids weren't listening. "You were completely out of it. I don't know what the hell you and Louise drank, but you weren't well." He hesitated. "You didn't quite make it."

"What do you mean?"

"To the toilet. I had to mop it up with a towel."

"Jesus fucking Christ." I could feel myself about to lose control. My head was pounding.

"Sweetheart, it's okay." He patted my leg. "It's done, I cleaned it up really well."

"Right, I get it, you cleaned up after me, just please stop talking about it."

In the long claustrophobic silence, the full scope of what I'd kept from Tom presented itself: a skein of petty lies and omissions stretching clear back to the day I met her. He'd taken the job, he'd worked all this time in order to give me the gift of this year, and in return, I'd taken myself away from him little by little, betraying him. And yet I had not been able to keep the accusation from my voice, as if by bringing up the disgraceful thing I'd done, he had failed in his duty to protect me. I shifted in my seat, perversely annoyed at Tom's proximity, his obliviousness, which I myself had created. I unclasped my seat belt, glorying in a vision of myself thrown clear through the windshield, imagining in minute detail the sound and feel of my body shattering on the road.

Around one o'clock, the kids, who had watched another full movie, began to complain about being hungry. At a roadside stand buzzing with flies, we bought bags of homemade potato chips and *tortas de jamón* and fruit sodas.

I stared vacantly at the scrubby field, the memories flooding back. I was looking at the Navarro of the two monkeys on the bed; then stumbling down the stairs, taking Tom's wallet from his dresser drawer, removing his bank card.

"Sally?"

"I think I've done something terrible." A convoy of trucks was passing, their air brakes whining into the din, the kids asking at once what was wrong, why was I just staring that way, Ida laughing that I looked stupid.

"What's that?"

I searched into his face, my heart fluttering wildly.

He pointed to his ears. "The traffic is so loud, I couldn't hear. What did you say?"

"No, nothing. Just, I'm sorry, Tom. For everything."

He smiled consolingly—hadn't he told me it was nothing? He caressed my leg again, saying with a raised voice intended for the children that it was time to get going, everyone should try to pee before getting back into the car. Henry refused to use the bathroom, which had no door and only a hole in the floor. Ida said pointedly she would, why not, glaring at him as she went. Then we all piled back into the dusty car. Tom resumed driving. Hours more passed, the view beyond the window remaining uniform as though we were moving to stand still.

At last, near four o'clock, we began the long steep descent into jungle. The road narrowed to a single twisting lane. The jungle spilled onto the asphalt, covering the tiny shoulder in vines. For forty minutes, we were trapped behind a truck heaving diesel. Dead dogs swelled in the roadside ditch, and even a dead horse, its legs like sawed-off saplings, its head mostly gone. All the windows were down, the air soupy, not yet smelling of the sea. I turned, looking back at my children. Ida was bent over Henry, who had fallen asleep again. They seemed alarmingly vulnerable, with the window gaped open above their limp bodies and tangles of green closing in on them. I reached back, caressing Ida's little head, smoothing the delicate wisps of hair. When I touched Henry's leg, damp with sweat, he awoke with a start.

"I need to pee," he moaned.

Tom looked at me. "It's not safe," he said. "There's no shoulder."

"I can't hold it!"

"What should we do?" I asked, and Tom said to give him an empty soda bottle into which he could pee.

"I can't!" Henry protested, hearing.

"Sweetheart, there's nothing else to do," I said. I had turned back to face him, holding the empty bottle steady. "It's okay," I said. I smiled at him coaxingly. A few seconds later, I felt the warmth meet my fingers, filling the bottle. "Good, Henry. Almost done?"

"A little more."

Feeling a swell of nausea, I lifted my eyes to the endless regress of green out the back window. "I don't feel well," I said to Tom in an urgent whisper.

"Face forward and close your eyes."

The hot bottle sloshed under my hands, releasing the smell of urine in waves. When I closed my eyes, the patterns of the jungle flashed and flickered sickeningly against the red of my eyelids. *It's blood*, I thought; *that's what makes it red*. "I'm going to be sick." I lowered the window, tossing the bottle spraying piss.

"It's only a few more minutes," Tom said.

But the last fifteen kilometers took three-quarters of an hour, winding behind a gas truck and, after we'd stopped in a tamped-down bit of jungle for me to vomit, a rusted pickup piled impossibly high with oranges. At every turn, one or two flew off and exploded, benign grenades. The air grew bloated, full of new smells, citrine and musky, rank. I braced my arm against the door, my head lolling to one side.

"What's wrong with Mommy," Ida said.

"She's just a little carsick," Tom answered her.

I had to vomit again. Only bile was left. I retched into a crumpled bit of napkin, not even bothering to lean out the window. As I arched forward, convulsing, through the damp thinness of my tee shirt, I felt Tom's hand rest against my back. I was humbled. Wordlessly, my back returned his gesture, softening beneath the slow pulse of his fingertips.

"Better?" he said.

"Yes, thanks, Tom."

A few minutes later, he put the turn signal on, calling out that we were there. Cheering from Henry and Ida. To my surprise, I really did feel a bit better. When we heard the first distant crash of waves, Tom looked at me just long enough for something mundane and ardently wished for to pass from his eyes to mine.

And then we laughed, like old friends reunited. In that single moment, one reality washed away another as outside, by coincidence, the low sun broke through the heavy curtain of leaves, and everything changed color.

46

There were six identical thatched-roof huts scattered in a clearing, the beach sweeping up behind them. At a cramped *oficina*, a woman gave us the key. Though it was only one small living area intersecting two cramped bedrooms, Ida and Henry rushed around excitedly, crawling under the dense mosquito netting wrapping their bed, clambering over the musty mismatched furniture, briefly holding hands as they stood staring up at the domed ceiling. When they began to bicker, tired from the long drive, Tom came to the doorway, frowning. I thought he was about to scold them, but he surprised me, saying, "Why don't we put on our bathing suits and see the ocean?"

Their shouts of joy were instantaneous. After the dank *casita*, the vast near emptiness of the beach was a revelation. I had been so long away from the East Coast of my girlhood that I'd forgotten how it feels to stand before the ocean, the salty coat of its humid air. It moved me to be sharing it now with my children, who had only ever swum in lakes, navigating weeds, stroking over glassy stillness. Henry ran screaming into the surf and then frantically back when the waves gathered and broke. Ida had assumed her ninja stance, legs bent, arms raised as if in preparation for battle, grinningly trying to hold her balance as the tugging ebb of each wave eroded the sand beneath her feet. Tom was the first to go in, battling his way past where the waves broke and then bobbing beyond them, waving to Henry and Ida.

"Do a somersault," they hollered.

He disappeared beneath the water. When he resurfaced, he folded up his legs so that only his toes poked out, a few feet from his chin. "Henry, Ida! Look at me! I'm a midget!" Like an ensuing drum roll, a wave crashed his head, and they roared with laughter.

"Take us out with you," they begged. "Take us into the deep!"

One at a time, he carried them on his hip beyond the waves, their little hands clutching desperately at his neck, their heads slick as seals, Tom releasing them for moments to paddle frantically. Ida had let Henry go first, watching closely as he was carried through the tumult into the enormity of the sea. When it was her turn, her face remained still as a statue. *Shall we go back?* I imagined Tom saying, his head bent close to her, Ida determinedly shaking her frozen face. When he took his arms away, for seconds, she continued to cling to him. When she let go, her face reanimated, charged with joy. "I'm swimming in the ocean!" she cried, gasping, her chin lifted high above the water.

Afterward, they were famished. They huddled shivering on the sand, asking for dinner; when would it be ready? I had nothing for them to eat. We decided to go into town, Tom dashing into our hut for some money, our discarded clothes. Aimlessly we walked along the beach, the sun almost setting. The walk took nearly twenty minutes. Henry kept running ahead to sit at the edge of the break, letting the waves tumble him backward, his hair and ears and bathing suit filling with sand.

The town was little more than an intersection of two gouged dirt roads. There didn't seem to be any proper restaurants, only a corner *tiendita* with a few sad-looking roast chickens and, in a glass case, some sort of sandwich meat of a brand called Fud, and some rubbery white cheese. We bought a bag of sliced white bread and some of the cheese, an assortment of other things Henry and Ida wanted, for once refusing them nothing: frosted cream-filled cakes sealed in plastic bags, chips, apple-flavored sodas; for Ida, pickles in a jar covered in a thick layer of dust. In a ramshackle park, we ate. We played on the rusted seesaw, still in our damp clothes and bathing suits, happy. Only on the way back did the kids begin to protest. It was pitch dark. They were tired, they moaned; they couldn't walk all that way again! Why hadn't we taken the car? Why couldn't we get a taxi like in San Miguel?

A taxi, I laughed to myself, thinking: *Now they will get stronger, tougher, less like the spoiled white kids they've been. Now there is only us, and the crabs scuttling over the sand, the moon, the ocean with its black depths.*

That night, after we had settled them beneath the mosquito netting, already half asleep, Tom and I went silently into our room. We kissed, standing at the foot of our bed. We took our clothes off without words. No thought, no preamble. I settled myself onto my back, the sheets damp with sea air, lifting my hands over my head. Tom held them firmly, his fingers interlaced through mine, our eyes opening and closing languidly. There was no need to rouse myself, Tom not careful or half apologetic. Nothing performative between us. We were only natural with each other, unhurried in all we did. In the final minutes, he lay on his back in the spot where I'd lain, and I climbed on top of him but faced away toward the black immensity of the ocean while he gripped my hips, every sense concentrating into the point at which we joined. We'd never made love that way before; after nine years, it was something new. We came that way, with my back to him. Afterward, we didn't reach to put our underwear on like we almost always did—as if to protect ourselves, regain some small bit of separateness—but lay side by side in the dampness with our feet touching, and slept.

47

I awoke the next morning not knowing where I was. Only that I had done something unforgiveable. Guilt bristled into sweat along my legs. With the crashing of waves, incrementally, it returned: the beach, the lovely night we'd shared. It wasn't so much an awakening as a lulling back asleep. A kind of lucid dreaming into which I willed myself, hearing the sounds of our children whispering in the room opposite us, the wingbeat of their consonants, the sudden high music of their laughter, thinking, *If I could hold it in my mind at all times—that we made them only from ourselves, our love—nothing would ever be wrong between us.*

In this way, I gave myself over to the new rhythm of my days. Their idleness and boredom, their heat. Each afternoon at two o'clock, we gathered beneath a palapa for whatever meal the proprietress, a fat woman in her fifties, had made for the guests. Only half the cabanas were rented. The other guests were all Mexicans, who insisted out of deference that our mealtime conversations be conducted in English, holding forth on the failures of NAFTA, the troubles of class stratification in Mexico, the serenity of this particular stretch of beach. Señor Melendez, a grandfatherly man with a barrel-shaped stomach and white panama hat, took it upon himself to teach Henry chess. After each meal, the two sat at a small concrete table in the garden, he with a cigar and a glass of tequila, Henry with a bottle of Coke.

Most evenings, we walked into town. Beginning in late afternoon, the townspeople sat in lawn chairs on the sidewalk, smoking or slowly drinking their liter bottles of beer. There was a dwarf who had no legs and was always in the same chair on the same stoop beside his paralyzed friend, as if the two had sprouted from the spot like potted plants. Henry enjoyed speaking with them when we walked past, wishing them good evening, telling them how he was learning chess. He would have been frightened by such characters at home, and certainly never thought to strike up a conversation with them—a fact Tom and I remarked to one another proudly. On our second night, making our way along roads rather than the beach, we had discovered the town's single restaurant, where a fisherman's wife sold marlin tacos and fried squid. A little farther, a man stood on the sidewalk before a *tienda* grilling *hamburguesas* and *salchichas*. There were ice cream treats in a case outside the launderette, half melted and stale. After we'd eaten, we would sit next to each other on a bench in the park, holding hands while Henry and Ida played.

It was as if we were discovering anew how to be an autonomous family. Pulling on damp suits and rumpled clothes. Eating cobbled-together meals with our hands, drinking soda straight from the bottle. Brushing our teeth together at the one big sink adjacent to the children's room, laughing and drooling white foam when we caught sight of each other's faces in the mirror. Climbing into unmade beds. These were pleasures that for six months hadn't been allowed us, in our large house with María tending to our needs. In certain ways, I'd never allowed them, and it occurred to me that making meaning—in life, in art—didn't have to be so effortful. Just as each night Tom and I made love, as miraculously free from complication and shame as it had been the first night here. Sometimes we spoke softly during our lovemaking. Or else paused and looked at each other, for whole minutes moving not a muscle, smiling with the guilelessness of children, before resuming more slowly than before. Other times, it lasted scarcely a minute. He parted me and in one slow stroke we arrived, shuddering together, after which we slept heavily in each other's arms.

48

I had let the Navarro slip more and more from my mind, half convincing myself it could be undone, things were returned all the time, people changed their minds. It vaguely occurred to me that in my drunkenness I'd neglected some crucial step—I hadn't specified the form of shipping, for example, or had incorrectly entered the card's security code—and so the sale had not gone through.

Neither did I think much of Louise, with a few exceptions. At the farthest corner of the beach, at the base of an outcropping of rock, Ida had discovered clay. I'd never seen clay in its natural form. It was orangey-brown and dried in the sun to a dull mud color. While Henry played in the waves, while Tom and I sunbathed or swam, Ida quietly went about her "work" sculpting small animals and other things, cups the size of thimbles, dice. She and Henry soon evolved a game that they played each day at low tide, deeply absorbed for hours. It involved harvesting hunks of clay and stacking them in a mysterious yet particular order on a flat, ovate rock they termed "the factory." The factory, about five feet from the ground, was accessible by a "staircase" of rocks. It was unclear what the purpose of the factory was, only that their livelihood depended upon it. "We're poor," I heard Henry say, adding the customary, "right, Ida?"

"Yes, very poor. With the money from this factory, we can go to the market and get things we need, like salt, and"—she paused—"maybe pasta."

"And candy!"

"No, Henry. You don't need candy."

"But I like candy," he cried in that piercing tone, as if this were all completely real; never again would he taste candy.

"Henry, we don't have time for this! We have a lot of work to do. Maybe we'd make enough for a lump of sugar," she allowed. "Once a year maybe. For Easter, or maybe Thanksgiving."

Listening to this back-and-forth, my initial charm morphed into agitation. I was affronted by the way she bossed Henry, his self-effacement in response. Her tacit endorsement of poverty and disdain of wealth reminded me unpleasantly of Louise; the way she was attempting to press those ideas onto Henry, who now said grudgingly, "All right, Ida," lingering on his thumb for a few more seconds before falling in line with the harvesting, rinsing, shaping of clay into cubes.

Ida smiled imperiously. I fought my urge to shout a warning to him not to go along, to stay true to himself, his own joy. *She'll crush you!* Beside me, Tom dozed on his towel, a straw hat propped over his face. Turning to watch him sleep, I calmed myself. I shook the thoughts of Louise away, promising myself again that I wouldn't see her anymore; Tom would never need to know how tangled things had gotten. I pressed my body to his. I lifted my face to the sunlight as if to let it bleach me clean. Now and then, a twitch passed along the length of Tom's leg. Except for this, I was alone.

49

Out of this time, one particular day stands out, both for its stark perfection and for its suggestion of what was to come. As it happens, it was Christmas, though it might have been any other day. We'd lost track, opening the few gifts we'd brought several mornings before: a set of pastels for Ida, an action figure for Henry, a hardcover copy of *The Borrowers* that Tom had already begun to read to them each night, sitting on the floor next to their bed. Henry had begun asking if there was a place where the water was calm enough for him to actually swim. On Christmas Eve, I learned of a place from the man who owned the laundry. "*Es mar tranquilo*," he assured me. He'd taught his own son to swim there.

The next morning, I packed a picnic and we all piled into the car. It was the first time we'd driven since arriving. The kids were excited, leaning their head out the opened windows. The man had drawn a map on the side of a brown paper bag, noting that the final turn was unmarked. "*Pero no se preocupe*," he'd said, don't worry; we would know it by a fat pig tied to the base of a tree. It was our joke the whole drive: Turn left at the pig. But then, unbelievably, there it was, sprawling in the dust. "God, I love this country," Tom laughed, Henry and Ida pointing out the window, hollering with glee, "The pig! It's him!" Then on for several more miles. The trees thinning and ending, the road narrowing. Until, without warning, it dissolved completely into dunes.

Tom shook his head, saying, "My God, we've actually found it: the end of the road."

The kids were desolate. "What do we do now?"

"Do we have to turn around?"

But there wasn't space even to turn the car around. We simply took the keys and left it, Tom and I laughing, Henry and Ida cartoonishly wide-eyed as we walked away.

"You're sure it's the right way?" Henry ventured.

"It's the way to *something*," Tom answered mysteriously, climbing up a steep dune.

"But what if we get lost?"

"We'll live off the land. We'll catch fish with spears. Mommy knows her way around a spear, how do you think she caught me?"

Ida roared at that, while Henry darted his eyes around, thrilled, terrified. Then, suddenly, as we crested the dune, the ocean appeared, vast and azure, gently lapping an endless stretch of white sand. It was like nothing I'd ever seen. Henry pulled off his shirt, whooping as he skied down the dune and bounded farther and farther into the water. Fifteen yards from shore, it remained only inches deep, clear and still. He crawled through it on his hands. He belly flopped, fell backward, sending huge splashes into the air.

"I want to take my shirt off, too," Ida said.

Tom had ambled ahead. I glanced around. The beach was deserted, and she was barely eight; puberty was still far off for her. Yet for a second, I hesitated.

"Can I?" she persisted. "Henry did it, why can't I?"

Because you're a girl, I silently answered, the thought immediately striking me as punitive and deeply fucked-up. I shrugged, said yes; she pulled her shirt off, bunching it into a tight ball that she handed to me before sprinting away, arms lifting at her sides. Even if someone came, I thought, why would they care? With her short hair and slender tanned limbs, she was as much boy as girl, trotting proudly along the beach beside where Henry swam. There was a new lightness to her, and catching up to Tom, I commented on it.

"Ida's doing so well." I wanted him to agree, to say he accepted her, he liked her hair this way, and I nudged him, saying, "Her hair really suits her, don't you think?"

"Yeah, she seems happy."

"Louise actually did a nice job."

I felt the thread that a moment before had spanned between us like sunlight snap. I'd often imagined it coming out; Louise might tell him herself in her bragging way, or Ida. Never had I thought it would be me.

"What do you mean?" Tom said sharply, stopping. "Sally! Hold on a minute. I need you to explain this. You told me you took her to get it cut."

"I—yes," I faltered. "That's true, in the sense I gave Louise permission."

"That's not what you told me."

"Okay, maybe I gave the wrong impression. But if you think about it, what difference does it really make? Louise knows how to cut hair. And Ida wanted it so badly."

"That's not the point."

"But, Tom—" It was his look that had made me stop; the way it interrogated me, as though I were a thing beyond understanding. I tried to shake it off, saying his name a second time, like, *Come on, you're making too much of this.*

"I'm just trying to understand why you lied," he said evenly.

"I didn't mean to!" Then, switching tacks, pleading with him, "It's only because I didn't want you to be upset."

"Upset at whom?"

It was all he said, in his correct way. It was enough. By now, the children had gotten far ahead, and I gestured that we should catch up. Not because I was concerned for them. All I cared about was diverting Tom's attention, invoking Ida and Henry to make him love me as he had a few moments before. As we slowly closed the distance, I found myself hoping someone would appear, to force him to pretend everything was okay, reassume the role of attentive husband.

Yet the farther we walked, the more impossible it was to imagine encountering anyone. We were like the world's first family, or its last. The car forgotten behind us, the children still far ahead, little dots of happiness. Eventually they stopped to wait for us at a rocky barrier. Climbing over it, we discovered a second beach, also deserted, where on a small outcropping of rock a group of buzzards as big as Henry were picking a sea turtle clean. They hunched over it, tugging ropes of rancid flesh from the massive shell. We stood very near to one another, engrossed. Whenever one of us stepped forward, the buzzards startled noisily up, croaking, landing back with a hollow thump onto the sand.

Eventually, in wordless agreement, we walked away, and a little farther on, we came upon the great discovery of the day: a huge fish more than three feet in length washed up on the beach, silver with an ice-blue eye and pointed nose, a vivid blue stripe around the neck. Its mouth was hinged open, the teeth like pearly thorns.

"What kind is it, Daddy?" the children wanted to know.

But he surprised us, for once saying he didn't know.

Unlike the buzzards and the turtle, this marvel was not forbidding. Ida knelt beside it, Henry peering from behind her shoulder. They took turns touching or nearly touching it, pulling their hands away as if burned. They fell into whispers, consulting.

"The souls go up into the clouds," Ida said.

"What are they?"

"Like, the part of me that's me and not my body, separate."

"You split up?"

"Sort of."

"But can it happen when you're alive?"

She was too intent to answer. She had bent very close over the fish, examining the one glassy eye with clinical detachment, and Henry said, his voice high with fear or excitement:

"Let's dig a hole and bury him."

After the hole was dug, at the kids' request, Tom took the fish by its tail. It lifted like a single tensed muscle. It must have been very recently dead because there was no odor to speak of. For a few silent moments, we all admired it, hanging from Tom's hand, its skin gleaming in the light. Once it had been buried, the packed sand slightly darker in color, Ida wrote some symbols with her fingertip. As she recited a prayer, tentatively, I took Tom's hand, feeling with relief the pressure of his hand in return. He had forgiven me.

After that, I set out our picnic beneath a tree: cheese and salami, a plastic tub of watermelon sprinkled with lime and chili powder, a dense loaf of bread bought from a man on the side of the road that we tore hunks from with our hands. Henry's tooth was loose, and because we had no knife, I bit off small pieces of meat and then passed them to him to chew, like a mother bird.

"Is there anything to drink?" Tom said.

I'd packed a bottle of beer and two bottles of soda, dewed and still slightly cool. Henry drank his soda sitting in the water, his shoulders dark as a nut, his hair sun-bleached. Ida bounded noisily through the water.

Merry Christmas, I mouthed across at Tom, suddenly remembering.

Merry Christmas, he mouthed back, his face tanned and handsome, creased about his eyes as he smiled. "Another sip?" he said, passing the bottle of beer.

When I rested my head onto his lap a moment later, inhaling his smell, I thought drowsily how nice men are. Men can forgive and move on; men don't lie in the same way women do, their meaning tangled in layers of subterfuge; if you ask a man if he is happy and he says yes, there is his entire truth.

"I wish I could take a picture of you right now," Tom interrupted my thoughts, and I smiled up at him, saying, "Just always remember the perfection of this moment. You will, won't you, Tom?" smiling dumbly at him, and he smiled back at me and said, “Only because I’m very gifted.”

Suddenly then, from far away, we heard a sharp cry. I jolted up, scanning the beach, my heart pounding.

But all was well. The kids were far from shore, huddled close together in waist-high water. Slender and small, backlit by the sun, they looked like a single strange being balanced on the surface of the sea—a praying mantis, a walking stick. Then one part disentangled itself and became Henry. He was holding one fist high in the air, calling out to us:

“Look! Look! My tooth came out!”

50

That night, when I came to give them their kiss, I found Ida standing rapt before the ugly painting in their bedroom—the requisite acrylic of a beach scene, complete with palm tree and low orange sun. I thought of the Navarro, but quickly pushed it aside: I would fix it; it was nothing.

"It's so beautiful," Ida said, as if issuing a challenge.

"It's magnificent," boomed Tom; he had stepped into the doorway. "It's probably the nicest painting in the town of Huasquitico, on the south side of the beach, on Altavista road." Catching my eye, "At least one of the ten nicest."

It was a way we often joked, only this time, I didn't join in. To my surprise, I discovered I had room in my heart for this tacky painting; that I, too, could love it, if only because Ida did. I kissed her on her head. I pulled the netting aside for her to climb in beside Henry, saying, "I'm glad you like it, darling."

After we had kissed them both many times, and put the tooth under Henry's pillow, Tom and I lingered a long while beside their bed, speaking softly of happy things, touching and admiring Henry as though he were still a baby, caressing Ida's sun-pinked cheek.

Finally thinking them asleep, I nodded to Tom. We could have our drink sitting on the beach chairs outside our door, as we'd gotten in the habit of doing. As we were shuffling out the door, out of the stillness, Henry said:

"How did that fish die, really?"

"Probably just old age," Tom said.

"You're sure it wasn't that someone caught him?"

"If they had, they would have kept him. Or set him free."

"They would let him go back into the ocean," Henry said wistfully. He'd been silent several beats, and in that time had chosen to let himself believe. Tom and I met the assertion with nods, assenting sounds, of course they would have, people here are kind!

Over our evening drink, we talked about this exchange, debating when it's compassionate to lie to children and when it's not. For some reason, I was hesitant and even upset lying about Santa Claus, whereas the tooth fairy held no such complication. Maybe because it's not so swept up in capitalism, Tom speculated, and I laughed: What could be more so? "It's just money, straight up, no pretense."

"Show me the money," Tom parroted, and I joined in his laughter. I was grateful he hadn't returned to the subject of the haircut; it felt like a gift he was giving me. I took a deep sip of my drink, relaxing into the knowledge that he had let it go, all was well.

As we were having a second drink, still musing, I said that perhaps I preferred the lie of the tooth fairy because the story felt less co-opted. I could evolve elaborate tales—that the fairies use teeth to build elaborate staircases, gleaming artificial limbs, weapons for drawn-out battles with their enemies—and what existing narrative would contradict them?

"People like their own lies," I concluded. "Maybe if they're yours, and if they're offered with love, they're acceptable."

Shortly after, I put the coins beneath Henry's pillow. I hid the tooth in a pouch in my cosmetics bag. Then I crawled beneath the mosquito netting, where Tom was waiting for me.

51

We spent our final night at the beach imagining a permanent life in Mexico. For once, it wasn't me who brought it up but Tom, stepping from our *casita* with a drink in each hand.

"Could you ever imagine living here?"

I laughed in delight. "Here in this town, this hut, what?"

"I mean, yeah, sort of. Having a different kind of life."

I looked at him, hesitating out of a fear our fantasies would diverge too starkly. As a boy, he'd been fascinated by books like *Robinson Crusoe*. His fantasy of life in Mexico would likely be about having less, living a simpler life. Whereas mine, it appeared to me with sudden clarity, involved having more, a richness not available to us in the States. I felt a quickening of anticipation, imagining his disappointment in me, even scorn. And as if to provoke him, also because we were leaving and I was suddenly frightened about what awaited us, I said:

"If I'm being honest, I don't want some alternative life. I want a house like Bill's, filled with beautiful furniture and art."

He didn't react the way I'd expected. He laughed warmly. "My beautiful little materialist," he said, as though it had all been a joke.

Shortly after, we went to bed and lay naked with our legs spread into wide Vs, sweating and holding hands. For the first time since arriving, we fell asleep without making love.

52

The drive the next day was uneventful. The children watched a string of DVDs. They slept. In the long spans of silence, I revisited the conversation with Tom about remaining in Mexico. To my surprise, I found myself questioning if I truly wanted to. My mind kept turning to Henry—maybe because he was more malleable than Ida, more adept at belonging. I imagined him married to a woman like those who waited with me in the courtyard, with their painted nails and elaborate makeup, their easy jollity. The thought chastened me; the idea that I would be replaced, and Tom, our culture of origin. Henry with a brood of Mexican children, their hair gelled and expertly braided, their ears pierced and little glinting gold crucifixes around their necks.

In such moments, I was haunted by my revulsion toward my own mother, guilty that, as a child of Henry's age, I'd cringed at the feel of her lips on my cheek. I couldn't stand for her even to smile at me, as though she perceived nothing amiss, clumsily attempting to love and care for me, beaming at me across the dining table. How undressed I felt by that smile. As though she deployed it solely to invade my thoughts, physical spaces that ought to have belonged only to me. So deep was my resentment that whenever I caught myself smiling at my own children with any semblance of longing, I chastised myself: *Don't smother them! Don't try to claim them as your own!* And if they ever looked at me with lingering adoration, I chastised myself also: *It isn't something you're owed. If they express love, don't grow to expect it. They didn't ask to be born.*

Yet it struck me, in the car beside Tom, that there must be a way for mothers and children to smile at one another that is correct. In my confusion and ignorance, all I could think of were certain moments with Louise: The time in the coffee shop when she praised my writing. The wordless seconds when we faced each other at the mouth of the tunnel, when the drops of water clung above her lip.

I was strangely calm as we made the drive back to San Miguel. I remember at one point, when we were again passing the huge wrinkled mountains, letting my hand fall onto Tom's thigh and saying something sappily banal. *I'm so happy. Everything is so wonderful.*

As we reached the outskirts of San Miguel, we rolled down all the windows and put on the *Star Wars* music full blast. "We're in the *Millennium Falcon*!" Tom proclaimed, and the kids hung out of the opened windows baying while Tom and I grinned like idiots.

In our absence, María had made everything perfect. All the bed linens freshly washed, the beds made up, the children's toys and stuffed animals arranged in tableaux as though at a beautiful toy store or on a movie set of a child's room. On the Saarinen table, a vase of flowers picked from the garden. In the refrigerator, homemade tacos carefully wrapped, two kinds of salsa. After the long drive, we were famished and ate hungrily. We opened a bottle of wine. Tom said he needed to check his emails; after that, maybe he would wade through the messages on the answering machine attached to the landline in his office. I went downstairs with Ida and Henry. I began to run a bath. I went to their room and found their heavier pajamas that we hadn't taken to the beach, laid them out onto their beds. I pawed through the toiletries bag for their toothbrushes. In the bathroom were big blue-and-white-patterned pitchers containing fresh filtered water, two clean glasses.

"Didn't María leave everything so nice for us?"

"I liked when we brushed our teeth together at the beach," they chimed. "Daddy, come brush your teeth with us!"

I went to the foot of the stairs, calling to him gaily, "Your presence has been requested." When he didn't answer, I ran up to the living room, eager to see him, to embrace and kiss him. As soon as I saw him, I knew something was wrong. *The lithograph*, I immediately thought. *He's logged into our bank account, found out about the money.* But that wasn't it. It was Bill Barnes. The previous Thursday, while walking through the airport in León, he'd suffered a massive heart attack. He was dead.

53

I stood attempting to metabolize the news, comfort myself that at least Tom had not discovered the purchase; maybe it hadn't gone through after all. Even if it had, I still believed I could undo it and, in a more amorphous way, everything, all that I'd impulsively set in motion—although it would have to wait, I reminded myself. Tomorrow was Sunday; the gallery was closed.

As I made these calculations, Tom continued to relate the details of the call he'd just ended. Several investors had pulled out in the wake of Bill's death. Fearing others would follow, it had been decided he would fly back to Minneapolis and spend Monday trying to assuage the gathering panic, meeting with investors, the firm's lawyer, a representative for the bank. And so, on the evening of our return, Tom repacked his suitcase, now with a warm jacket, a shirt and tie. I sat on our bed distractedly, making occasional comments: *Don't forget your toothbrush. Did you remember something to read on the plane?*

Sundays were María's day off. With no one to watch the children, we again loaded them into the car so I could drive Tom to the airport. We'd kept the reason for Tom's departure secret from them—why trouble them unnecessarily?—turning the radio on in an attempt to gain privacy. As Tom and I spoke in half whispers, it occurred to me that our decision not to tell them that someone they barely knew had died was evidence of a misstep on our parts, that we'd erred in our duty by buffering them too completely from the harsh realities of life.

"Do you think there's a chance we'll have to leave San Miguel?" I said under my breath.

"I don't know."

"But if you had to guess."

"It's possible, I suppose. Yes."

"Tom, no!"

He glanced a warning—whether because it was callous to be considering my own happiness when someone had died, or simply that I'd been too loud and could be overheard, I wasn't sure. "This is wasted energy," he said. "Let's wait and see what transpires in the meetings."

"Even if the worst did happen," I said, "and you lost your job and the project fell apart, would it really be so bad?"

"What are you saying? Of course it would be."

"Maybe it doesn't have to be." I paused. Ever since hearing the news, I'd been pondering how we could stay. "What if we took it as an opportunity to rethink things, restructure our lives, like what we talked about on the beach?"

"Come on, that was a fantasy. Even if I wanted to, we don't have the money."

"Just hear me out." I began to speak eagerly, saying that there were other neighborhoods where we could live, mentioning how little Louise had paid for the house in Montes. "And it's a really nice house, Tom, it's nicer than our house at home." When he didn't respond, I threw out figures, what we currently had in savings, what we owed on our mortgage and what I thought we could sell it for.

"Hold on," he said. "We're not selling our house." I heard by his tone, how he'd lifted his hand from the steering wheel as if to hold me back, that I'd gone too quickly. Absently he said, as ever hewing to facts, "We have considerably more than what you said in our bank account. It's actually closer to twenty-five thousand."

It was the difference of the cost of the Navarro. I made a half gesture with my arm, an equivocating sound, hmm, feeling my stomach lurch. "The thing is, Tom, yes. Technically, yes, you're right. I mean, we *will* have it."

"Will?" he said, laughing strangely.

"It's just, I spent some money. But I'm going to get it back!" I smiled in an attempt at confidence.

"I don't understand."

"Tom, okay, I want to tell you something. I was impulsive. I fucked up. But I can fix it."

"You're freaking me out right now, Sally. What are we talking about here? Like, you gambled, you loaned someone money?" A pause. "Does this have to do with Louise somehow?"

"No, not at all! It's that I bought something. A work of art. It's an amazing piece, Tom. It was supposed to be a surprise."

I sat in the wake of silence, thinking with absolute clarity, *I am a fucked-up person. I am not a person that a healthy person should love.* In the back, the kids were quiet also. In the mirror, Henry was making the superhero figure we'd given him for Christmas talk and move his legs jerkily, a white bead of spit on his lower lip. Ida was staring ahead in her contained way, her mouth pursed into a small O, and I suddenly thought she had heard and was reading the silence, a tiny witness to my disgrace.

"I don't even know what to say."

"It doesn't matter, I can undo it. I can get it all back, the piece hasn't shipped yet."

"Shipped? This is insane. How much are we even talking about?"

"Fifteen." There, I'd said it.

The impact was instantaneous. "*Oh my God.* Fifteen *thousand*?" His face had contorted in disbelief. There was a silence. "Just to get this straight, I'm losing my job, and you're talking to me about selling our house and moving to Mexico and spending fifteen thousand dollars on a—on a fucking painting."

"It's a lithograph."

"You're actually correcting me."

"No—I'm sorry!" I saw myself then as Tom must: not merely deceitful but selfish. This whole year had been an elaborate gift, and still I'd wanted more. "I can fix it. Look—I can get our money back. Tom, please." I glanced at him. "I love you."

"Yeah," he said, as though the fact was a burden. Or a lie.

We were by now entering the airport. I followed the signs reading SALIDA, the traffic slowing, one lane only for taxis. Tom glanced over his shoulder several times to the children, his mouth tight. We pulled behind a black BMW sedan with DF plates. I sat speechless while he patted Ida's and Henry's knees and reached back and tousled their hair and told them he would miss them. Then we both stepped outside and briefly stood facing one another at the back of the car with the trunk open.

"I'm completely floored." He shook his head. "I'm just—I'm not even sure I recognize you anymore."

"I know."

"I mean, what the actual fuck, Sally?"

"I know, Tom," I repeated. "I'm so sorry. I love you."

His eyes had filled with tears. People were moving around us, speaking animatedly, waving goodbye. He lifted his suitcase from the trunk, set it down, pulled up the handle. "Look, I'll call you tomorrow afternoon," he said. "We can talk about it then."

54

I stood watching him pass through the sliding glass doors, waiting for him to turn back, but he never did. Numbly I drove home. In the back seat, Henry and Ida argued. Because it was Sunday, the gallery in Mexico City where I'd bought the lithograph was closed, as was La Conexión, our mail service. I checked my email, hoping for news that the purchase hadn't been completed, the piece had been returned unopened. But there were only several unread messages from Louise, beginning on Friday, presumably in anticipation of our return, each typed in her customary exhorting capital letters:

COME SEE ME AS SOON AS YOU'RE BACK.

MISSED YOU TERRIBLY, XOXO.

SURELY YOU MUST BE HOME BY NOW? YOU TRAMP, WHAT ARE YOU PLAYING AT?

I'LL WRING THAT PRETTY NECK FOR MAKING ME LOVE YOU AND WORRY.

The most recent, written that morning, struck a note of intrigue:

COME WHENEVER YOU GET THIS. HAVE HAD A RATHER STUNNING REALIZATION.

I didn't respond to any of them. I spent several hours instead drafting emails to the gallery. Some had a vaguely confessional tone: long pleas, slow prostrations professing ignorance, foreignness, a failure to secure my husband's agreement. Others were terse, entitled: *To whom it may concern, I purchased a lithograph from your gallery in error. Kindly refund the full amount to my credit card upon its return.* I agonized over these drafts for hours, shifting commas and periods, making the sentences more and then less emphatic, only to put them in the trash. At five o'clock, for dinner, I drove the kids to Pollo Feliz, a chain with a big indoor playground, and sat slowly sipping a beer while they ran through the elaborate maze of tunnels and slides and jumped in the ball pit, and with the coins I gave them bought handfuls of candy at the machines.

The next morning, Monday, I woke the children early. I had barely slept. A sense of anxiety had been building in me that left my throat dry, my stomach queasy. It was both a relief and a burden to see María again.

"*Los extrañé, señora.*" She kissed my cheeks.

Lowering my eyes, I muttered shyly that we'd missed her, too, it was good to be back, all the while thinking about what I'd done, how I'd been an unworthy wife; I was not the loyal and good woman she took me for.

"Everything was tidy on your return?" she asked.

I nodded, thinking of her cleaning when we were gone, oblivious to Bill's death, wondering—did she know even now? Worrying next that Tom would lose his job and Bill's children would sell the house, and then what would become of María and Rocío and Antonio? How would they survive without the income, the weekly tips, the money we gave at baptisms and holidays? We had become a part of their family, if only in the sense of a family as a hierarchical structure, their lives more secure since our arrival. But we also felt a deep love for her, as I believed she did us. I had told her we wanted to remain in Mexico, perhaps buy our own house, and she had held both my hands when she told me she wanted to stay with us, she would come to whatever house we bought.

"Please," she had said as insistently as I'd ever heard her, "please allow us to stay with you."

Yes, I had answered, of course we would stay together as long as we were here! Perhaps for that reason, I found myself agreeing now to her suggestion of a comida that was a favorite of Tom's, not saying that Tom was away, as though the preparations and our eating of it could cement our inseparability.

After dropping the children at school, I went to the market. This took longer than usual, both José Luis and Enrique asking how the beach had been, were we pleased to be back home in San Miguel, had we missed it? At last, home again, having deposited the bags into the kitchen to be washed and sorted and cooked, I pulled up the website of the gallery and found the telephone number. I paced around the living room, working myself up, rehearsing phrases in my mind. Any telephone conversation was in itself stressful, my Spanish always worse when I could not read the cues of the person to whom I was speaking. At last, I called. It rang several times before a woman answered. I gave my name; she asked several questions to which I listened with razor focus, answering with deliberate care. At length, the gallery owner came onto the line, speaking in English, introducing himself as Señor Menendez. I'd recently made a purchase, I began.

"Yes, yes," he said eagerly, "we were so pleased to ship this particular piece to you. If I may compliment you, *señora*, you've chosen a very powerful work. *Muy bien lograda*."

"You've sent it?" My heart had begun to pound.

"But of course," he said with an air of assurance.

I couldn't speak. My mouth seemed filled with ash. Finally, barely above a whisper, I managed to say, "The purchase was made in error."

"Pardon me?" he said, all suave solicitousness, as though he hadn't heard. Maybe he hadn't. Suddenly I couldn't bear to disappoint him, this fatherly man I'd never met, whom I had imagined seated at a dark wood desk in an elegant suit, holding the telephone urbanely to his ear.

In a fog, I plucked up the envelope upon which, the night before, I had written a few phrases: *Would it be possible to return the piece? What is the protocol for that? Am I able to get a full refund if I return the artwork unopened?* They were written in Spanish; I hadn't counted on being able to speak English. As I stared now at the words, they seemed to no longer be relevant, as if I'd neglected crucial interim steps required to be able to speak them. Frantically my eyes scanned down the list.

"*Señora?*" the man prompted. "How may I be of assistance?"

I cleared my throat. "I'm sorry," I finally managed, "please excuse me, I'll have to call you back. I need to pick my children up from school."

55

In fact, it was nearly noon. I would need to take the car if I was going to be on time for Henry. As I approached the bridge, slowing to look for a parking space, with a bloom of dread, I saw Louise. She was waiting for me. At least she was outside of the courtyard, I consoled myself; we wouldn't be overheard.

"Mia, at last; I've missed you," she called warmly as soon as I began across the street. Then, seeing my face, "What's wrong?"

Impulsively—she always managed to get my guard down—I was about to tell her Tom was in the States; I was worried about the future of the project. Catching myself, I said only, "It's nothing. I have a lot of errands I have to run after being gone so long."

She had been studying me closely, in a way that made me want to reclaim myself, shrug away her hand when she set it onto my shoulder. But it had been such a punishing twenty-four hours, so isolating, that I was at the same time comforted, Louise squeezing my shoulder gently now, saying, "I know it's difficult, but these moments are opportunities."

I nodded. Stupidly I began to cry.

"Why don't you let me take the children for you?"

"No, no"—wiping at my face. "I'm fine, really."

"At least let me take Ida. It would give you some time to get your errands done, settle in a bit."

I hesitated.

"Say yes."

"Okay, yes, then," I said, thinking how happy Ida would be to see her, how much she loved Louise's house. The kindergarteners were already being brought out, and to draw the conversation to a close, I asked if I could give Louise a ride back home or into town. No, she was stopping by the gallery to say hello to Hector and Fabiola; she'd be back for Ida at two o'clock.

"Here, then." I handed her a fifty-peso note. "This way you and Ida can take a cab home."

"I couldn't possibly."

"You're helping me so much, *please*." I pressed it into her hand, hurried to collect Henry. He'd been tired, his teacher told me. I carried him, heavy-lidded, to the car. At home, we watched television together on the couch while María cooked. I tried to think what I was going to say to Tom when he called, indulging the thought that after our conversation, he would call the gallery for me and fix everything; contriving how I could orchestrate that to happen, impress upon him his strength and my incompetence so that he would offer without being asked. My body felt leaden, as if I had the flu. I curled tightly against Henry, longingly listening to María pad back and forth in her plastic sandals setting out the dishes, knowing she was setting the table for four and saying nothing.

"Is the *señor* bringing Ida?" she finally asked from the top of the two gentle stairs that led into the living area, seeing me still on the couch.

"No, María, *lo siento*. He has business, and Ida is with a friend; they won't be home for comida." As I spoke, I'd cowered a little, but she had no discernable reaction. She simply said:

"*Bueno, señora, la comida está preparada.*"

A half an hour later, as María was clearing the dishes, the landline rang.

"It's me."

"Tom." I had run into the living room, coiling the phone wire nervously around my finger, my head lowered as if about to receive a blow.

"It's over."

"The meeting? Did it go okay?" I knew from his voice that it hadn't; that wasn't what he'd meant.

"I just told you, it's *over*. The backers pulled out."

"But will you find other ones?"

"No, we won't find fucking other ones," he said, in a voice laden with mockery. Then, pointedly, "And what about you? Have you gotten our money back?"

I was quiet for a moment, thinking.

"I'm in Houston, by the way."

I started. "What, already? But when does your plane arrive in León? I'll pick you up."

"Don't bother," he said, explaining shortly that two other partners and the firm's lawyer were with him to help wrap things up in Mexico; they'd get a car together; the firm would pay.

We hung up. After a moment, I asked María, could she watch Henry for half an hour? It had suddenly occurred to me that I could return the lithograph unopened. "*Sí, sí, señora, no hay problema.*" Henry had gone back to watching television, perhaps sensing that I didn't have the bandwidth to refuse him anything. I got in the car and drove into town, circling for a parking spot near Parque Juárez and finally finding one. I hurried up the street toward La Conexión, seeing the rose seller at the corner on her wooden stool, irritated somehow by the predictability of her presence, her oldness and meekness, the deference with which she always wrapped the roses in newspaper. I stepped inside the narrow door; before I'd even reached the counter, I said tersely, "I'm here for my mail. Number 189A."

With a smirk, the girl turned and disappeared into the back. I craned forward but couldn't see anything. A few moments later, she reappeared, carrying only a bundle of envelopes.

"Wasn't there a larger package?"

"Larger package, no," she said, her eyes wide in a pantomime of innocence or else stupidity that nevertheless reassured me, because it meant I hadn't yet received the lithograph, there was hope.

I said, trying to infuse every word with authority, "I'm expecting a work of art from a gallery in Oaxaca. However, I don't want to accept it. I want it returned." Her expression had shifted, and I repeatedly loudly, as though speaking to a dimwit, "*Quiero devolverlo.*"

"*Sí, señora, pero este paquete ya ha llegó.*"

I gaped at her. "What do you mean, it already arrived? Then where is it?"

"Don't worry yourself, *señora*," she said. "*No se preocupe*, your mother signed for it."

56

Driving to Louise's house, I had a particular, familiar sensation—a tingling in my arms and legs accompanied by a quickening in my chest—that I had often had in childhood. It was a distillation of rage, a hardening of will. A preparation for battle. "Who the fuck do you think you are?" I said aloud. "Who do you think you're playing with?" I barked out a jagged laugh, then tried to slow my next exhalation, to calm myself. *She's not worth it. Don't make a scene. Just get the lithograph, get Ida, and leave.*

At the door, she was all smiles, happy to see me. The bracelet that Tom had given me shone on her wrist as she lifted her hand in that now accustomed gesture of love and welcome, saying in a ringing voice, "I'm so happy you've come, Mia!"

"Don't call me that."

"What in the world has gotten into you?"

Quickly I stepped past her, scanning the room for Ida. I saw it then, hanging in plain sight, right beside Allan's painting. The Navarro. My breath caught, as if I were staring down the barrel of a gun. After all the hours of studying and rejecting and fetishizing it, I wasn't even curious to see it in person. I only wanted it gone.

I turned, trying to move away. But Louise sidestepped, blocking me, smiling and signaling with a nod that we should admire it together. I stared at her mouth, her white teeth, petrified by impotent rage. Ida must have heard us; presently she trotted into the room, shouting at me that she wasn't ready to go, then went onto the back patio, where I saw that Louise had set up the infamous easel, no doubt filling her with stories about who had used it and the mystical powers it conveyed.

Thinking this, I suddenly imagined Louise showing Ida the Navarro print, the two of them standing in front of it just as she and I were now doing, Louise perhaps explaining the lurid act in some way to make it seem normal to her. At the thought, disgust washed through me.

"What are you doing with this?" I said, pointing to the lithograph.

"Doesn't it look wonderful beside Allan's? But you knew how much it would mean to me, Mia; truly, I'm so touched." She beamed at me—that loathsome smile suddenly so like my mother's in my dreams it made me start. Her eyes had filled ridiculously with tears. "Oh, and now that you're here I can finally tell you: I've found us a house—in La Cieneguita."

I had scarcely heard it—found "us" a house—before cutting her off, coming straight to the point: "We're leaving Mexico. Tom lost his job."

"Has he? I wondered how long that would take. Obviously it's been in disarray from the start."

The mildness of her reaction flustered me slightly, but I kept my resolve. I stepped to the print. "And I'm taking this."

"To Tom? I hardly think so." She laughed lightly. "I don't really think he would understand it, any better than he does you and me."

"Shut up."

"Oh, *please*! Enough melodrama. Tom's going back to the States? Good. Now you'll see what you're actually made of. Now it truly begins, Mia."

I couldn't stand it any longer, her smiling at me, asserting a reality in which Tom and I were no longer together, calling me Mia. She moved as though to draw me into an embrace, my bracelet riding up her arm, and suddenly I grabbed at it, tugging frantically. When I couldn't pry the bracelet off, I shoved her, sending her stumbling backward. I began to hurl insults at her. "Liar! Bitch!" More spewed from me, I don't remember what, only that she didn't defend herself. An odd expression had come over her face, almost pleased, her gaze fixed on a point behind me. On an impulse, I turned.

It was Ida. She was standing stock-still in the doorway that long ago Louise had struggled to unlock, where I'd stood helpless watching Henry wail.

"Sweetheart," I began.

"Don't speak to her like that," Ida said.

I shook my head. My mouth opened dumbly. I was trembling, still consumed with rage. "We're leaving," I panted out.

"No."

"Ida, come here."

Her lips puckered with distaste, as if I was a bad smell. She took a few steps closer. As she drew near, I reached for her, but she darted past me to Louise, pressing her body against Louise's, the two of them looking at me with the smug expression they shared, the haughty set of their mouth I wanted to slap off. Looking to Ida, I said in a quavering voice, "Go get your things. We're going home."

"No. I want to stay with Nonna."

Nonna. A sour sound escaped me. I couldn't believe my ears; when had she begun calling her that? Slowly I moved my gaze between them, their cropped hair, ugly little replicas of each other. I thought of grabbing Ida. I was still much bigger than her. I could have dragged her to the car and hit her and slammed the door and driven off as she screamed.

But I didn't. I didn't want to give Louise the satisfaction of seeing that she had successfully turned her against me; I didn't want her to watch me battle with my firstborn child, about whom I had once naively thought, holding her perfection at my breast, that if I love her as my mother never loved me, if I love her father, if I give her a beautiful home in which to grow and stability and support, if I myself am beautiful and joyful and beyond reproach—if I can do all of this, then she will not grow up to hate me.

Yes, I had been stupid enough to believe that. Just as I'd believed I could have the lithograph that now hung on Louise's wall; I could have the life Louise had, and then discard her and have a better one, Tom and Henry and Ida and I, when it was Louise who had taken my life, ruined my marriage, made my daughter despise me.

More than anything, it was this last thought—Ida's despising me—that I couldn't stand. I cast my eyes over the bald concrete patio, thinking, *If I find an egg on the ground, so help me, I'll crush it and let the yolk drip through my fingers. I'll smash it against the painting Ida was working on at the easel, hurl it at her face. If she wants to hate me, I'll give her a reason.*

But there was no egg. There was only me, myself the beginning and end, the sole focus of Ida's hatred. So I removed myself. *Fine*, I silently chided her, *be without me, if you detest my company so much.*

As though I was watching a movie, completely outside of myself, I turned and walked to the front door, pausing only when I opened the car door, hearing the chiming, glancing around in bewilderment. Men were working in the building site across the street. Silhouetted against the horizon, I imagined I saw Tom—his height, the curve of his back, the gracious authority with which he gestured—speaking to someone, and I briefly thought to call to him, enlist his help.

But no, he wouldn't want to help me with this or anything. He wasn't even here. He was on an airplane, far above the earth. The project was finished.

57

In jerking motions, I backed my car into the pitted dirty street with the thought that I was returning to the only person in the world who still loved me, whom I'd not yet disappointed. I drove seeing no more than the few feet ahead of me, thanking God for Henry, repeating to myself like a mantra, *Henry will always love me.*

He was sitting on the couch, exactly as I'd left him.

"Henry, my darling," I said, wrapping him into my arms. His eyes remained on the television while I kissed him extravagantly, his plump cheeks smeared with ketchup, his fist pressing his lips as he sucked his thumb. I inhaled his breath. A mostly empty plate of homemade *papas fritas* sat on the coffee table—María always made them to spoil him.

"Do you want to go to the old hacienda?" I asked, holding him tightly.

He nodded.

"Only the two of us, won't that be fun?"

Soon we were walking through the botanical gardens. There was the exquisite huff and whip of bird wings that I've only ever heard in Mexico, maybe because the air is thin and pure and the altitude so great. We listened silently as they beat the air. We walked single file over the viaduct. When we'd moved here in the rainy season, it was submerged in an inch or so of water that perpetually fell, crashing over its edge, but now it was bone dry, the reservoir a moonscape of pocked mud.

"Is it this way?" I asked when we reached the fork on the other side, uncertain of myself.

"No, the other path," he said. "Come on, let's run."

We ran through the tall grasses, Henry leading, my sole life guide a five-year-old boy. Sometimes he would disappear for a moment, and remembering him bounding into the shallow sea on the day we found the end of the road, diving and falling backward, I had to bite back the urge to ask if he would always love me.

We stayed for a long time at the old hacienda, or so it seemed. It was only the remains of a building, only its outlines, like the half-built structures in the field. But we pretended it was our home, gathered sticks and built a "fire" and cooked food over it. We played that there were people coming to take our home away from us, and so we had to defend it with other sticks that were swords and spears. I kept wanting to assert that it was fun; wasn't it fun? Didn't he love this? Mexico? Me?

But I controlled myself. I looked at him and thought, *This memory belongs to you. I give it over to you, I erase myself from it, I'm nothing. I'm nothing like my mother.*

58

It was dusk when we finally retraced our steps. Rounding the last corner toward home, I saw Tom. He was pacing the driveway, furious. He'd been looking for us, he scolded me, as Henry called and began to run to him. He was beside himself with worry. Where had we been? What on earth was going on? Where was Ida?

"With Louise."

"What do you mean?" he demanded.

"Just what I said."

"But it's getting dark," he said, as if the statement definitively answered everything, all life's enduring mysteries and catastrophes.

"Yes," I said. "Henry, should we go brush our teeth?"

I moved to the door, which was slightly ajar, and held it wide for him to run inside. I lingered on the threshold. Tom fixed me with a look, and after a moment, I followed him inside and up the half flight of stairs to the living room. He opened his mouth, closed it. I watched the muscles tense up the side of his face.

"Sally, what is going on here? You knew I would be getting back. Don't you see it's getting dark?"

"Yes," I said, nodding dumbly. "It's dark; that's true, Tom."

He stared as if trying to fathom me, the situation. *Don't bother*, I thought. *You don't know me, what I'm capable of. You don't know the half.*

Seeming to arrive at a decision, he shook his head. "I don't trust that woman. You shouldn't either."

I laughed. "Believe me, I know that."

"So, what, it's down to me, then?" he said furiously. "I'm supposed to go get her—me, after everything I've been through today."

I just looked up at the ceiling, like, *Whatever, it doesn't matter. I've already lost her.*

In the next second, reconsidering, I said I would go.

59

My first thought at finding the house dark and locked was that they'd gone up the road for dinner. I sat on the stoop, reasoning that it was a matter of time before they came back, not wanting to chase them down. I could hear the television blaring next door. After twenty minutes or so, I knocked on the neighbor's door.

"Who is it?" came the voice that I'd first heard asking Louise if she needed a maid.

"I'm looking for my daughter and the old woman."

The door cracked open. "Your mother?"

I hesitated. "Yes. Where are they?"

Through the crack in the door, she smiled thinly, her face permeated with dislike. "How would I know?" Then the door shut.

I stood for a moment, trying to decide what to do. I climbed back into the car and drove into the small neighborhood beyond Louise's, slowly passing the bodega, the tiny churchyard. Several people were queued up outside the woman's house for tamales, and stopping, I rolled down the window, calling to her with an acrid taste in my mouth, "Has my mother been here?" "Not tonight," the woman answered. Unable to think of anywhere else to look, I went back to Louise's. Finally, at half past eight, I drove home alone. Tom was having a drink in the living room.

"Where's Ida?"

"They weren't there," I said. "They must have gone out somewhere. Maybe she took her to a friend's or something."

"No," Tom said. "This is completely unacceptable."

"What, then?"

We would go back together. Henry was sound asleep and never awakened in the night; besides, we'd only be gone a short while. I sat in the passenger seat, distractedly twisting my hands in my lap, starting to speak and then stopping. I was anxious about leaving Henry, but also taking Tom somewhere I'd been without him, where I existed as someone else.

"It's just there," I said as we neared the building site.

Tom cast me a look, widening his eyes. I could see a vein working tensely at the side of his neck. The house was still dark. After we'd parked, I knocked at Louise's door, after which Tom nudged me aside, banging his fist loudly.

"What the fuck?" he said.

"Maybe the back patio door is open," I suggested. We went around the side, standing at the tall wall that enclosed the patio. Along the top edge, at random distances, jagged pieces of glass were affixed in the concrete. "You'll have to hoist yourself over."

He looked up, assessing the possibility, shifting his position left and right. There was a small shrub of some kind and, stepping on top of it, he was able to place his hands between two shards. With a heavy effort, he swung a leg up.

"Careful!"

He had managed to hoist himself over, his fingers still clinging on for seconds; then I saw them release.

"Did you cut yourself?"

"No," he answered in a strange voice. A pause. "It's open. What now?"

"Come through to the front door and let me in."

There was another hesitating silence before his voice came back, still from the same place, "Should we be doing this?"

It seemed like a false question to me; we'd already crossed a crucial line. And so, without answering, I walked back to the front, and after a few seconds, he opened the door. Stepping past him into the darkened, empty house, I was gripped by a terrible foreboding. A crushing emptiness, as though I had ceased to exist. I switched on a small table light, the room coming dimly into focus.

"We need to get back to Henry," Tom said.

"Yes."

"I can't believe this."

"Should I leave her a note?"

"Yeah. Tell her to call as soon as they're home."

"She doesn't have a phone."

"This is utterly fucked; who even does this?"

We went back and forth like this. Since coming inside the house, my voice and manner had become increasingly cowering, his terse and pressing, so that it was only as I was turning toward the small, hidden room to look for a piece of paper that I noticed: Allan's painting was gone. The Navarro also.

Seeing my face, Tom said, "What is it?"

I ran to the stairs, taking them quickly. I threw open her closet, her dresser, ran into her bathroom to check the cabinet. She hadn't taken everything; fleetingly I comforted myself with that fact: *She's not vanished; it isn't permanent*. Tom was calling to me from the bottom of the stairs. I hurried back to her bedroom, roughly pulling aside the covers, searching her bedside table. There it was, beside a stack of books: my bracelet. She'd set it atop a small piece of paper on which was written in her domineering hand: *FOR MIA, WITH LOVE*.

I was numb, struck through with terror. The bracelet, the words of parting. My first thought was that she had killed herself and Ida. I ran back down the stairs, into the living room, searching frantically for anything to reassure me: her cigarettes, the record of La Niña de los Peines, her black leather bag. All gone.

Tom kept repeating the same phrases: *Talk to me, what's happened, what's going on?*

As a last hope, I ran onto the patio, searching for Bella. When I saw she wasn't there, I felt all the blood leave my face at once, replaced by ice, ice filling my limbs, my legs buckling.

"What is it? What's happened?" He had grabbed hold of my shoulders and begun shaking me, like in an old movie where the man slaps the woman. "Speak to me!"

Still I couldn't dredge up the words, *Ida's gone.* It had occurred to me that saying them would make them irrevocably true. Whereas if I continued to say nothing, it might prove otherwise; Louise would walk through the door, calling to me warmly, *Mia, my love, you're here!* And I would let her call me that. To get my daughter back, I would pretend to love her.

60

When I was a girl, imprisoned in the grim mill town to which my mother had taken me, I briefly had a friend who lived in one of the few grand homes. A girl ensconced in a respectable family very unlike my own who used to grill me about terrible eventualities. It was a titillation for her, a fun game to imagine such things. Sitting on the floor cross-legged and smiling, she would ask: What if you were kidnapped, and you were locked blindfolded in the back of a speeding truck, what would you do? What if someone had you pinned down, and they were tearing at your clothes? What if . . . On and on it went. With a kind of ancient resignation, I would dutifully project myself into each scenario, knowing she was a fool, thinking but not saying—because to do so would have ended the game and marked me as unacceptably different—that there was nothing to do but submit. Close my eyes and hope that death came quickly, the rape climaxed quickly, the bloody ripping of hair and tearing of delicate openings and the knocking out of teeth passed quickly, I became worthless quickly, so that whoever had me would tire of me and leave.

In Louise's dimly lit living room, Tom was still shaking me, his face rough red, mine bloodless. "Say something!"

"Ida's taken" was how I finally put it.

"What do you mean?" His face had clouded. "Taken where?"

How could I make him understand when it seemed so personal? As though everything that had happened, the entirety of my life, had been carrying me here. This exact moment, this room that had seemed like a sanctuary, that I had loved and now hated. I felt an ancient dam abruptly give way. And then, at last, I began to wail.

61

What happened next exists in a fog. I remember the ice in my limbs. How my head shook from side to side as I wailed like the disabled people in the factory town where my mother had taken me as a girl, who shuffled along the sidewalk making noises I didn't want to associate with human beings.

When at last I'd quieted, Tom spoke with new gentleness, perhaps frightened of me. "One of us should go home to Henry. You stay, you have your cell phone. Call me as soon as they come back."

I felt a tide of indignation, wanting to scold him—Tom, of all people!—*Don't be stupid, she's gone, she might as well be dead.*

Still, after he'd gone, I stared feverishly up and down the road as if to conjure their two figures out of the darkness. I banged again on the neighbor's door, repeating my questions more urgently, demanding she get the boy who had played with Ida on the day Louise cut her hair—I didn't know if he was her son or grandson—asking him, had he seen Ida or Louise, noticed anything at all? No, I gathered from something other than words, no longer able to articulate reality to myself. I went back inside Louise's.

I lay shivering on the daybed until Tom returned the next morning. It was five o'clock, he said, seeming confused at finding me still alone, time to come home; Henry needed to wake up and get ready for school.

We went home. In a stupor, I performed those tasks, leaning into their dull regularity. Henry was eating cereal when he suddenly asked where Ida was.

"She stayed overnight at Louise's," I said, smiling, astonished at my ability to pretend this to Henry, how calm I sounded. "Louise is taking her to school."

But when we reached the courtyard, seeing Henry start across the grass amid all the other children, I was suddenly afraid. "We have to call him back," I whispered wild-eyed to Tom.

"No, school's the best place for him," Tom said. "It'll give us time to sort things out."

We drove back to Louise's. Finding it empty, Tom announced we would drive to the police station. He must have looked up the location the night before. His foresight unsettled me; that, despite assurances to the contrary, he had anticipated this need.

A woman in a gray-and-white uniform greeted us. She remained emotionless as we explained our purpose, afterward showing us into a room where we repeated in greater detail to a police officer, an officious man with fat lips who had introduced himself as Díaz, that a woman had kidnapped our daughter.

"Excuse me, this woman is known to you?"

"Only casually," Tom said.

He cocked his head in a show of confusion. "And has she ever had the child in her care before?"

Tom looked to me. "She's watched our children a few times," I said.

"Then . . . surely." He spread his hands, smiling knowingly at Tom as if sharing a private joke, *Mothers.*

The affront cut me, that I should be grouped with women who fussed over their children with no true sense of danger, and I looked quickly at Tom, pleading for him to intervene, be a man in this country of men. And for once, when he began to talk in his pedantic way, in the language men share, stacking sentences like heavy blocks into an incontestable meaning, "Our daughter has been taken without permission," I found it wonderful, gloried in him, thinking, *He's succeeding; they're going to find Ida now; order will be restored.* It seemed to me it already had when, the instant Tom stopped speaking, Officer Díaz pressed a button and the woman we'd first spoken to entered in her gray pencil skirt and starched white blouse, holding several pages of forms. With a new formality, seating herself at an electric typewriter in order to record our answers, she asked us Ida's full name; her age; her hair and eye color; her height, which we didn't know, Tom turning to me with a cowed expression, as though being asked to describe a ghost, "Would you say four foot six, four foot seven," lifting his hand in approximation. Next I gave Louise's address, the names of her acquaintances I knew and of the gallery where she worked. When the questions were done, I stayed seated as everyone else stood, wanting for there to be more, to prolong the illusion that steps were being taken to restore Ida to me.

We must have gotten Henry from school. Turned on the television for him. Eaten comida, made conversation. Since the night before, I had been waiting for Tom to demand I explain how I could have let this happen, say definitively it was my fault, break something, yell at me. I had longed for him to be the kind of husband who would hit me, and taken his withholding of anger as a demonstration of his superiority: He was a good man; I was an animal unfit for life among human beings. It was what I had long suspected, after all, only intermittently considering I might be the person he'd thought I was.

I hadn't slept in nearly forty-eight hours. I sat inside time in a fog. At some point, a knock came at the front door. Seeing Officer Díaz alone in the stark sunlight, I grew panicked. Where was Ida? Why wasn't it dark; wasn't it the middle of the night? I had the impulse to keep him from coming inside. But María had already held open the door for him to pass, Tom asking him to please sit, would he care for anything to drink, some coffee?

No, he shook his head, saying affably, "But you didn't tell me that the alleged kidnapper is your wife's mother."

Tom's first reaction was to laugh. "Mother? We hardly know her."

"Really?" He looked to me. "You are Mia, are you not?"

I shook my head slightly, no.

"*Señora*, please." He made a show of smiling, as though he'd indulged me long enough. "I've made some inquiries at the school, with some of the parents, and at the art gallery where the old woman works." Tom was objecting—*it's not true, there must be some misunderstanding*—and Díaz raised his hand to silence him, saying, "If the *señora* could please clarify."

Cringing, I tried to reason what to say. "They *think* that's my name, yes."

"And the woman?"

Tom had gone silent, stiffening beside me.

"This woman is your mother," he pressed, "the girl's grandmother?"

"They think so, yes."

"And why would they think so?"

"Because I let them," I whispered.

"I'm sorry? Can you speak louder?"

"Excuse me," Tom interrupted, "have you found our daughter or not?"

"I have not," the policeman said without concern. "But I will be very surprised if she does not return soon. The woman is known here, she has no car, she cannot have gone very far."

The two of them locked eyes. As if agreeing silently to continue without me, they took several steps away, speaking in lowered tones. As he listened, Tom leveled his gaze at me and gave an almost imperceptible shake of his head that I first read as *This guy's a complete incompetent*, and then understood to mean *I know what you've been doing, and you are so fucked*.

When the policeman left, Tom called down to the courtyard where Henry was playing, telling him to go to his room. Next he went into the kitchen and told María she could leave for the day; he needed a private word with me. When she came to the top of the steps, her apron off, I was too ashamed to look at her, knowing I had lost her esteem, that I was an unworthy wife, mother, mistress. "*Todo va a estar bien, señora*," she said when she passed me, lifting her clasped hands before her heart, and I began to weep, hearing as if for the last time her footfalls on the stairs, the overhead light in the laundry room being switched off, the front door closing.

Once she was gone, Tom's questions began: What, when, how could I? There was a cruelty to his tone I found gratifying, that I believed I deserved.

"I warned you. I told you not to get involved. What did you think?" he sneered. "You would have a life here, with Louise as your mother? We would all move out to the *campo*, one big happy family?"

I lowered my head.

"Was that your fucked-up little fantasy?"

"Yes."

He exploded. "You know what? It's true what you said. You're damaged. You're just a fucked-up little girl who wants a mommy, and because of that we've lost our daughter."

"I know, I— Where are you going, Tom?"

He had stepped past me. I stood glued to the spot, watching him cross the living room, pass through the tall glass doors and onto the patio. At the gardener's closet, he stopped, fumbling with the padlock, rummaging around inside. He emerged carrying a crowbar. A sharp jolt of fear struck through me. Still, I waited at the foot of the three steps leading to the dining area. Tom strode purposely back inside. At the coffee table, he paused, his mouth twisted. For what seemed long seconds he stared down at it, the beautiful walnut table that Bill had designed specifically for this space, which Tom and I had always admired. Calmly he lifted the crowbar above his head, then brought it down. Again. Again. At the sounds of the vase falling and shattering, the wood splitting, shouts rose from Henry's bedroom. Several more blows brought it heavily to the floor, like an animal with a broken back.

"Mommy! What's happening?"

"Don't come up," I begged, darting to the top of the staircase.

"I'm scared!"

Tom was still hacking at it, occasionally heaving the shattered pieces aside.

"It's all right, Henry. It's only Daddy."

At that phrase, in the sudden shrill silence, our eyes met. There were tears all down Tom's face. His shirt was soaked through with sweat. It occurred to me he might have a heart attack, like Bill. Because of me. Because he'd tried to love someone who couldn't be loved.

"Tom," I said.

He shook his head. He had begun to cry in earnest, the way children cry, ugly and uncontained.

"Please, Tom, it's going to be all right. We'll find her. We'll get Ida back." I was speaking very quietly, words I didn't believe.

"Why did you do this?"

Meaning the name, I supposed, the charade of being her daughter, and I began gropingly to explain the things that had led me here, my forays into another life—only I couldn't put them in order. Couldn't find the beginning, which I sensed was further back, before Mexico or Louise.

When I began again, reaching to him, he brushed my hand away. "Go comfort Henry. He's frightened. He needs his mother." The words like a book being shut.

I found Henry crying on his bed, curled sideways beneath his covers, hiding himself. I climbed in behind him and held him tightly, patting his back, caressing his head, repeating over and over the phrase that had become my faithless prayer, *It will be okay, it will be okay.*

Somehow, with his stuffed animals piled around me, his small back heaving rhythmically, hotly pressed against my belly, I slept. Not for long. Maybe fifteen minutes, in which I dreamed of the day my mother took me to the cottage to meet her lover. We were driving along the dirt road. She was looking into the mirror, adjusting her expression, arranging her hair with her hands, just as she actually had. Except the trees were in full leaf, and the branches met above the car forming a tunnel of green, and she said, "You're going to be a good girl, aren't you?" And then we were outside the cottage door and it had become fall. I wanted to run, but where? From within and beyond the dream, I thought, *This is your only mother.* And so, when the lover answered the door, I gave him my hand, and when he took it, his hand was as cold as a dead man's.

With a start, I awoke. For a few blissful seconds, I glanced happily at Henry's things, his stuffed animals, the rug littered with toys between his and Ida's beds, all of it filling me with joy—*Mexico! We're still here!* Then, all at once, oblivion left me, displaced by a nullifying grief. I ran upstairs, searching for Tom.

"Is she back?"

He was sitting on the couch. The remains of the coffee table had been cleared away. I could tell by the light it was late afternoon.

I flung myself at him. "Is Ida here?"

He only put his hand on my shoulder. It was cold, like the hand in the dream. As soon as it touched me, I knew about Louise. I knew before I fully understood the scope of what she had done. I stared into Tom's eyes and said simply, "There's a man."

62

I had thought, of course, of the man from the path. The man Louise kissed, who stood in the sidewalk beneath our house and later seemed to know me. I wasted no time. I found the car keys, my phone, Tom following me to the driveway.

"Stay with Henry. I'm going to find Ida."

I drove without direction, searching the streets for his face. Past the Plaza Civica. North along the Obraje road, past Louise's. *Think*, I commanded myself. *Think what's here!* But there were only unmarked turnings, a few crude structures, two horses hobbled at the side of the road. I doubled back, skirting the Jardín to the other side of town, funneling somewhere beneath Parque Juárez. I moved as one does in dreams, with that same illogic, that sense of ineffectiveness and fate. Once, I thought I recognized him by his gait, only for the gait to change, the face to morph.

I was now far beyond the historic center, yet somehow the traffic had become denser. On a crowded one-way street, I heard amplified music, growing louder. I pulled over as best I could. My temples throbbed. Squinting through the brightness out the rear window, I discovered the source of the music: a truck with a bullhorn affixed to its roof. As it came scraping past, I saw that it was towing a cage in which a tiger paced lethargically. Children ran behind, yelling and laughing. Now and then, one would snatch something off the street and hurl it at the cage: an empty chip bag, a gum wrapper, a shard of plastic. A tap at my window made me start. A clown with a red plastic nose peered in at me, his Popsicle-red mouth moving exaggeratedly as he exhorted me.

Confusedly I shook my head. "*¿Qué quieres?*"

"*¡Veinticinco!*"

It was like watching a poorly dubbed film. I studied the huge kidney-shaped mouth, comprehending the words at a slight delay.

"*¡Solo veinticinco pesos!*"

I gestured with my palms, no money.

Ignoring me, with a thump, he pressed a paper ticket against my window. The circus was in town. He lifted his gloved fingers one at a time—how many tickets did I want? He mimed laughter, holding his hands to his sides.

"*¡No!*" I screamed at him. "*¡No quiero nada!*" My head was spinning. I was suddenly desperate to get away from it, the impoverished merriment, the appalling abuse of the animal. "Leave! Get away from the car!" I revved the engine. Before he had even stepped away fully, with a jerk, I began to drive, blaring my horn. I pulled onto the first street, a narrowly winding *callejón*, then onto a broader thoroughfare, passing a grocery store I'd never seen, large and windowless, all the shoppers in the parking lot fat and laughing stupidly. Not long after, I found myself on the road that led toward the hot springs, and suddenly the clouds parted. Tears filled my eyes. I remembered Louise telling me of her friend in La Cieneguita. I pressed my foot to the gas, seeing the insistent set of her mouth, her eyes when she said:

You ought to visit him; he'd enjoy meeting you.

63

It was another six miles before I exited the highway. After the clamor of San Miguel, the hushed verdure astonished me. Fields of soybeans, their green iridescent in the late-afternoon light, pastures dissected by twisting paths of darker green that traced the edges of creeks. A few cows bent, still as statues. A man on a bicycle pedaled by. Two women walked at the side of the road, balancing baskets on their heads. A field ahead was filled with people. All women, perhaps thirty of them, sitting or bending forward on squatting legs, gathered into groups.

I parked. Stepping from the car, I approached the nearest clutch of four women. They seemed completely uninterested in me, absorbed, their arms moving ceaselessly. They were washing clothes, I realized, the field a marshland in which the thermal waters had been funneled into stone basins.

"*Buenas tardes, señoras*," I began.

"*Buenas tardes*," they chorused, barely looking up.

"I'm looking for a couple. They have a young girl with them."

In unison, they shook their heads; no, they didn't know of any such couple.

"You're sure?" I pressed. "They're old; the woman has short gray hair." After a pause, "The girl has short hair also."

"A girl with short hair," one said, and they all laughed. I felt myself stiffen but held my smile.

Reining herself in, the tallest said, "No, but there was an older woman and a child at the house of the painter."

I had translated her words, *la casa del pintor*, in that literal way, my stomach tightening at the mention of a painter.

"Impossible," the fattest of them was saying, "the painter lives alone, he sees no one. *Es muy solitario.*"

"*Sí, en la casa del pintor*," the first insisted. "I saw them together, walking along the road with a small dog."

My heart quickened; it had to be them. The women had begun to bicker, who'd seen what, who was the greater authority, and I cut in, "Please tell me where he lives, *el pintor*." It was as though I hadn't spoken, I wasn't there. "Where is the man's house?" I repeated loudly.

"Ana cleans it," said the one woman who hadn't yet spoken in a dull voice.

I wanted to scream at her—what did it matter who cleaned the house? But they were all calling to her at once, "Ana, come speak to this lady, *ven aquí*," as at the far end of the field I saw a girl detach herself from her gaggle and begin across the field. She was much younger than the women to whom I'd been speaking, no more than sixteen, but with a woman's voluptuous body, all heavy breasts and broad swishing hips. A thick braid of reddish-brown hair swung behind her as she walked. The women were still calling to her, the tallest gesturing at me, saying primly:

"This lady wants you to show her the painter's house, do you think it's correct?"

"What has the painter ever done for you that you're so concerned to protect his privacy?" the fat one rebutted, laughing contemptuously. "What business is it of yours, anyway? What are you, the empress?"

Ana was near now. I appealed to her with my eyes, attempting to secure her sympathy, this teenage girl who, in an instant, had assumed the full measure of her power and was looking at me as from a judge's bench. A crucifix glinted at her throat. I thought, *Deny me and I'll rip that bit of gold from your neck*. Then, unable to hold myself back any longer, I ran to her, panting, "Can you help me?"

She regarded me as if amused, lifting the corner of her mouth skeptically.

"Please!" I was nearly crying. "I need to find my daughter; she needs to come home."

With a small gesture, she turned and began to lead me away, both of us retracing the distance she had just crossed. In the road ahead, I could see two small boys riding a dirt bike. The one behind was lifted up slightly, as though standing out of a saddle above a galloping horse, his mouth opened wide. Nonsensically, I searched their faces for Ida, then the faces of the older girls Ana had been speaking to, Ana stopping now to tell them without emotion, "I'm taking this lady to the painter's," while I stood crying and trembling in impotence.

She resumed her sluggish progress. We reached the edge of the field, stepped onto the road. The boys on the dirt bike had turned around. As they shot past us, spraying gravel, Ana shouted curses at them. They were barefoot, not more than ten or eleven years old. "The one driving is my cousin," she told me. As if I cared who they were! She was standing motionless and I wanted to shove her forward, deride her, *You don't need to stop walking to speak*. But in the next instant, she bent forward, drawing aside a branch, and I saw a narrow, overgrown road.

"*Aquí*," she said, with the universal boredom of teenagers, pointing to a primitive-looking house at the end of the lane. Crude cinder blocks without any stucco over them; lengths of rebar stuck from the tops of each corner.

"*Es la casa del pintor, ¿estás segura?*" I asked, my heart fluttering up again.

"*Sí, claro*," she answered with that same bored manner, looking at me as though daring me to walk away. In the low sun, she appeared gilded, like a Renaissance painting of a Madonna. For the first time, I saw that she was pregnant. She had that shape, swollen in only those places, her legs and arms slender. She seemed on the point of saying something, and it crossed my mind she wanted something for her troubles, a few pesos. Instinctively I felt at my pockets, though I'd left the house without my wallet.

"Now you can bring your daughter home," she said.

"Yes," I said. And for a second, it filled me with terror.

64

Once I began to walk, I became steadier. There were no windows on the front of the house, no chance of being seen. My mind was working now. I narrowed my gaze. I honed my focus to a single point, Ida, alert to her voice, to Louise's. But no, there was only birdsong, the droning of insects, the distant whine of the dirt bike.

At the door, as I was about to knock, I changed my mind. Better to arrive unannounced. I tested the knob. It was unlocked, and I pushed it open, stepping inside. As my eyes adjusted, I saw that I was standing in a long hallway hung floor to ceiling with paintings. Ahead was a bit of light toward which I cautiously shuffled. A short step, another. The floor was uneven; I stumbled. At the sound of my heel striking down, a man called out in Spanish:

"Hello? Who's there?"

Hearing his voice, deep and forceful, I involuntarily edged back.

"*¿Quién es?*" he repeated more loudly.

"*Estoy buscando a mi hija*," I said. I'm looking for my daughter. Then, "I'm looking for Ida."

"Mia?" came the quick response.

It might have alarmed me, hearing that name called by a stranger into the dimness in which I stood. Something in the way his voice softened around the syllables reassured me. I stepped forward, stopping at the edge of a large open room where books lay scattered, a few teacups and saucers of a blue-and-white-patterned ceramic, potted plants arranged on a heavy wooden table. Mostly I noticed the paintings that covered every wall. In particular, my eye was drawn to a series that, though I'd never seen them before, were familiar by their palette and the whispery limbs sprouting from geometric shapes. I thought, strangely: *Ida must like it here.*

He had remained beside the large back window—the room's only visible source of light—looking at me uncertainly: the man from the path, whom I'd later seen from my balcony. Presently he said, "Mia, is that you?"

"Yes." I had decided it was the best way. "It's me."

For moments, we stood looking at one another, reticent, each with our separate hunger.

He was the first to break the silence. "It's so good to finally meet you."

"Yes," I agreed. "It's nice to meet you, Allan."

As soon as I spoke his name, it was as if he'd been called into being. Timidly at first, then with increasing liveliness, warming to his subject, he began to speak of his life here since returning from Italy, his hope of sharing it with me, all the ways we would make up for lost time. I held my smile, careful to let him think this was a beginning and not an end. It was difficult, keeping my desire in check, although it was a long-practiced skill. I was good at it.

"Can I see the house?" I said when the moment arrived. It would be useful to understand how things were laid out.

"Yes, of course," he said, pleased.

Following him across the room, I noticed the Navarro propped beside a doorway. Allan was still explaining things to me. I let his words spool out, strands of the story. Louise had not told him she was pregnant; he had not known he had a daughter until recently. My eyes flashed to the windows, the front hallway. He gestured to a back hallway, saying there were only some bedrooms there, a small enclosed courtyard.

"Is Bella here?"

"Oh, yes, she's about."

"And Ida?" I asked, careful to maintain my warmth and ease. "Where is she?"

"Out with her nonna, buying a few provisions. Actually I'm surprised they haven't come home yet."

In sudden panic, I thought of my car at the other side of the field. What if they had seen it? What if they were in the field now with the women to whom I'd been unable to conceal my anger, making plans to disappear once more?

"Carol—" He checked himself, casting me a beseeching look. "Your mother said that you and Ida might come and live with me."

I smiled my agreement; yes, we would see.

"I want you to know that your mother and I only recently reconnected. We were estranged for many years. If I'd known about you, I never would have stayed away—"

We had not moved for several minutes, and to relieve my tension, I looked again at the Navarro. Noticing, Allan brightened, saying, "Carol tells me this was a gift from you. It's very generous."

I opened my mouth, but instead of answering him, inexplicably my body betrayed me. I began to cry. "I'm sorry," I said, sniffing, averting my face slightly. "I'm just so happy we're together, and I'm going to see Ida again."

"You've missed her," he said knowingly, patting my arm. "I have, too, and I didn't even know I had a granddaughter."

For a bizarre moment, I thought, *But what about Henry?* and was wounded on his behalf, that Louise had excluded him, discarded him because he'd proven un-useful.

"They'll be home soon."

"That's nice," I said, mustering a smile to keep everything from dissolving. He was staring at me longingly, as if I should fall against him, let him hold me. No, it was too much. I began to tremble, admonish myself, *Pull yourself together! Don't be weak; it's only a little longer.*

"Shall I get you some water?"

I nodded, clumsily wiping at my face. "May I use the bathroom? I just want to freshen up a bit before they come home."

"Of course, of course," he said in a tone almost of rebuke, *It's your home, too*, gesturing along the back hallway.

I hurried to the bathroom, closed the door, turned on the tap to mute the sound, took the phone from my pocket.

Tom answered immediately, "Well?"

"I've found her."

Quickly, in lowered tones, I gave the necessary facts: Our daughter was being held in a house in La Cieneguita. She was with Louise and her lover; his name was Allan Pearlman, I thought. There was a field nearby where people washed clothing. As I panted out these words, I was aware of what I kept back, that I had yet to see or touch her, telling Tom only that I was here at the house, to go to the police, to hurry.

"Ida's okay, though?" he interrupted me. "She's all right?"

I could hear the fear taking him from his purpose. "Tom, listen to me," I whispered urgently. "The house is at the farthest end of the field, at the end of an overgrown dirt road. Tell them you need to find the house of the painter. Say it back to me."

As soon as he repeated the words, we hung up. I replaced the phone in my pocket. Seeing my face in the mirror, I had a horrifying moment of unrecognition—not of myself exactly but reality. A sudden sense that this was all an illusion, the field full of women, the house full of paintings; I had slipped into a pretend land where Tom would never find me, and from which I could never escape.

Allan had begun calling to me. Was everything all right?

I turned off the tap, answering, everything was fine! I was able to smile and thank him when he handed me the glass of water a moment later. The first sip I remember vividly. The feel of it washing into me, cold, leaving an aftertaste of iron.

I was still drinking when I heard the dog begin to bark. I couldn't contain myself then. I ran to the door, threw it open. I could just see her at the narrow opening of the lane. Not Ida, Louise. She was speaking, presumably to Ida, though I didn't yet see her.

"Why not wait inside?" Allan said behind me. "It will be nicer that way, we'll surprise them."

"Yes," I agreed, thinking: *That's better. The house is more contained. Once they're inside, they won't be able to get away so easily. They won't be able to see Tom arriving.*

65

We had returned to the living room. On a small sofa of the kind you see a lot in Mexico, made of leather and unvarnished wood, I sat facing away from the door. My feet on the ground, ready, my fingers tensely interlaced. I could hear their voices getting closer. I couldn't yet make out the words. Ida chattering away, happy in her particular way of being happy, the merciless trajectory of her thoughts. It was Louise's words that arrived first, in that haughty, scorning tone:

"You made it heavier with the rocks."

Then Ida's piercing voice, reaching me through the dusky interior: "I needed the rocks."

At the sound, my chest constricted painfully. Allan was pressing something into my hand, "This was taken when your mother was pregnant with you—not that I knew it then." I must have muttered something, *Oh* or *Thanks*, not looking because I'd heard the door open, their voices suddenly loud, Ida's continuing unabated even when Louise called tersely:

"Is someone here?"

She must have seen the back of my head. I sat frozen, too choked with emotion to turn and conclusively verify their presence. Instead, I looked at Allan, reading his hopefulness. My body had gone rigidly alert, and to reclaim myself—there was only a second in which to regain my self-control—I glanced at the photograph in my lap. They were all standing on my balcony—that is, Bill's—huddled before the backdrop of sky and descending clay rooftops. Bill was at the far right of the frame. Beside him was Fernando Navarro, whom I recognized from the many images I'd searched up online, his arm thrown around a beautiful woman who must be Nuria. Next to Nuria, a much younger Allan, handsome and tanned and sexy. And leaning her head at his shoulder, Louise, young, unscarred, smiling in the sunlight.

The dog had trotted up, sniffing at my legs. Unsteadily I stood, turned toward the hallway. Hungrily my eyes took in my daughter, my firstborn, whole, alive! My face flushed with joy. Ida shifted closer to Louise.

Smiling at me, "So, you've finally come," Louise said. "Good."

"I don't want to go!" Ida interjected before I could answer. "I want to stay here with Nonna and Grandpa Allan."

"Of course you'll stay," Allan said.

"It's your home," Louise said. "Both of yours."

A small sound escaped me. My eyes met Louise's, her smile broadening, exultant in her achievement, her hand resting on Ida's shoulder. Ida clung to her, encircling her waist with her delicate arms, attaching herself in a proprietary gesture of love as if to protect them both, wrapping her in a pantomime of the very affection she kept from me. Did they cling together like that at night? Did they lie nested in sleep, Ida's sharp body softening as Louise caressed her head, her back?

"I'm amazed it took you so long to find me." Louise made one of those laughs that are just a quick intake of breath, adding to Allan, "We have such a strong connection, Mia and I. From the very first moment she was born, we've had a remarkable bond."

Allan had taken the bright plastic shopping bag. As he retreated to the open area that served as a kitchen, the dog trailing behind him, the thought of grabbing Ida and bolting for the door flashed across my mind. But the car was too far. She would fight me, thrash like an animal, and I would not be able to contain her for such a distance.

"Go to them," Allan was urging me. "I'm sure you've missed them these last few days. Give Ida and your mother a hug."

I scanned Ida's face quickly. It was unchanged by this reference to Louise as my mother. She looked at me as if awaiting the answer to a question. But I was unable to go any closer, sickened by the certainty that my reclaiming her would not be a consolation but a wound. Never before had I been so sure of her separateness, that she was not something I could hold and tame.

Louise shook her head at me, releasing a long, generous laugh: *Silly girl, why so shy?* Aloud she said, "You've seen your room? Allan's shown you?"

"I've done the basic tour," Allan called. He had removed a large shoulder of lamb or goat, heaved it onto an enormous cutting board, and begun to trim the fat from it with a large butcher knife, absorbed by his task.

"Ida, why not show your mother what you've been working on?" Louise said, taking from Ida the smaller bag that I could see by its outline held a bundle of tortillas and some limes.

"Yes, I'd love to see it, Ida!"

At this, finally, Ida smiled. With immense effort, I kept my face open, hiding my desperate need, crouching slightly so that I might receive her. When she reached me, wrapping her in my arms, I couldn't help myself; I said quietly, "Should we step outside, maybe? You could show me the outside of the house?"

She seemed to hesitate.

"Her project is in the back bedroom," Louise said, fixing me with a gaze that stopped me in my tracks.

I nodded, permitted myself to touch back a strand of Ida's hair.

"After you've seen Ida's project, you can help Allan with the dinner," Louise announced, tilting her head toward the kitchen, where Allan was hacking at the white ligature that binds muscle to bone, sorting the fat and the flesh into piles.

"Yeah, help out your old man, why don't you?" he joked, pointing the thick blade at me. His brow was knit in a way that recalled how he'd looked when I'd first seen him, when he'd followed and then caught Louise from behind on the arroyo path; how they'd shoved and struggled, then kissed. I felt something give way then. A kind of resignation. A loathing, not of her but of me; all the ways I'd coveted and enabled her, like a child craving limits, punishment.

"Of course," I said, taking in the room again, the long front hallway and the bolted door. I smiled. I lifted my shoulders in a show of ease and warmth. "Yes, that sounds nice."

Ida took my hand, and I allowed her to lead me back toward the bedrooms.

66

Shortly after, I stood at the kitchen sink rinsing salad greens in a big bowl. Louise had put the flamenco record on. I could hear Ida moving in one of the rooms down the hallway. *Not much longer now*, I told myself, followed by a wave of uncertainty, a wash of terror at what might happen when we were found. Beside me, Allan stood patting at the meat with paper towels, the muscles in his forearms twitching as he salted and seasoned it, caressingly coating it with flour as though powdering a baby's bottom.

"Mia adores this music."

"Is that right?" Allan answered with unconcealed delight, gazing into my face. "Your mother and I used to listen to this, once upon a time."

I made an assenting sound, as though the fact charmed me.

"And now you, too," he said, his eyes glossing with tears. I let him caress my cheek with the back of his dirtied hand. Louise had begun to totter around, gathering cloth napkins and silverware from a woven rectangular basket. I chatted and smiled as I performed the tasks Allan asked of me: fetching down a jar of olive oil from a shelf, tearing the remainder of the bread he'd baked yesterday into hunks, lighting the flame beneath the big pan. All the while, I was vigilantly aware of Ida's position within the small house. Moving in and out of view, dashing here and there but always skirting back to Louise, in the way the dog had scampered and barked and circled Louise's legs on that first evening. Periodically I glanced at my watch, keeping up a mental calculus of where Tom might be. Could he and the police have arrived at the field? Were they at this very moment making their way to us?

In these moments of glancing at my watch, I felt the margins creep nearer; the fact that everything would end, had already ended somewhere—love, family, our life here.

With a kind of serene authority, Louise had begun setting a small cloth-covered table. "Should we open a bottle of wine?"

"I think we should," Allan said. "Mia, why not do the honors?"

Ida had returned to the living room wearing a tiny artist's apron speckled with paint that Louise must have sewn for her. "I'm hungry."

"You'll eat when we all do," Louise answered in that harsh tone that Ida improbably seemed to like and be soothed by, astonishing me by saying:

"Yes, Nonna."

Did she actually believe that Louise was her grandmother? In a way, it didn't matter. Ida had an active imagination; whatever she played at became real to her.

"You can go and wash up," Louise instructed, as if making a small concession. "Maybe take a bath, if you want," she added, and I was seized with dread at the thought of her nakedness, wanted to scream for her to stay dressed, stay near me. I suddenly thought I glimpsed, through the back window, the red pulsing of police lights. But it was nothing. Only the last remnant of sun that presages night.

"What's gotten into you?" Louise chided, taking the still unopened bottle of wine from my hands, uncorking it. As she was pouring, a sudden noise made me start.

"What now?"

"No, it's nothing," I said, turning from her and managing a laugh. The sound was only Allan laying the meat into the hot pan, searing it. "I'd love that glass of wine."

Louise handed it forward to me, her body pressing my back, her breasts and bony chest, as for what seemed many minutes I listened to the sizzling and the sporadic pops of grease, those insistent little detonations.

A new song began, Ida reappearing, crying excitedly, "Nonna, I love this one!" She had changed into a dress I'd never seen before, white satin trimmed in bits of lace, resembling the dresses girls wore here to their first communions.

Louise clapped her hands, shouting merrily, "Dance for us!"

"Yes, do your dance!" echoed Allan.

Without hesitation, Ida lifted her arms and began to twirl in the white dress with that overweening confidence that is particular to children. The dance wasn't a girlish princess's dance, but that of a woman, a sorcerer. Intermittently she would stop her twirling and stomp a bare foot against the floor, still holding her arms above her head with fierce eyes, her small mouth set into a proud expression. There was something queasily intimate in her performance, like witnessing a person enact a fantasy of love in the privacy of their bedroom.

Wrapping her arm around my waist, pulling me tighter against her, Louise cooed, "Isn't it wonderful, being together like this?"

"Yes, I'm so happy."

"I love you," she said, lifting her voice in invitation for me to say it back, Allan turning to us expectantly. Somehow I managed to say it, the words weightless, barely more than whispers. Then, more loudly to make sure I'd been heard:

"I love you, Mother."

With the phrase, I felt cleaved. My face placid, smiling; my mind a black, disordered fury.

67

The dance had finished. The meal was finally ready. We sat at the table, Ida perched across from me in her white dress attempting to cut the piece of meat Allan had placed before her, Allan prompting me, "Mia, why don't you help her?"

It was only a table knife. Still, I weighed it in my hand before I began to slowly cut the meat into bite-sized pieces. I'd not finished the task when the first knock came at the front door. Maybe I'd imagined it, the sound immediately subsumed by the percussive rhythms of the flamenco.

But the second was sharp, startling the dog, who had been sleeping in a chair beside the back window. In the interval between knocks, no one moved. At the next insistent rap, the dog erupting into barks, Allan pushed his chair back, saying, "What's this?" directing his question to Louise, me. I felt Louise's gaze on me as he moved off, calling, "*¿Quien está aquí?*"

"*La policía. Abra la puerta, por favor.*"

Briefly then, my eyes met Louise's. She was still seated, her cane leaned against the edge of the table, regarding me with a cold, lacerating hatred.

"You stupid girl," she said lowly. "What the fuck have you done?"

But I was now looking only at my daughter: her hands clasped before her, the pooling white satin of her dress hanging from her slender shoulders. We could hear Allan arguing in the hallway, the contained chaos of men being men, refusing to stand down, issuing commands. There was something implacable and resigned in the police officers' tone and demeanor that struck me, with a twinge of longing, as distinctly Mexican.

"*Venimos a llevarnos a la niña*," one of them said. We've come to take the girl.

At that, Ida's eyes grew wide. Her hands unclasped and pressed the table, and I made a quieting gesture with my palm, *Stay calm, this will soon be resolved*. Allan was speaking with exasperation, his voice rising, "What's the meaning of this? She's my granddaughter!" Calling to me, "Mia, come explain to them!"

I didn't answer. Only smiled at Ida, nodding to her, *All is well, we're fine*, in the way mothers do when a flight hits rough air and the jet lurches and drops.

"Mia, come tell these men I'm your father!"

Seeing my refusal, with an ugly smirk, Louise got to her feet and began hobbling over to them, spewing her absurd lies, perhaps already understanding it was over.

"Ida," I said softly, "Ida, my sweet, let's go get some shoes on, what do you say?" I half rose from my chair, then froze, not wanting to spook her. Her eyes were as large and black as a deer's paused at the edge of the field, head raised, every nerve tuned to listening.

The sounds in the hallway had swollen and become less legible: short huffs of breath, scuffling noises, something clattering to the ground. Then Allan scolding furiously, "This is Carol, my wife, the grandmother of the little girl!"

His emphatic tone told me he'd begun to understand. The police were still speaking in their imperturbable Spanish, Allan saying to Louise in desperation, "Explain to them, why don't you?" A beat. Then a longer pause as the realization arrived. "You bitch."

"Be quiet, Allan."

"Lying bitch—"

"I said shut your mouth!" Louise hissed, the dog barking shrilly above her.

Her reverie finally broken, Ida sprang from the table, running blindly for the door. I followed, both of us momentarily arrested by the sight of Allan gripping Louise's oversized shirt in two fists. Louise was clawing at his face, her nails contorting it, the uniformed officers ineffectually trying to pry them apart, seemingly cowed by the sight of two old people fighting violently. With a shove, Allan wrenched free of Louise, redirecting his rage at the police, "Don't touch me, I've done nothing wrong," raising his hands, the dog leaping and snapping. In the confusion, Ida shot past the tangle of bodies and was gone.

Somehow, in the chaos, I managed to follow. I remember being through the door, my legs taking a moment to find purchase, to navigate the night's darkness; how frantic I was in my slowness to catch and contain her, hollering her name in a voice I didn't recognize. I saw the police car turned sideways where the overgrown lane met the road, a few townspeople gathered there straining to see. And then Tom, towering beside Officer Díaz.

At the sight of them, Ida pivoted, darting through the cypresses that edged the overgrown road, sprinting nimbly between the branches and into the fields. I took after her, leaning into my stride, pumping my fists. Ida was pumping her fists also, her dress a strange white blossom floating in the dusk. She had seemed to acquire a different kind of motion, to hover within the white satin that billowed behind her, to fly rather than run. Then I, too, was airborne. I felt the ground tilt and lift away, and for seconds, the earth become sky, and just as suddenly, my face and shoulder struck the ground, my body skidding and somersaulting.

I lay gasping, the wind knocked out of me.

"I've got her!"

I searched toward the sound, seeing the tall figure of Tom wading back through the grass. His strong arms held Ida aloft, her white dress like a cloud he'd somehow caught between his hands.

"I've got her," he bellowed again, up to the great, fathomless dome of stars. "I've got my daughter!"

He was calling to Officer Díaz, I realized. I heard the triumph ringing through Tom's voice. An odd calm fell over me, a numb relief that I felt as a kind of dying, as I watched him carry Ida, her limbs still kicking, toward the waiting car.

68

Once I've fully awakened from my dream, I put the kettle on. I wrap myself tightly in a sweater. The apartment is drafty, the day colorless, brutally cold. I drink my tea. I check my phone. There's a text from Henry from the night before: *Do you know where my copy of The Great Gatsby is?* At his high school, the teachers speak of toxic masculinity and white privilege. He and his friends tease one another about their baseness and irrelevance, mocking that version of maleness that our current president exemplifies. With his girlfriend, he is deferential in a way that reminds me of his younger self, habitually acceding to his sister, *Right, Ida? Like this?*

Then, too, I think of him asking María to make him *papas fritas*; how she doted on him, beaming when he galloped away on his imaginary horse. *¡Muy guapo, Señor Haynree! ¡Eres un vaquero!* All the townspeople gifting him sweets, holding him on their laps, the handsome boy, the prize. When he was speaking Spanish with his friends, I couldn't tell them apart, young princes in the courtyard of their kingdom.

On our final day in San Miguel, I had walked into town, descending the steep hill alone, wandering pointlessly through the throngs in the covered market. Nothing to buy for María, no meal she would be preparing. Still, I bought a few things that caught my eye, as if by this act I could reenter the dream: another housewife going about her shopping, happy. I bought dish soap; a piece of marzipan candy wrapped in cellophane; an avocado, not quite ripe. "*Para hoy o para mañana*," Enrique's father asked, the customary question, and I told him it was for tomorrow. Ordinarily I would have asked after Enrique: Was he well? Somehow, in the span of a few days, it had come to seem inappropriate; too intimate a question to put to an old man whose name I didn't know, with whom I'd enacted a fantasy of belonging.

Before ascending the Cuesta for the last time, I stopped in to see José Luis. Only to say hello; I'd not told him we were leaving. With him, for a few minutes, I almost succeeded in pretending it was a normal morning, my son and daughter in school, my maid waiting to prepare the day's big meal. "*Muy bien*," I answered when he asked how I was. "*Y tú, ¿cómo estás?*"

"*Vivo*," he kidded, alive. As our laughter died, he pulled a serious face. "You've heard about the American banks?" he asked, referring to the mortgage crisis that had just begun to unfold.

I shrugged—what did it matter? I no longer lived there.

"We have a saying: When the US gets a cold, Mexico gets the flu." He smiled equably, reminding me of what Louise had said, that Mexicans understand justice doesn't exist. "Ah well. The world will always be in turmoil. When you have God . . ." He let the sentiment hang unfinished.

Not wanting to leave quite yet, at the doorway, I inquired after his wife; had he read to her today? Oh, yes, he said, *como siempre*; he only wished he could be certain that she heard.

"Why? Is there something wrong with the phone?"

"No, because of her impairment."

He had used the word *discapacidad*, and at my questioning look, he clarified:

"*Sí, Es-sal-lee, está en coma.*" He sighed. There were people who eventually came out of them, who had reported hearing their loved ones speaking to them. Still, he confessed, sometimes it was difficult to believe.

For moments, I was speechless, terrified I would commit the sin of beginning to cry.

"And what about you, Es-sal-lee? You are happy here, you and your husband?"

"*Sí, estamos muy contentos.*"

"You don't miss your home?"

I have none, I started to say, then caught myself, and told him that San Miguel was my home. "*El hogar de mi alma*," I elaborated, the Spanish permitting or else excusing the mawkishness of the phrase, *the home of my soul.*

Since leaving, the years have only burnished that sentiment, sharpened my longing, although I rarely talk about it. Not to Henry. Certainly not to Ida, who will be eighteen in two months, who has one of those haircuts that are popular among a certain kind of person with a point to make: asymmetrical, shaved on one side of her head. Because she is preparing to strike out on her own, or as a way to express her displeasure with this country and the extent to which she feels ill at ease here, perhaps in her own body, she has occasionally begun to speak of San Miguel. When she does, I fall silent, lost, overcome. I allow my questions to refocus on her. I indulge myself in wondering whether, when she and Louise greeted one another in the school courtyard with uncanny familiarity, they had somehow already met. Or was it that they shared a less tangible connection? A dark current of love already flowing between them, linking them even still? Sometimes, when Ida adopts a certain angle of her chin or set of her mouth, it can be like seeing a ghost.

This weekend, it's my turn to have the children, in my apartment that used to be the upstairs of a single-family house. Tom kept the bungalow that I'd once thought cramped and faintly depressing—unworthy of our dazzling lives, the enviable love we'd authored out of nothing—and that now seems handsome and spacious. Soon after Tom drops the children, Henry tells me he's meeting friends, glancing shyly at me, hoping it's okay, I won't be hurt? No, of course not, I tell him. *Go! Have fun!* I make dinner for Ida and me, the pasta she likes. I offer her a glass of wine, and she declines. She is uninterested in losing control, still contained, intensely private. One waits in her company for the rare moments when she gives a bit of herself away, unexpectedly breaking into a pitch-perfect imitation of a character from television, moving her body to comic effect. Then it's like a dazzling jewel dropped onto the table.

After we eat, Ida wants to watch a movie. We stream an Almodóvar film she's heard of, about women in comas seemingly lost to the world, and the men who reach them or abandon them in their isolation. In the end, one of them, a toreador gored by a bull, dies; the other, a dancer, awakens by bearing a child. It's a complicated movie, full of deceit and violation, loss and longing, beauty and ugliness, and we sit afterward talking about it. A rambling conversation, in which I mention that there once was a yearly running of the bulls in San Miguel, before our time; Louise had claimed she'd seen it.

"Can you imagine bulls charging through Centro?" I laugh.

Ida doesn't respond beyond a long, unreadable silence in which I reproach myself: I've spoken too freely; I shouldn't have mentioned Louise; I've scared her away. I am about to give up, to clear away our plates, when she says:

"I dream about it sometimes."

I am so afraid of making her retreat again that I don't even nod.

"I miss it. The way it smelled, and how you could hear the roosters in the morning. And how free it was compared to here, riding around without seat belts. Remember when we rode to school in the back of that girl's pickup truck?" She laughs, narrowing her eyes over the memory in that familiar way she has had since girlhood. "I loved it there."

I exult, *She loved it! It wasn't all for nothing!* I wait, motionless, hoping greedily for more, that the trick will work again. This time, no. The silence between us expands. But it has become companionable; I sense we are both remembering tendrils of the same dream. The smell of roasting corn and lavender soap. The field beyond Louise's house. The serenity of María's face when she called us to the table, everything drenched in sunlight.

After a little while, Ida announces that she's tired. She withdraws to her bedroom. I stand in the hallway outside her closed door, wanting sharply to tuck her in as I did when she was still mine—or when her smallness could support that illusion, and I could hug and kiss her, pull the covers up over her shoulders, fill my lungs with her scent.

Once I've cleaned the kitchen, I bundle up and go out into the frigid winter night. I pull the collar of my coat up, my eyes blurred from the stinging wind, the snow chirping beneath my feet. It's something Tom told me when I followed him here: When it is truly cold, the snow doesn't crunch underfoot; it squeaks. Other things I've observed to myself, in the years without him. That by November, the sun remains low to the horizon, the daylight like weak tea. That on winter's coldest days, the air is odorless, pure, baptismal, the snow turning over and over itself like a white dog licking its wounds. Occasionally these observations find their way into my writing, though less and less. It's no longer what interests me: the poetically observed detail, the beautiful turn of phrase. Those luminous moments that can distract and lie.

Before I go back inside, I light a cigarette. I smoke, shifting from foot to foot in a vain effort to stay warm. When I fling the butt into the snow, I scold myself that I'm being a bad citizen, littering, even though I've never wholeheartedly believed in the endeavor of belonging. And then, for a moment, something of the old irreverence that even the ruin I set in motion did not destroy flares back, and I laugh, *Fuck it.*

Inside, I pour another glass of wine. I write, without self-censure, without thought or preamble, as once, for a brief time, I had made love to my husband. I don't stop to reread. I don't refill my glass. After many hours, when I've finally spent myself, I climb into bed. I read restlessly, page after page. When I turn out the light, to my surprise, I fall asleep quickly, entering a version of the same dream I'd had the night before.

It is San Miguel, of course. The street where La Conexión is located, and on the corner, the old woman sits atop her wooden stool selling bunches of roses for ten pesos that she wraps in newspaper. I first catch sight of her from a distance: her slightly lurching gait, her cane clutched in her hand, her head erect and chin slightly lifted as she shuffles from the sidewalk through the narrow doorway. In the cramped room, she gives the numbers briskly, *número ciento ochenta y nueve, letra A*, in that accent that is so difficult to place, that could be German or Italian. When the girl hands the package across the counter, she says nothing. Her eyes only widen before she turns to leave.

But in the entryway, she pauses. For the first time since she's been collecting the mail for the young couple who are gone on vacation, she steps into the adjoining café. I know these things as one does in dreams, though I don't yet know who I am, or that I am everyone, the cripple, the absent wife, the girl who fetched the package, and the people passing busily along the street.

In the café, she sits at a table beside an open window. It's late morning, and the café—a tourist place mostly—is empty but for her. Unwitnessed, then, she unties the string, undoes the thick brown paper wrapping. As it's revealed, a look suffuses her face. Impatiently she gestures to the waiter: *A cappuccino!* When the boy arrives with her coffee, she instructs him to set it on the adjacent table, away from the art. "*Aquí*," she commands, gazing onto the framed picture that's resting in her lap. There's a glint of tears on her cheeks. She touches back her short hair, smoothing the skin beneath her eyes, like a legendary actress before her final curtain call.

And when, a little later, she rises to leave, she no longer needs her cane; she doesn't even need her legs. She simply drifts, out along the cobbled street, through the sunlight, head aloft above broad shoulders, the package tucked under her arm.

"*¿Qué color, señora?*" asks the wrinkled rose seller when she stops there.

"Orange."

The *campesina*, who seems as small as a child perched on her rustic wooden stool, gathers up the roses dripping from the plastic bin. "A lovely color," she observes, wrapping them carefully in newsprint.

"Yes."

"Delicate, like the color of sunsets."

Her bracelet flashes as she reaches to accept them, her perfect white teeth when she says,

They're for my daughter. My daughter loves this color. Her father used it in a painting of her once. He made it the color of her little limbs. She was only a thought then, a whim. Mia. She wasn't even born—